MURDER IS A PROMISE.BAK2017-07-30T10-14

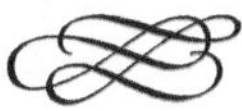

GIACOMO GIAMMATTEO

INFERNO PUBLISHING COMPANY

INTRODUCTION

As always, this book is told using first- and third-person points of view. A gun image means it is in first-person POV, that of Nicky Fusco. A badge means it is in third-person POV—anyone else. A badge does *not* mean it is from the POV of a person on the "good" side of the law.

Much of the time, the badge will represent the POV of Frankie (Bugs) Donovan, but it may also be anyone else. Also to note, my characters use nicknames frequently. Nicky is "The Rat" and Frankie is "Bugs," but usually only to each other.

I tell my stories this way because I think it adds to the depth of the characters. Each POV switch is indicated by an image, so it should be easy to follow.

If you just see an ornamental scene break (and no image), it means it's the same POV, though it may have switched scene locations or even changed characters, but with the same POV. If there is only an extra line or two and no scene break, then it usually indicates a lapse in time.

*W*hat is a promise?

You *promise* your child you'll protect them, or you promise to take them to the zoo.

Is one promise more important than the other?

To you, they are. To the child, I'm sure the zoo is more important.

But a promise is a promise, and *all* promises should be kept. If you're not going to keep a promise—if you think something might interfere —don't make the promise. And if you *do* make a promise—keep it.

AND REMEMBER—MURDER **is a promise**.

WELCOME HOME

Paul and Jake sat next to each other on the plane. Jake looked at Paul when the stewardess announced that the pilot had turned on the seat belt sign.

Jake leaned toward Paul and whispered. "Go through this again. What do we do?"

"It'll be a piece of cake. We've talked this over this several times. Just sit still, and we'll go over it again before we hit Customs."

"Ladies and gentlemen, we are now on our final approach to New York. Welcome to America, or welcome home, whichever is appropriate. We'll be landing in approximately twenty minutes."

Jake tapped Paul on the arm. "Maybe we should reconsider."

Paul frowned. "Jake, I told you before. We'll talk about it before we hit Customs. Now shut the hell up before someone hears you."

"But suppose we…"

"Wait till we get off the plane," Paul said through gritted teeth.

Half an hour later they exited the plane. Once in the airport, Jake said, "Can we talk now?"

"Yea, but don't worry about it, Jake. We won't get caught, but if we do, we stick to the plan. We say some guy in France approached us in a café and agreed to pay us for smuggling them in. He paid us half up front, and we were supposed to wait in Central Park at 4:00 for someone to show up with the rest of the money. We're supposed to give him the goods, and he'll give us the rest of the money."

Jake didn't seem to buy it. "And what happens when nobody shows up?"

"Easy," Paul said. "We say they must have spotted the cops and took off. If we stick to our story, they can't prove it's wrong."

"I still don't like it," Jake said.

Paul got angry. "Then you shouldn't have agreed to do this. But you're not spoiling my payday. You're going through with this if I have to kick your ass. Now, get hold of yourself before we get to Customs. And remember, your name is Felix, and I'm Philip."

DANIEL WAS WATCHING each person as they walked through the line. Most of them seemed nervous, but it was "normal" nervous; however, one young man appeared extra jittery. Beads of sweat were on his forehead, and he continually shifted weight from one foot to the other. Twice, he leaned forward and whispered something to the young man in front of him. Something wasn't right. Daniel made a mental note to probe further.

When the two young men reached the front of the line, Daniel stared like a man peering over the rim of his glasses. One of them seemed calm and collected, but the other grew more nervous by the moment.

"Anything to declare?" Daniel asked.

"We put everything on the form," the first young man said. The other man shook his head.

Daniel wanted to hear him talk, so he glanced at the form, then pointed to the second man and asked again. "How about you, Felix? Anything to declare?"

Jake/Felix shook his head again. "No. Nothing."

Daniel stood. "Why don't you come with me."

"Where?" Jake asked, a concerned tone noticeable in his speech.

"Just to answer a few questions," Daniel said.

Once inside the room, Daniel had a guard search them, then he asked the young men to sit.

"What do you want?" Jake asked.

"Why are you so nervous? I just have a few questions."

"But why the questions? We've already told you what you needed to know, and you've got the declaration forms."

Daniel smiled. "As far as the forms, anyone can write nothing to declare. We're here to determine if that's true or not."

Jake shifted in his seat, nervousness showing. "But you already searched our bags, and you just searched our bodies with that wand thing."

Daniel smiled. "Yes, we did, but that wasn't a thorough search. The next one will be. If you'd kindly begin by taking off your shoes followed by the rest of your clothes."

"What? I'm not getting naked," Jake said.

Paul placed a calming hand on Jake's shoulder. "Don't worry, Felix, just take off your clothes."

"You don't have to remove all your clothes. Shoes, pants, and shirts will be enough and don't worry, it's just us guys."

Daniel put on a pair of latex gloves and began inspecting the clothes. The pants and shirts were checked by feeling, and then by turning the pockets inside out. The shoes required more work. After a thorough search inside the shoes, Daniel turned them upside down and tapped them on the table several times to lodge loose anything that may have been stuck near the toe. On the second shoe belonging to Felix, Daniel noticed the heel twisted a little.

"Sorry about that," he said, but then looked closer. The heel was hollow and contained numerous identity cards—blank licenses, credit cards, and social security cards. A smile came to Daniel's face. "Well, what have we here?"

"I can explain," Paul said.

"I'd like to hear that," Daniel said while he sat.

Paul sat in the chair and motioned for Jake to do the same. "A guy approached us in Paris and asked us to bring these cards back."

"Asked you? Did you know him?"

"Asked is not the right word. He offered to pay us if we did it."

"Ah, I sense we're getting closer to the truth. Who are you delivering these cards to?"

Paul shook his head. "I don't know. We're supposed to go to a park and sit on a bench at 4:00 o'clock. A man will bring us the rest of the money, and we're supposed to give him the cards."

Daniel nodded. "Okay, stop right now. Don't say another word." He reached across the table and got two tablets and two pens. "Philip, I want you to move to the other end of the table. Felix, you stay here. When I say so, write down which park and which bench you are to meet this mystery man. Also write down how you'll recognize him, or how he'll recognize you."

Jake shot a glance to Paul, who was attempting a signal. "No talking," Daniel said. "And no signaling. Start writing now."

A few moments later, Daniel collected the tablets and read the answers. "Looks like you got Central Park right, but nothing else matches."

Paul leaned forward. "I can explain."

Daniel shook his head. "I think you've done enough explaining for a while, Philip—if that's your real name. Now it's time to go to prison. Maybe while you're in there, you and your buddy, Felix—if that's his real name—can learn how to tell good lies."

"But we're not..."

"Yes, Felix. You are lying. And everyone knows it."

"What can we do? I can't go to prison. I'm still in school."

"You should have thought about that before agreeing to bring the cards back. Besides, I don't believe that story either. These shoes have been expertly crafted to conceal the cards; that took a lot of time. It's not something done on a moment's notice."

"It took weeks," Jake blurted out.

"Really? That's odd because you have only been gone for eight days according to your passports."

"I mean, it would have if..."

Daniel laid his hand on Jake's arm. "Felix, it's probably better if you stopped talking."

"Yeah, just shut the hell up," Paul said.

Daniel pushed his chair back from the table and stood. "I'll be right back. I've got to log this in as evidence."

"Wait!" Paul said. "Isn't there something we can do?"

Daniel turned and stared. "Like what?"

Paul looked around the room and lowered his voice. "We can give you money."

"How much money?"

"Five thousand dollars."

Daniel shook his head. "Not enough."

"That's half of what we were paid," Paul said.

"Make it ten thousand, and we've got a deal."

"What? Really? You want all the money?" Jake asked.

"That's what I said."

Paul got some of his confidence back. "You're saying if we give you ten thousand dollars, you'll let us go?"

Daniel whispered. "If you've got the money on you, you can walk out the door now. If not, have someone bring it."

Paul got excited. "We've only got five thousand now like I said, but I can get the other five in two days."

Daniel shook his head.

"Wait. Wait. I'll give you five now. We'll be back in two days with the rest, or you can turn us in. You've got our names and addresses."

"What am I supposed to turn you in for? Failing to complete payment on a bribe? Besides, I have no idea if these names and addresses are real."

Paul stifled a laugh. "Okay, how about this? I give you the five now, and you keep the cards. If we don't return, you can sell them for way more money. These are new identities for people who need to disappear. They've been farmed from birth, so they're solid: bank records, social security numbers, credit cards, license renewals, all of it. If someone needs to disappear, they'll pay a fortune for one of these."

Daniel smiled. "Based on what I'm hearing, you know a lot more about this than someone who was simply approached to smuggle in a few cards."

Paul shrugged. "Maybe."

"No maybe about it. Who do you work for?"

"That wasn't part of the deal," Paul said.

"The deal is whatever I make it," Daniel said. "Otherwise, I'll call in the guards, and you and Felix, or whatever his name is, will spend some quality time in one of our fine jail cells."

"And I'll tell them of your little shake-down attempt."

"Who are they going to believe? You and Felix—who are trying to smuggle illegal identities into the country—or the valuable employee who caught them?"

Paul remained silent for a moment, then said, "His name is Professor Reed. He's our history professor at Columbia."

Daniel smiled as he pocketed the cards, and then held out his hand. "Deposit five thousand dollars on my palm, and you're free to go. But remember, come back within two days with the rest of the money or these cards disappear."

"Don't worry. We'll be here before the day is over. Those cards are worth a lot more than five grand."

"Good, I'll be here until five o'clock each day. You can go now."

* * *

After Paul and Jake left, Daniel pulled out his cell phone. When it was answered, he said, "Viktor, please."

"Who is it?"

"Daniel from Customs. He'll want to talk to me."

A moment later, Viktor got on the phone. "It better be good."

"It is. I just spotted the best fake identities I've ever seen. I ran a quick report on a few while we had them in interrogation."

"And?"

"And the kids I caught with the cards said they were brokered by Professor Reed from Columbia University."

"Professor Reed? And you think I should pay him a visit?"

"These identities are better than any you've shown me, and the kids who were smuggling them into the country said they were farmed from birth. I'd pay him a visit if I were you."

"And the kids?"

"I have no idea. The identities they were using listed them as Felix Marsh and Philip Dubois, but I'm sure they were fake. I didn't bother digging. I figured the person behind the scheme was more important than a couple of runners."

"I agree. You did good, Daniel. I'll have someone visit the professor."

A TALK WITH THE PROFESSOR

*P*rofessor Reed finished his class, then put away his notes in the desk drawer. He picked up the phone and dialed Paul's number, but got no answer. *Odd that he doesn't pick up.*

The professor placed a few papers in his briefcase, locked it, and headed for the door. Five minutes later he was exiting the building, enjoying the robust weather.

He walked across the parking lot and was about to unlock the car when someone approached him from the side.

"Professor Reed?"

"Yes. Do I know you?"

"Not yet," the man said, and then he pulled his jacket aside to expose a gun. "It would be wise if you followed me."

The professor stood erect. "What's this about?"

"Just follow me. All will be explained."

More curious than afraid, the professor followed the man to a car at the opposite end of the lot. It was a dark-blue sedan. "Get in the back," the man ordered.

"Not until you tell me what this is about," Reed said.

"It's about your daughter," the man said.

"My daughter? What about her?"

The man sighed. "If you don't get in, she's going to die."

"What? Why? What do you want?"

"All your questions will be answered later. For now, get in the car and keep your mouth shut."

Reed got in the car and took note of where they were going. They crossed the Brooklyn Bridge and went past Prospect Park, and they continued all the way to Brighton Beach. The man pulled in front of a restaurant, then stopped, got out and opened the back door. "Time to get out, Professor."

As Reed exited the vehicle, he said, "How do you know who I am?"

"Your job is to answer questions, not ask them." He walked to the front door, then escorted Reed inside and to a table in a back room. "Here he is, boss."

A man stood and spoke in what seemed to be a thick Russian accent. "Good to meet you, Professor Reed. Please sit."

Reed sat, then said, "Who are you? And what does this have to do with my daughter?"

Viktor laughed. "I like a man who gets to the point, so I will too. You have students smuggling identities into this country. I like the looks of them. You will tell me who is doing the work and introduce me to them."

"And why would I do that?" Reed asked.

Viktor pulled a phone from his pocket and showed the professor a picture of his daughter. "Because if you don't, I will have the three men standing behind you rape her before they kill her."

"You wouldn't dare. You know if you hurt her, I'll tell you nothing."

Viktor appeared to give it thought. "Yes, I know that. It seems we have a problem. I know you won't talk if we hurt her, and you know we'll hurt her if you don't talk. The question is, who will break first. I think it will be you. You know why?"

"Tell me."

"Because I also have your students—Paul and Jake. If you don't talk, I'm sure they will. But in case you're not convinced, let me show you what we have planned for them." Viktor nodded to a man positioned behind Reed. "Make sure the professor can't leave the table."

The man gagged the professor, then placed his hands on the table. He hammered nails through the back of Reed's hands into the table, then stood aside."

Reed screamed long after the man stopped, but it was difficult to hear his cries through the gag. Viktor leaned forward and whispered. "That was just the beginning. If you do not tell me what I need to know, your feet will be nailed to the floor, and if that doesn't work, we'll nail your balls to the chair."

Reed's eyes went wide. He nodded.

"Are you going to tell me what I need?" Viktor asked.

Reed nodded again.

Viktor looked to the man behind Reed. "Take his gag out. Let's see what he has to say."

The man untied the gag, and Reed began to speak immediately. "Her name is Jean Marie Solange."

"A woman?" Viktor asked.

Reed nodded. "She has been doing this for many years."

"Write down her full name and all contact information," Viktor said. "And don't make a mistake. If you do, I will find you no matter where you go."

"Don't worry. It will be correct. Just don't tell her where you got the information."

"You have nothing to worry about."

Reed finished writing and set the pen on the table. "It's all there," he said. "Now I need to see my daughter."

"I'm afraid that won't be possible," Viktor said. "I can't risk you calling your contact and warning her about us."

Reed thought quickly. "Then keep me here until you find her. Afterward, you can let me go."

Viktor shook his head. "I don't think so. The weekend is coming up, and the restaurant gets crowded. There isn't any room."

"What are you talking about? You can't just kill me."

Viktor smiled. "Yes, we can. And we will." He shot a glance to one of the men standing beside the professor. "Make sure he doesn't run anywhere, then tonight, get rid of him."

The man put the gag back into the professor's mouth. Then he knelt and nailed his feet to the floor. The professor screamed, but he couldn't be heard due to the gag. "I'll take him out tonight, boss. Where do you want him?"

"Drop him in the water. And tell Petrov that I need him to go to France right away. We need to pay Ms. Solange a visit."

WRITING THE WRONG THINGS

$\mathcal{S}$hawna Pavic put the finishing touches on her money-laundering piece, then printed it out and took it to the editor. It may have a mistake or two, but the content was sizzling—good enough for the first page if she were to judge. Second page at worst.

She sat in the chair opposite her editor's desk while he read the article. "Damn, Shawna, this looks good. Maybe good enough for the front page."

"Maybe good enough for the headlines," Shawna said. "You know it will raise a few eyebrows."

Jackson, the editor, nodded. "It'll raise a few eyebrows all right. I just hope it doesn't raise the wrong eyebrows. Some of the people you mentioned have powerful friends."

"All the more reason to start a fire," Shawna said. "If we don't let the little fish get away with things, we can't give the big fish a free pass."

"You've verified all this?" Jackson asked.

"Every bit of it. The money goes straight from the Mafia-controlled banks in the form of loans to corrupt politicians, who use the money to buy bars and nightclubs. The Mafia uses the clubs to launder their cash, and sooner or later, the politicians declare bankruptcy, forfeiting on the loans. In the interim, the Mafia gets favors from the politicians, and the politicians get the cash skimmed from daily operations."

"Seems pretty complicated."

"It is. I only gave you the short version, but the facts are in the report."

"And you've got witnesses who can verify the claims?"

"If we can keep them alive, yes."

"What else have you got in case the boss gets cold feet?"

Shawna shot him a threatening look. "Don't do this to me, Jackson. I've worked hard on this."

"I know you have, but I don't make the final call around here. If the boss thinks there's too much exposure, he won't run it. You know that."

Shawna leaned back in her chair. "I've got a used-car scheme in the Bronx, and a concrete scam in Midtown. But that one's dealing with the same damn people. If the boss won't run the money-laundering story, he sure as shit won't run the concrete scam."

"I hear what you're saying," Jackson said, "but just in case, give me what you've got on both of them. I need to have backup."

"I'll have it before I leave."

"I'll be here, so just drop it off. By the way, did your ex have anything to do with this?"

Shawna had her hand on the doorknob as she turned. "You mean my ex-husband or Donovan?"

"Either one," Jackson said.

Shawna shook her head. "Neither of them had anything to do with it.

This is all me." She turned the knob to leave, then said, "That's good, right?"

"Depends on how you look at it. One of the people you named in the article has a brother who sits on our Board of Directors. If you're wrong, I can't imagine that it'll be good. Hell, if you're *right*, I can't imagine it'll be good."

Shawna sighed. "You going up there tonight?"

"As soon as you leave. It shouldn't take long. He'll either love it, or shut it down, but I'm guessing the decision won't take more than a minute."

"All right. I'll be at my desk. Let me know when you hear something."

"If I'm smiling when I step off the elevator, he's running it. If not…"

"Yeah, that's what I'm afraid of."

Jackson walked toward the elevator. "See you shortly."

Shawna went through her mail while waiting on Jackson. One letter stuck out—it was addressed to her maiden name, and it was hand-written. She opened the envelope and read the letter.

Stop writing the wrong things, or you'll suffer the consequences.

Confused, she read it again and wondered what "wrong things" they were speaking of. It couldn't have been any of her new articles because no one knew about them. Even with those articles removed from the equation, it left a lot of topics that may have offended some-one. *But which ones?*

Shawna thought about her most controversial articles over the past month, but when she heard the elevator bell, she forgot all about it.

She got up from her desk and raced to meet Jackson. He was smiling. "He okayed it?"

Jackson's grin grew wider. "He did. Front page too."

Shawna wrapped her arms around him and hugged. "I can't believe it. Thank you so much."

"No need to thank me. You're the one who wrote it. And now congratulations are in order. We should celebrate. Drinks at the bar?"

"Why not?" Shawna said. "I'm buying."

"Damn," Jackson said, "If I'd have known you'd be so magnanimous, I'd have chosen somewhere nicer."

Shawna laughed. "Don't push it. I can barely afford drinks at the bar. Anyplace nicer and I'd be forced to ask for a raise."

Jackson picked up his coat and slipped his right arm into the sleeve. "You're on your own for that. I'll fight for your articles, but I draw the line at requests for more money."

"I figured as much," Shawna said. "But that's all right. It's fun being broke."

"Don't I know it," Jackson said. "You should try it with two kids."

"I'll pass on the kids. My cat is enough trouble. I can't imagine the things kids get into."

They got into an elevator and pushed the button for the first floor. "You're right again, Shawna. You *can't* imagine. They're into something new every day. And if they weren't so damn funny, it would be tragic."

Shawna and Jackson sat at a corner table and chatted for almost an hour, then Shawna said she had to go. "I need to go home and get some sleep. Some of us have to work."

Jackson gulped the rest of his drink and grabbed his coat from the back of the chair. "If you run into any of those people who have to work, tell them I'll be in the office bright and early."

"Go to hell, Jackson. See you in the morning. And thanks again for backing me up."

Jackson held the door open for Shawna. "No worries. Good writing makes my day. I'm just glad he went for it."

Jackson turned left, then hollered back. "Shawna, I didn't think of it before, but do you need a ride?"

"Not after seeing you down so many Scotch and waters. But thanks anyway. I don't live far from here. I can walk."

"Suit yourself," Jackson said. "See ya."

Shawna walked home, climbed the one flight of stairs to her apartment, unlocked the door, and set her purse on the sofa. Afterward, she got into more comfortable clothes and settled in to watch TV.

ACROSS THE STREET, a man peered through her window using a pair of binoculars. She seemed at ease on her sofa, maybe too at ease. He'd have to remedy that. First, he'd see if she listened. If she were smart, she would.

ANOTHER DAY

I got up at 5:30, got dressed, and quietly left the house. Sometimes I hated working out so early—and today was one of those days—but I knew it had to be done if I wanted to stay in shape. And staying in shape was mandatory if I wanted to remain alive.

I jogged down Beech Street, hit the park, then headed toward the woods. My daily jaunts had made a path through the woods, and it was a good one—enough obstacles to help me keep my balance: logs to jump over, rocks that protruded from the ground, and railroad tracks to force me to maintain agility on a thin structure. The trail simulated all the obstacles I might find in the normal course of a run through the city streets.

When I finished my run, I went home and worked out with cinder blocks and bags of cement to maintain strength as well as grip. Afterward, I went upstairs to shower.

Angie was up when I crept into the room. "Have a good workout, babe?" she asked.

"Always," I said. "But it's chilly today."

"Didn't you wear a jacket?"

"I should have, but I didn't."

"Kate called. We got the wedding invitation. She said the formal one will arrive shortly, but she wanted to call and let us know beforehand."

"What? An invitation?"

"For the wedding. Don't tell me you forgot."

"I didn't forget, but I guess I still don't believe it. I figured Bugs would find some way to delay it or something."

"Kate's not going to let him do that. Unless I misjudge her, she's going to keep him on track."

"Well, if anyone can do it, it'll be Kate. How long are we going up for, by the way?"

"I figured we'd stay a week—if you can manage it, and if we can swing it financially. I'd like to take Rosa to see some sites before or after the wedding."

"A week's fine by me, but two weeks would be better. And before you object—don't worry about the money. Bugs said we could stay at his place."

"We can't do that. They'll be newlyweds."

"They'll be on their honeymoon, for God's sake. Besides, Bugs said they needed someone to watch Alex."

"Really? That would be perfect. He can come with us when we go sightseeing."

"He has school, you know. We can't just take him out of school."

"Actually we *can* take him out of school," Angela said, "and he'll love us for it. What kid doesn't want to get off school?"

I laughed. "I know that. I was just giving the kind of answer you usually give. Of course we'll take him out of school, and of course, he'll love it."

"What do you need to do for work?"

"Not much. Everybody knows what to do. I may need Moresco to bid a job for me."

"And you're okay with that—with him bidding a job?"

I nodded. "It's a small job. We can't go too wrong on it."

"Then it looks as if we're all set. I'll tell Rosa when she gets up."

Rosa walked in from the other room. "I heard, and I'm ready. I've already got a few places I want to see—Ellis Island, the spot where the Towers were, Grand Central Station, Wall Street, Broadway, Central Park."

"Whoa! We're only going for a week," Angela said.

"Two weeks, Angela. Remember?"

Rosa kissed me on the cheek. "Two weeks? Then we won't have to be so quick," she said, and laughed.

"Shh. Be quiet, or you'll wake your brother," Angela said.

"It's time he got up anyway, Mom. I can't believe he's sleeping this late. I bet you didn't let me sleep this late."

"If you just—"

"—worry about yourself, you'll have more than enough to worry about," Rosa said, finishing Angie's sentence.

I stifled a laugh, and Angela shot me a glare. "That's right, young lady. Now go upstairs and get ready for school."

"I will. And don't forget, I have the dance tonight."

"I *did* forget. Who are you going with?"

"Lee Comegys, remember? He's the boy from—"

"The boy from Forty Acres," I said. "I remember."

After Rosa left, Angie turned to me. "You could have helped me by not laughing when she said that about—"

"About *worrying about yourself?* I tried, but you've got to admit, it *was* funny. She knows you too well."

"The problem is, she's too much like you. You need to teach her some respect."

"She's got plenty of respect, Angie, but she also has a sense of humor. Now please step aside while I make more coffee."

"I can make it for you."

"No thanks. You always make it too weak," I said.

Angie grabbed the grinder and the beans. "Coffee is expensive. And you don't need that much caffeine."

"So says the woman whose coffee is like muddy water."

"Hush up and go to work. Let me enjoy the day with my son."

I went upstairs and dressed for work, then came back down. As I was leaving, Rosa called from the kitchen.

"Wait up, Dad. You can drop me off on your way in."

"As long as you hurry," I said. "I don't want to be late."

"You run the company, Dad. Who's going to say anything about you being a few minutes late?"

"I think your mother's right; you need to learn respect."

Rosa caught up to me, leaned over and gave me a peck on the cheek. "You wouldn't have me any other way. You love me, and you know it."

I laughed as she raced to the car. "Get in there before I kick your butt."

As I drove toward school, Rosa said, "So Bugs is finally getting married?"

"That's Uncle Frankie to you, young lady."

"Now you sound like Mom. Besides, he tells me to call him Bugs."

"I know what he tells you, but that's to make him feel younger. And he doesn't give a damn because he doesn't have to live with you. Listen to your father and call him Uncle Frankie."

Rosa smiled. "You're doing that to tick him off, aren't you?"

"Maybe."

"If that's the reason, I'll go along, but—"

"No buts. Do as I say."

"When is the wedding?" Rosa asked.

"I don't know the exact date, but it's still a few weeks away."

"A few weeks—so soon?"

"Yeah, Bugs wanted it done quickly, and the reception hall had a cancellation. He grabbed it, mostly because I think he wanted to force himself to go through with it. He was probably afraid he'd back out."

"What's Kate like?"

"She's nice. Good sense of humor, and a hard worker."

"What does she do?" Rosa asked.

"She's the medical examiner."

"So she works cases with Bugs?"

I turned and glared. "With *Uncle Frankie,* yes."

As we passed the St. Francis hospital, Rosa said, "You can drop me off here, Dad."

"I'll take you all the way. I don't mind."

"That's all right. I don't want everyone to see you drop me off. Having your parents drive you to school isn't cool."

I pulled to the curb and said, "At the risk of sounding like your mother, you need to stop worrying about what's *cool*. And tell that Irishman he better mind his manners tonight. If you don't tell him, I will."

Rosa stretched over and kissed me on the cheek. "I will, Dad. Thanks."

I shook my head as she walked up the street, wondering how she'd gotten so old. Once I saw she was safely at school, I drove to work and started putting things in place for my so-called vacation. A couple of weeks wasn't long to be gone, but if you had to leave your business for even a day, it seemed like a long time.

I entered the office to find Sharon hard at work. "Good morning, Mr. Fusco."

"Morning, Sharon. And it's Nicky, not Mr. Fusco. You know that."

"You got it, Nicky. Nice day, huh?"

"Too damn cold, but other than that, yea, it's a nice day. Sharon, when you get a chance, will you get Johnny Moresco on the phone? The number may be listed under his father's name: Teddy the Tank."

"Will do."

A few minutes later, Sharon buzzed to say Moresco was on the line. "Johnny! It's Nicky Fusco. How the hell are you?"

"Great, Nicky. How you doing?"

"I got a favor to ask."

"Shoot."

"I've gotta go out of town for a couple of weeks, and it might be when

I have to bid on a small strip center out in Newport. Think you can handle that for me?"

"No problem. You'll have somebody call me?"

"Yeah, assuming it comes in while I'm gone, Sharon will call to let you know. She'll have all the details."

"Got it. Don't worry about a thing. And I'll guarantee you make money on it."

"Thanks, Johnny. I owe you one."

"I'll mark it down, Nicky. I'm keeping track. But I won't call the favors in until you get to owe me three or four."

"That's fine, Johnny. You know where to find me."

A NIGHT TO BE MUGGED

The dance couldn't have gone better, and Rosa's date had been a dream. He dressed nicely, and his manners were impeccable.

"Can I walk you home, Rosa?" he asked afterward.

"I don't know," Rosa said. "I'm supposed to call my father so he can pick me up."

"Don't worry. It's not that far, and I'll make sure you get home safely."

Rosa gave a mock bow and smiled. "If you insist, Mr. Comegys. Consider my honor in your hands."

Rosa and Lee left St. Anthony's and started walking home. About three blocks down DuPont Street, two young punks approached them.

"What have we here?" the taller punk said.

"Looks like a couple of brats on their way home from the dance," the other one said, then pulled a switchblade.

Lee raised his hands. "We don't want any trouble," he said. "Take what you want."

Rosa shot him a glare. "The hell with that. You're not getting anything."

The shorter guy placed his knife to Rosa's throat. "Give me the purse, or I'll have to cut you."

"Wait till after I fuck her," the other one said, then you can cut her.

Rosa handed her purse to them. "You'll regret this," she said.

"Yeah, I know," the taller one said, and turned to Lee. He held out his hand. "Your wallet, brave boy."

The shorter mugger laughed. "Brave boy! She's got more balls than he does."

With Rosa's purse and Lee's wallet in hand, the muggers ran off.

I was mugged. I was mugged, for God's sake. Miracles do happen. Rosa turned to Lee, shaken up by the incident. "Lee, are you all right?"

"I'm okay," he said. "But let's get you home before they come back."

THE MUGGERS TOOK off down 7th Street, then up Franklin. Halfway up the block, the shorter one rummaged through Rosa's purse while the other one watched for cops.

"What have we got?" the taller one asked.

"Not much. Normal girl shit, a ring, a bracelet, a coin—"

"A coin? What kind of coin?"

"I don't know. Some fake shit. Probably from a board game or something."

"Let me see," the kid said. He grabbed the coin and looked at it. "You stupid shit. This is one of Monroe's coins."

"I don't care whose coin it is."

"You'll care if Monroe finds out. But why does a white girl have one of Monroe's coins? Give me the license. Who is she? Monroe doesn't give his coins to just anybody, especially not white people."

The first kid handed Rosa's wallet to the taller kid, and he removed the license. "Rosa Fusco! Holy shit!"

"Who's Rosa Fusco?"

"You dumb fuck. That's Nicky the Rat's daughter."

"The Rat? As in the guy who killed those drug dealers in Hockessin?"

"And the one who supposedly rescued Monroe's cousin."

"So what? He doesn't know who we are."

"He doesn't now, but he will. If you like beating off, we better return this purse and hope that's enough."

"Enough for what?"

"Enough to keep our dicks. If we don't 'The Rat' will have 'em cut off."

"Cut off? Is he the guy who—"

"One and the same. Now let's get this back to her before she tells him."

"She doesn't know us. There's no way he can find us. I say we get rid of the purse and run."

"You willing to bet your balls on him not finding us because that's the least he'll do when he catches you. And I did say *when* because he *will* catch you."

～

ROSA WALKED south on DuPont Street slightly ahead of Lee. She had walked about three blocks when she saw one of the guys who had mugged her. He was standing on the sidewalk holding her purse. *What the hell?*

As she approached, the guy walked toward her with his eyes held low, and his voice not as brazen as before. "Are you Rosa Fusco?" he asked.

"Yeah, why?"

He handed her the purse. "I'm sorry. We didn't know who you were until we saw the license."

Rosa rolled her eyes and lifted her head up. "Good God, I can't even get mugged."

The guy looked at her as if she were crazy. "My sister would kill for your problems. She's been robbed twice this year. Just do me a favor and don't tell your father what happened."

"Don't worry," Rosa said. "Nothing will happen."

After the mugger left, Lee grabbed Rosa's arm. "Did that really happen? Did that guy give you your purse back?"

"Not just the purse," Rosa said, while she went through things. "Your wallet too." She handed Lee's wallet to him. "Get used to it if you hang out with me. No one dares to mug me or anything."

"Shit! That's cool. I wish I had that problem."

"No, you don't," Rosa said. "It's not as cool as you think." She walked another half a block, then said, "You might as well go home, Lee. I'm fine by myself as you saw."

"You sure?" Lee asked.

"Yes, I'm sure. You can either walk home from here, or you can finish walking with me, and I'll get my dad to drive you home."

"I guess I'll walk home," Lee said and started to leave. He returned quickly. "On second thought, I'll walk you. I don't want your dad to think I abandoned you."

Rosa raised her eyebrows and looked to the sky. *God, no. We wouldn't want that.*

When they reached Rosa's house, she went in and asked Nicky if he would drive Lee home.

"No problem," Nicky said. "You want to ride along?"

"I'm fine," Rosa said, "I'll just say goodbye." She went outside said goodnight to Lee and gave him a peck on the cheek. "Thanks for everything, Lee. I'll see you tomorrow."

"Okay, Rosa. See ya."

Rosa went inside and fixed hot tea while she waited for her father to return. About twenty minutes later, he walked through the door.

"Lee seems like a nice boy. Did you have a good time?"

Rosa sat at the table, head hung low. "I guess."

"You guess? What's the matter? Why the long face?"

"Because everybody is afraid of me, that's why. Girls want to walk home with me after a dance—not because they like me—but because they know no one will bother us."

Rosa pushed her cup of tea aside and said, "You know what they call me at school? 'The girl who can't be mugged.' They say I don't need to carry a gun, just a license."

"That's a good thing," Nicky said. "Why wouldn't it be? Do you *want* to get mugged? I'm sure I could arrange it if you do."

"Don't be an ass, Dad. I don't *want* to get mugged. But it would be nice to know that I *could* get mugged—like anyone else."

"I don't understand it," Nicky said. "Why would it be nice to know you *could* get mugged. I would think the opposite would be true."

"You don't understand, Dad. It's fun to do something daring, knowing there could be consequences. With me, it doesn't happen. Nobody wants to do anything with me. The worst that could happen is I'd get hit be a car or something."

Nicky got up and poured a glass of wine. "Well forgive me for providing a safe environment for my daughter. I'll see if I can arrange to have you hit by a speeding car—if that's what you want."

Rosa sat up thinking after Nicky went to bed. She thought about what the one mugger had said—about no one wanting to be mugged.

Maybe he had the right of it, she thought. For a couple of minutes tonight, she experienced what it was like to be mugged, and she didn't enjoy it.

Perhaps I don't have it so bad after all. Maybe being Nicky Fusco's daughter is a good thing.

A NEW CASE

Frankie got up and considered the day. It was both good and bad. Good because of his $700 Moreschi shoes and his Brioni pants and shirt. Bad because of the shit job he had—dealing with the scum of the earth.

Then an image of Kate popped into his head, and that made him smile. If there was anything besides new clothes that could bring a smile to his face, it was Kate or Alex.

Frankie finished breakfast, gave Kate a kiss and Alex a hug, then grabbed his coat as he walked out the door. "See you guys later."

"Don't forget about tonight," Kate hollered.

Frankie hesitated. "What's tonight?"

Kate sighed. "I knew you'd forget. We're going over the invitations. That's where I scratch off most of the people you want at the wedding, and you scratch off the ones on my list."

"At least nobody's scratching off the names on my list," Alex said.

"Why don't we get married in a civil ceremony? It would be easier, not to mention a lot less expensive."

"Because the woman decides where to get married, and since I'm the woman, I'll decide."

"Why is that?"

"Because it is. Now go to work and make a lot of money to pay for this elaborate wedding."

Frankie laughed. "Okay, my bride-to-be. I'll see you tonight. You too, Ace."

Frankie drove to the station in a relaxed state of mind. Everything was going great at home, and it wasn't even bad at work.

In the past, either life at work or life at home were in a state of flux; now both of them seemed stable. It was nice.

Lou greeted him at the top of the stairs. "Hope you're ready, Donovan."

"Ready for what?"

"A body washed up by Red Hook. Got the call a few minutes ago."

"Shit. All right, let me get more coffee. I'll meet you in the car. You're driving."

"You may not want me driving," Lou said. "I was up half the night with kids making noise, then woke at five to more noise. Damn kids."

"A lot of kids in your complex?"

"A lot? Probably ten thousand of 'em."

Frankie laughed. "That's your fault for living in such a shit-hole building."

"Well, maybe there aren't ten thousand, but there are a lot of kids."

Twenty minutes later, Lou pulled in to a warehouse fronting the river. He drove to the back side where two uniformed officers stood next to a body.

"What have you got?" Frankie asked as he got out of the car.

The shorter officer said, "Christ's sake, it looks like he was crucified. He's got holes in his hands and feet. Looks fresh though. A few days old at best."

"Any ID?" Lou asked.

The taller officer shook his head. "Nothing. But he doesn't look like a junkie or anything. Looks respectable."

"Respectable people get murdered too," Frankie said. "Anyone call the coroner?"

"She's on her way. Should be here any minute."

Five minutes later, Kate showed up, her whole crew with her. "I see you didn't come alone," Lou said.

"When they said they found a body in the river, I presumed it wasn't a fish, so I brought what I needed."

"Looks like you're still the smart ass you always were."

"I learned long ago that if you use your intelligence, it tends to stay with you. You should try it, Lou. You may even solve a few cases."

"Just look at the body and tell us what we've got. Looks like he was shot in the back of the head."

Kate knelt next to the body and examined it. A few times, she asked her assistants for instruments to probe the wounds.

Frankie knelt next to her. "The wounds in the hands and feet almost look like a crucifixion."

"Almost," Kate said, "but the entry wounds are wrong. It appears as if nails were driven into the backs of his hands, not the frontside. His feet were done separately."

"How do you know?"

"Look at the way the skin is pushed out on the palms of his hands. That's where the nails exited. If it had been done crucifixion style, it would have been the reverse. As far as the feet, the holes are in different spots, not overlapping."

"So this was torture?"

"Torture was part of it, but I don't think that's what killed him. I'd bet he died from the gunshot wounds to the back of the head. Looks like .22 caliber wounds. As far as the rest, he was definitely tortured. Your job is to figure out why."

"Okay. Get me what you can as quick as you can, then Lou and I will get to work."

"You better be quick. I can't imagine this guy didn't tell his captors what they wanted to know. That means something else will be going down."

Two days later, a missing persons report matching the ID of the dead man came in. It belonged to a Professor Reed from Columbia University.

Lou called the professor's wife, who came in and identified the body. She said she had no idea why anyone would want to kill him. The daughter had a different story to tell.

"Someone grabbed me coming out of the mall a few days ago. They only held me for a few hours, then let me go."

"Did you report this?" Lou asked.

She shook her head. "They said if I did, they'd kill me, so I didn't do anything."

"Did they ask you anything? Do anything odd?" Frankie asked.

"Nothing. They held me in the back of a van, then let me go a few hours later."

"And you have no idea what they may have wanted with your father?"

"No idea," she said. "He was a damn history professor, for God's sake. Who tortures a history professor?"

"That's what we're trying to figure out," Frankie said.

After the daughter left, Lou turned to Frankie. "We need to talk to his students. See if any of them know anything."

"Look at that. Using your head already. I'll have to tell Kate."

"Screw you, Donovan. Just for that, you're driving to Columbia."

On the way over, Frankie said, "You know they're going to want a warrant."

"Screw them too. Tell them it's an emergency. That some nutbag is targeting professors and we need to talk to Reed's students."

"You mean former students."

"Yea, say former students. When you put it that way, it always creates a sense of urgency."

"You're a wicked man, Mazzetti."

"You must have heard that from my wife."

Forty minutes later, they were in the administrator's office at Columbia. "We're going to need all the students who had class with Professor Reed," Frankie said.

"I can't do that," she said. "Not without a warrant."

"Look, the professor is dead," Lou said. "We have reason to believe that whoever did this is targeting other professors, so unless you want to be the one named as the person who hindered our investigation, I'd produce a list of students and quickly."

It didn't take her long to come up with a list. "This is organized by class times. It has everyone in it."

"Okay, thanks," Frankie said. "This helps. Your cooperation will be noted."

"I don't want to be noted. I don't even want to be mentioned. Just stop this lunatic before he hurts someone else."

"We will," Lou said. "This information will help."

On the way to the car, Frankie said, "That was pretty slick back there, Lou. I didn't know this guy was targeting professors."

"Do you know that he isn't?" Lou asked.

"I guess not," Frankie said.

"There you go. Case closed."

"And you accuse me of bending the rules."

"Whatever works," Lou said.

"I'll remember that," Frankie said. "Now let's get to work."

"Let's start tomorrow," Lou said. "I promised my wife I'd take her to dinner."

"What about the professors? I thought you were concerned the killer may be targeting others."

"Yea, and if we're lucky, he'll get a law professor. Now drop me off so I can get my car."

"You're a callous old shit."

"You're listening to Kate too much. I'm a softie at heart."

A short while later, Frankie dropped Lou off to get his car. "I hope your meal is bad," Frankie said.

"Yea, and I hope you have pot roast for dinner."

"I like Kate's pot roast," Frankie said.

"Tell me that in five years. And do it with a straight face."

Frankie laughed. "See you tomorrow, Lou."

ANOTHER LETTER

Shawna got into work early, eager to start the day. As she went through her mail, one letter stood out from the rest. It was done in similar fashion to the one she received about a week ago —the one that had threatened her if she continued writing the "wrong things."

A sick feeling rumbled in her gut, but she persevered and opened the envelope. The letter was written with the same odd font. Her anxiety grew worse as she read.

We told you to stop writing the wrong things. Now, you'll pay for it.

She picked the letter up and started toward Jackson's office, but stopped. All reporters receive threats at some time during their career —all good ones anyway. If she reported this to Jackson, he'd think her a lightweight. He may even frown on her reporting on the tough cases.

With that in mind, Shawna turned, walked back to her desk and placed the letter in the top drawer. She'd wait and see if things got worse. Right now, all she had were a couple of letters, and she didn't even know which articles they referred to.

She met Jackson and a few colleagues for drinks after work. They talked mostly about the business: what was changing, how the digital age was affecting reporting, and fortunately, she had the opportunity to bring up threats when one of the old-time reporters mentioned it.

"You ever been threatened?" Shawna asked.

"Hell yes," he said. "About half a dozen times. The first time was about twenty years ago. I received an anonymous call telling me to stop working on a case."

"What kind of case was it?" Shawna asked.

"It was a Wall Street scam," he said. "The guy was taking money—mostly from retired people—using the old "pump and dump" scam. And he was good. Had a damn silver tongue. I don't know why he resorted to a scam 'cause he could have made a fortune honestly."

"That seems to be a problem with a lot of them," Jackson said. "The more talented they are, the more they lean toward the con. Always looking to make a fast buck."

"Did anything ever happen with any of these threats?"

Fernandez started laughing. "I see where this is going. You got a threat, and you're poking around to see if you should be worried."

Shawna could almost feel the embarrassment. She imagined her face had turned several shades of red. "If it's that obvious, I guess I'd better not play poker."

"Definitely not," Jackson said. "Why don't you tell us what happened."

Shawna brushed her hand in the air. "I'm sure it's nothing. I just wanted to check."

"Nothing or not, tell us," Fernandez said. "I still remember my first threat. It turned out to be nothing, but at the time, it scared the shit out of me."

The older reporters confirmed that they'd been scared upon receiving their first warnings also. It made Shawna feel more comfortable.

"Come on, Shawna. Spit it out."

She took a sip of her drink and leaned forward. "Last week I got a letter that warned me to 'stop writing the wrong things.' I didn't even know which things they were talking about, so I ignored it. Then today, I got another letter, and it appears to be from the same person. It said:

We told you to stop writing the wrong things. Now, you'll pay for it.

"Was it handwritten?" Jackson asked.

Shawna shook her head. "No, it was typed, but it was typed using a different font. Unique. The envelope was handwritten though.

"Anything else strange?" Fernandez asked. "Any problems with your car, or signs of things disturbed at home?"

"God no," Shawna said. "You don't think they'd come into my home, do you?"

"They better not," Jackson said. "Not with that lunatic cop you used to date."

Shawna laughed. "You mean Donovan? That's been over for a long time. Besides, I swore when it ended that it was over. I have no intentions of calling him."

"Maybe you *should* call him," Fernandez said. "If you still have his contact, that is."

"No way. Maybe someone else, but not Donovan."

After a few more drinks, Hernandez said he had to go. Shortly afterward, they all decided to go home.

Shawna turned down offers for rides and opted to walk. "It's only a few blocks," she said. "And it's well lit. I'll be fine."

She unlocked and opened her door, then went to the sofa, took her shoes off, and kicked her feet up on the coffee table. As she did, she noticed an envelope sitting on the table. Her heart raced, fear gripping it. She picked it up and instantly recognized the writing. It was the same as the other two letters.

She moved quickly to the door, checked that it was locked, then sat back down on the sofa to read it.

By now you've figured out that we know where you live. We decided to provide a simple example by leaving this letter for you. It could have just as easily been a bullet through your window. Next time...who knows?

By the way, don't bother giving this letter to the cops. They won't get anything from it, and it will piss us off.

Shawna froze for a moment, then she reached into her purse and got the pepper spray she always carried. She stood and slowly made her way through the apartment, checking every room and every potential hiding place.

Once convinced no one was inside, she sat back down on the sofa. She read the letter again, focusing on the part that mentioned the bullet through the window. She got up, moved to the side, closed the blinds, then took a seat in a chair away from the window.

Her heart was beating so fast she could barely breathe. *What to do? What to do?*

After struggling with too many options, she did what she swore she'd never do—call Frankie for help.

A PLEA FOR HELP

Frankie wrote the last name on his side of the list for guests at the wedding. "Why is my side so much shorter than yours? I didn't know you had so many friends."

"I wouldn't call them all friends. Let's just say they're necessary invitations."

"I would say this is going to cost us a fortune, but you're worth it."

"Good Lord, you're finally getting it. Now you're almost broken in."

Frankie laughed, then said, "Kate, the phone's ringing. Would you grab it please?"

"Who the hell is calling this late? It's almost one o'clock in the morning."

"If you answer the damn phone, you'll know."

Kate reached behind her and grabbed the phone. "Hello?"

"I'm sorry, I was looking for Frankie Donovan. Did I reach the wrong number?"

"No, this is his number. Who is this?"

"Shawna Pavic. He might know me by my maiden name—Shawna Ellis."

A scowl formed on Kate's face. "Hang on; I'll get him."

She handed the phone to Frankie and whispered. "It's a woman. Shawna Ellis."

Frankie raised his eyebrows. "Shawna! What the hell is she doing calling? And at this hour." He took the phone from Kate. "Shawna? What's up? Is something wrong?"

"No. Yes. Hell, I don't know. That's why I'm calling."

Frankie winked at Kate, who seemed intensely interested. "Settle down. Back up and tell me what's going on."

"Someone's threatening me. Actually, it's beyond threats,; they broke into my apartment."

"Are you certain it's the same person?"

"It's the same person. They left me an identical letter to the ones they'd been mailing to me at work. And they as much as said: Look, I can get into your house."

"When did this happen?"

"I found the note when I got home a few hours ago. The first letter came to my work address a little more than a week ago."

"Did you report the break-in?"

"I thought that's what I was doing."

"No, Shawna, you're calling a friend. This isn't my department."

"Can't you do *something?*"

"There's not a damn thing I can do right now, but I'll tell you what you should do. Call a cab, wait until you can see it outside, then take it to a hotel. Get a room for the night, then come to the station in the morning. And bring the letter and whatever other evidence you have."

"Will you be there?" Shawna asked.

Frankie noticed Kate was giving him a sideways glance. "No, Shawna, I won't be there. I just caught a homicide, and I need to be working that. But when you get to the station, ask for Sherri Miller. Tell her I sent you, in case I haven't talked to her yet."

"Sherri Miller?"

"Yea, she's good. She worked with me for a couple of years."

"She's in homicide?"

"She used to be, but she moved out not long after she got shot. I still talk to her, and I see her at the station."

"Is this a brush-off, Frankie? Am I being shoved aside because of … you know, what we had?"

"No, Shawna, this is not a brush-off. Sherri's good, and she's a friend. She's invited to my wedding for God's sake."

"Wedding? You're getting married?"

"Yes, I'm getting married. And yes, my lovely bride-to-be is the one who answered the phone."

"Who's the lucky person? Do I know her?"

"Probably. She's the medical examiner—Kate Burns."

"Kate Burns! I know her. I interviewed her a couple of years ago. Well, good luck to both of you. And don't forget to say something to your friend."

Frankie hung up the phone and looked to Kate.

"Was that Shawna, the news reporter?" she asked.

Frankie nodded. "It was. She said she interviewed you a few years ago."

Kate nodded. "Young, brown hair, gorgeous? Am I on the right track?"

"I don't know if there's a safe way to answer that."

"So I'm on the right track?"

Frankie nodded again.

"Now I'm jealous. What did she want?"

"She's being threatened about something she wrote, and they broke into her apartment to make a point."

Kate sighed. "As much as every bone in my body protests this, I'm going to say it anyway. You should help her. I know Sherri's good, but you're better. If someone went to the trouble of breaking into her apartment, it's serious."

"I don't know, Kate. I think Sherri can handle it."

"I'm sure she can, Frankie, but you'd never forgive yourself if you let Sherri take care of it and something happened to Shawna."

Frankie lit a smoke and went and sat in his chair. "I'll think about it after I talk to Sherri."

"Think hard. I don't want this on my conscience."

"All right. Let's go to bed. I'll figure it out in the morning."

Frankie thought about what to do all the way to work. He left a message for Sherri, then thought some more. He still hadn't made up his mind by the time he arrived at the station. After trudging around for a few hours, he walked down the hall or more coffee. Mazzetti was sitting at the table.

"Donovan, what the hell's wrong with you today? You've been walking around like a damn zombie."

"Nothing."

"Don't give me that *nothing* shit. Something's bugging you. Is it Kate? Wedding date getting too close?"

"Nothing like that. You remember Shawna?"

"Shawna. Of course, I remember Shawna. Every time I think of her my dick gets hard."

"Lou, your dick hasn't been hard in five years."

"Hey, wait a minute, Donovan. It's been more like three years, but that's between me and the girls I dream about."

Frankie laughed. "Well, Shawna's getting threats from someone for an article she wrote. I'm thinking of giving it to Miller, but I'm worried about it. What if something happens to her?"

"Miller or Shawna?"

"Shawna. Miller can take care of herself."

"Then take the case on yourself. I'm gonna have this other case busted in a matter of days."

"I know, but I'm also concerned about Kate."

"Kate jealous?"

"Probably, but it's not that. I'm not concerned about her or her jealousy; I'm more concerned about how I'll be around Shawna. I don't want to ruin things with Kate."

"Okay, now I've got you. Can't say I blame you for feeling that way either. Shawna is the kind of woman who makes you want to do things regardless of the consequences."

"Exactly. It's like a gambler vacationing in Atlantic City or Vegas."

"Or an alcoholic eating lunch at the local pub."

Frankie tossed his coffee cup in the trash. "I can't risk it, Lou. I can't."

"Then don't risk it. Let Miller run with the case. She'll get to the bottom of it."

"What if she doesn't?"

"Then you're still solid. Either way, you're good. If Miller does a good job, your problem is solved. And if Miller screws it up, your problem is still solved."

"Yea, but it would be solved because Shawna is dead."

"Then you'd have a murder case to solve and nothing to worry about with Kate. See, it'll work out fine."

Frankie shook his head. "Anyone ever tell you that you're an ass?"

"Yea, but I didn't pay attention. Being an ass is how I've lived as long as I have."

Miller waked in the coffee room a moment later. "Frankie, I got a message that you wanted to see me. What's up?"

"I've got something I wanted you to check out.. A reporter friend of mine has been getting threats due to something she wrote, and she asked me to look into it."

"Don't reporters get threats often?"

"They do, but this seems more serious than most. It started with letters to her office, but now they've broken into her home."

"Damn. Okay, give me her name and address, and I'll get right on it."

Frankie handed her a folder. "It's all in here. Thanks, Miller. I appreciate it. I'd have done it myself, but Lou and I just caught a new case."

"No problem. Timing's perfect as I'm just finishing one up. I'll call her today."

"Miller, you're the best. Thanks again."

"As I said, no problem. See ya, Frankie. And please take care of Mazzetti. He looks like he's got one foot in the grave."

Mazzetti sat upright. "Thanks, Miller. You could look good too—if you had four more pounds of makeup on."

After Sherri left, Mazzetti got a bottle of water from the fridge and sat back down. "Okay, Donovan. I solved that problem for you, now what are we doing with the professor?"

ANALYZING THE LETTER

$\mathcal{A}$s she drove through Williamsburg, Shawna got a call. "Hello?"

"Shawna, this is Detective Sherri Miller. Frankie Donovan asked me to give you a call."

"Damn, Frankie is quick. I told him I'd come to the station this morning; in fact, I'm on my way now."

"Do you have the letter?"

"I brought all of them; there are three. I'll be at your place in about five minutes."

"Okay, just tell the desk sergeant you're here to see me."

Ten minutes later, Shawna sat with Sherri while she examined the letters. "The only one who's touched them is me," Shawna said. "And that was only when I opened them. The rest of the time, I wore gloves, the same kind you're wearing now."

"That's good," Sherri said. "I doubt if we'll get any prints or DNA, but it's worth a shot. It doesn't hurt to be cautious."

"The problem with this is I don't know which article or articles they're talking about. It could be any of them. Even the seemingly innocent ones usually name someone as a guilty party to something."

"We'll have to take a look. In the meantime, let me ask a few questions. First, did you report this to your local precinct?"

"No, I called Frankie, and he said to talk to you."

"They're going to want to handle this, and since it's their turf, they may have a better idea of who it may be."

"But I don't—"

"Hang on, Shawna. I suggest filing a report with them, but in the meantime, I'll continue working it. Tell me who's working your case in Manhattan, and I'll coordinate with them."

"That won't be a problem?" Shawna asked.

Sherri shook her head. "That won't be a problem." She placed her hand on Shawna's shoulder. "Don't worry. We'll get to the bottom of this."

Shawna tried smiling, but she didn't succeed. "Okay, thanks. Tell me what else you need."

"Manhattan will want to see your apartment while it's reasonably fresh, so file that report as quickly as possible. And as soon as you can, I'll need to see all the articles you wrote in the past four weeks. We'll start with that. I'm guessing it's something you wrote in the past couple of weeks, but we'll check four weeks to be safe; I can't imagine it going back prior to four weeks."

"All right. I'll send them over, but I'll need—"

Sherri handed her a business card. "Email address and phone number are on the card. My cell number is on there too. Call me at any time."

Shawna looked at the card, then placed it in her purse. "Thank you, Detective. I'll stop by the Manhattan precinct on my way home."

"Not working today?"

"No. I was too upset after discovering they had been in my home, so I stayed at a hotel last night, and I took off today."

"Then you may want to wait until the police have gone through your home before going there. The less that's disturbed, the better."

"Do you think they'll find something?"

Sherri smiled. "Shawna, you've been reporting a long time. You know as well as I do that the chances are we'll find nothing, but you can't be sure. If you don't have anywhere to go, you're welcome to come back here."

"I'll be okay, Detective. I'll file the report, then go to the office and send you the articles."

"I thought you took off today."

"I did, but I need to get this done. You'll have the files before noon."

"Before you leave, I'd like to let the forensic team have a look at the original envelopes and letters, then they can make copies of them. Manhattan will want to see the originals too."

"Let's get it done," Shawna said. "I'll follow you."

Shawna waited several hours while the forensic team examined the letters, then they made copies and sent her on her way.

"Keep them in the envelope until you get to Manhattan," the tech said and handed her his card. "And you can tell them we already checked for prints and DNA, so they can call me to get results."

"But you still think I should go there?"

"Absolutely," the tech said. "It's their jurisdiction, so they'll want to run the investigation. Just tell 'em that Donovan is a relative or something and that's why you called him. If you say that, they won't get worked up about it."

Shawna left Brooklyn and headed to Manhattan to file a report. An hour later, she was on her way home with an officer who inspected her apartment. After he was done checking the lock on the door, inspecting the windows, and dusting several areas for prints, he said he was going to leave.

Shawna walked out with him and went to her office where she emailed the files that Sherri wanted regarding the articles she had written.

Shawna took some time reviewing them. Most were standard, but a few drew her interest. Two, in particular, stood out. *Frankie will want to see this.*

Frankie stopped by Sherri's office after receiving her message. "What's up, Miller? Get anything on the threats?"

"Yes and no. The techs weren't able to get any evidence, but there are a couple of articles Shawna was writing about that raised some flags."

"Like what?"

"She writes a lot of inflammatory stuff, but two stood out: one on money laundering, and one dealing with corruption in the construction business—concrete, in particular."

Frankie nodded. "Organized crime."

"That's right," Sherri said. "My best guess is that those articles will piss off the Russians and the Italians, or both."

"Will? The articles haven't bee run yet?"

"They're written and approved, but they haven't run, or hadn't run when she received the note."

"If it's one of those articles, that means whoever doesn't want them to run has inside contacts."

"Having inside contacts could point to either one of them, Donovan.

You know that. It may favor the Italians, but it doesn't preclude the Russians."

"Goddamn problems all the time," Frankie said. "I need to talk to Shawna."

"And tell her what?" Sherri asked. "She doesn't strike me as somebody who's gonna back off."

"She better," Frankie said and turned to leave the office.

Frankie called Shawna while he drove. "Shawna, where are you?"

"I'm home, why?"

"Stay there. I'm on my way."

"What for? Did you find something out?"

"Just stay put until I get there. For once in your life, listen."

Half an hour later, Frankie knocked on Shawna's door.

"Frankie!, that was quick."

"I read the articles you gave to Sherri."

"All of them?" Shawna asked. "That was even quicker."

"Don't be an ass. I'm talking about the two that matter—the money laundering and the concrete."

"Why do you think only those two matter?"

"Because they are bound to piss off people you shouldn't piss off."

"Such as?"

"You know damn right well who I'm talking about. I'm curious, though, why you didn't mention your ex in the article about money laundering. Wasn't he sent away for that? And wasn't he affiliated with the Russians?"

"You know he was sent away. You were helping to keep my bed warm while he did his time."

"I'd ask if you knew he was released a month ago, but I'm certain that you knew."

"And if I did?"

Frankie locked onto her eyes and stared. "Did you write that article to piss off the Russians, or to rehash your ex's embarrassment?"

"Let's say I was killing two birds with one tiny stone."

"A stone that could get you killed, Shawna. You need to lay off this shit."

"That's the last thing I expected from you as far as advice goes. You've always been against organized crime. What happened? Did they get in your pockets?"

"I ought to smack you," Frankie said. "You know I wouldn't do that. If it were me, I'd take them on, but I'm not telling you to take them on. You'll end up dead. They may think twice about killing a detective, but they won't think more than a millisecond about killing a reporter, especially one who's seen better days as far as popularity goes."

"Fuck you too, *Detective* Donovan. I don't see you wearing a captain's badge."

"No, you don't. And you never will. I don't want a captain's badge, and I probably couldn't get one anyway. But I don't regret it. Learn to be happy with what you've got, Shawna. That was always your problem. You always wanted what you didn't have."

"I guess some things never change," Shawna said.

"I'm telling you, Shawna. Lay off. These people do not mess around. They'll stuff you in a barrel and toss you in the East River."

She sighed. "All right. I'll lay off, but just this once."

"Smart choice," Frankie said.

"And thanks, Frankie."

"For what?"

"When I heard you were getting married, I was almost jealous—almost. You just reminded me why I shouldn't be."

Frankie grabbed her and pulled her to him. He leaned in to kiss her, then stopped and stared. "I don't know if it's some newfound willpower or if it's guilt, but something kept me from kissing you. I still want to, but I'm glad I didn't."

Shawna lowered her head. "Me too, Frankie. I couldn't have stopped at a kiss, and Kate deserves better."

"Yes, she does," Frankie said. "I'm glad you recognize that. Anyway, be sensible and lay off those stories. At the very least, lay off them for now."

On the way home, Frankie thought about what Shawna said regarding Kate. What an ass he was. He almost ruined it.

When he got home, he asked Kate to take a walk with him.

"Take a walk? What wrong with you? You haven't asked me to walk with you in six months."

Frankie stretched his hand toward her. "Come on, Kate. We'll only be a few minutes."

"If this is to break off the engagement, you can do that here," she said.

"Don't be an ass," Frankie said and opened the door.

Once they were on the sidewalk outside, Frankie leaned close and said, "Kate, there's nobody I love more than you."

"But..." she said, raising her eyebrows.

"But I almost blew it today. I had to see Shawna about those letters..."

"And...?"

"And one thing led to another, and I almost kissed her."

Kate closed her eyes tightly. "That's all you did was *almost* kiss?"

"Yeah, I wanted to do more, but then I thought of you and Alex. I'm sorry it happened. It won't happen again, but I had to tell you. I didn't want to start off with an unspoken lie."

They walked almost half a block in silence. "Well?" Frankie said.

Kate stopped and turned to face him. "I despise you for wanting to kiss her, but I love you for telling me about it."

Frankie exhaled and squeezed her hands. "We're okay, then?"

"I don't know about *okay*, but we're better than we were ten minutes ago. Now I know I can trust you to be honest with me."

"I will always be honest, Kate. I promise."

"Is your promise to me as good as that ridiculous oath you and Nicky have?"

"Absolutely," Frankie said.

Kate smiled. "In that case, we're okay."

THE STUDENTS KNOW

Frankie pulled into the lot just as Lou was getting out of his car. "No need to go inside, Lou. Hop in."

"Where are we going? I haven't had coffee yet."

"That's your fault. I had mine hours ago."

Lou buckled his seat belt and said, "That's because Kate made it for you, and she only did that because she wants to get married. My wife is long past that emotion."

"I'll say it again, that's your fault."

"Wait until you've been married for thirty years. Then you'll cry for station-house coffee."

"Lou, there are a lot of things I might cry for, but station-house coffee isn't one of them."

"We'll see about that. Mark this day on your calendar and in 2048 you'll look back on it and say, 'A wise man once told me I'd cry for this shit.' And you'll say it just before drinking it."

"That's why I like working with you, Lou. You're full of shit, and you say something to make me laugh every day."

"Glad I can help. Now you want to tell me where we're going—besides a coffee shop that is."

"Now that we've got a list of names at the university, I thought we'd better check them out."

"Remind me of what we're checking out."

"See if we can find out why the professor was tortured. I'm guessing one of two of his students may know."

"And what makes you think they'll share this forbidden knowledge with us?"

"Because they don't want to end up like the professor. I'm sure you can spin some kind of tale that would back that up."

"You have a lot of faith in an old man who hasn't had his coffee."

Frankie laughed. "Don't worry. You'll get your coffee. There's a shop by the university. We'll stop there."

Twenty minutes later Lou and Frankie were in the classroom. "How you want to play this, Donovan? One at a time or the whole class?"

"We'll have to start with the whole class. There are too many to interview one at a time. Besides, if we give out cards to everyone, we could get lucky and have someone call us."

"I hope you got a lot of cards. I only got a few."

"Some of us are prepared, Lou."

"Yea, and some of us are still sleepy."

Two classes went by without a hint of cooperation, then shorty after the third class, Frankie's phone rang. "Donovan."

"Detective," I'm one of the students from the first class. You asked for help regarding the professor. What do you need?"

"I presume you don't want to come in."

"No, I'd prefer if we could keep this anonymous."

"No problem. Here's the situation. I didn't tell everything during class, but the professor was tortured before he was killed—like someone wanted to try to get information out of him. You have any idea who might want to do that, or what they would be looking for?"

"I don't know who would want to do it, but I have an idea what they might be looking for."

"What would that be?"

"About a year ago, I heard rumors that Professor Reed was using students to smuggle things into the country. Illegal things. I don't know if it was drugs or diamonds or what, but I heard he did it often. My guess is that someone found out about it and wanted in on it."

"But you don't know who that might be?"

"Not a clue."

"How about the students? Any idea who they might be? I'd hate for anything to happen to them."

"No idea about that either. Like I said, it was just rumors."

"Okay, that's good enough for now. You've been a big help. If you think of anything else, give us a call."

"I will. Thanks."

Lou stood next to Frankie. When he hung up the phone, Lou said, "Got something?"

Frankie nodded. "He said he was in on the first class. He didn't want to talk, but he did."

"What's that supposed to mean?"

"He said the professor was smuggling something into the country using his students. If the kid was telling the truth, all we need to do is check and see which students have been out of the country for the past year or two, then talk to them. I"ll recognize the voice when I hear it. Besides, unless I miss my guess, this kid will be scared shitless. He won't be hard to identify."

"My guess is organized crime—of one ethic persuasion or another—is involved."

"That's always your guess, Lou, so forgive me if I ignore you."

"What bright ideas do you have?"

"Finishing up with Reed's other classes to see if we get any more leads, and then going back to the station to see who's been traveling."

Frankie and Lou spoke to two more classes, but at the end of the day, had nothing more to show for it. The only lead they'd gotten so far had been the one from the anonymous caller.

On the drive back, Lou rolled down the window and lit a smoke. "What do we know so far, Donovan?"

"Since he said he was in the first class, we can presume he wasn't. And since he called shortly after the third class, it's a good guess that's the one he was in, though it could still be the second class."

"And since he mentioned drugs and diamonds, the chances are it isn't one of those things," Lou said.

"Exactly," Frankie said. "That doesn't leave much that he'd be smuggling in using students. Maybe ancient artifacts?"

"I don't know about that," Lou said. "They keep track of that stuff pretty closely. It might be difficult to smuggle them on a regular basis."

"What's your guess then?"

"I don't know," Lou said. "Based on who's doing the smuggling, I'd vote against anything related to violence which rules out human trafficking, drugs, diamonds, arms, money, and all the stuff like that."

"Doesn't leave much," Frankie said.

"Could be food," Lou said.

"Food? Why the hell does anyone want to smuggle food?"

"Remember that case a while back where the guy was smuggling rare white truffles from Italy? Or the one where someone was smuggling expensive wine from France?"

"No. I'm not familiar with either one."

"Yea, it's a big deal. The truffles sold legally for $3,600 a pound, and they could be dumped off at almost any decent restaurant for not much less in cash, so getting rid of them wasn't hard. With the wine, they put fake labels on rare vintages to avoid the import fees and license requirements."

"Damn! I may have found a new occupation, Lou."

"You better stick to detective work. You're not very good at it but knowing you, you'd eat the damn truffles and drink the wine before you sold them."

"When is it you're retiring?"

"A year ago. Now quit bugging me. You're beginning to sound like my wife. I'll retire when I retire. How's that for a definitive answer?"

"About what I'd expect from you. If you don't turn your papers in soon, I'm gonna do it. I need a young partner, and preferably a pretty one."

"You had Miller, and you got her shot. Now quit complaining and get back to the office so I can solve this crime. I'm tired of pulling your weight."

Frankie got a parking spot close to the office entrance, and he and Lou got out and went inside. After going upstairs, he handed Carol a list of names. "Carol, I need you to get someone to cross-reference the names on this list with anyone who's gone out of the country in the past year. I want everyone who's left, including dates and how many times." Frankie walked away, then turned back. "Oh, and I need it yesterday, please."

"Good thing you said please."

"How long do you think it'll take?"

"If it were me doing the work, you'd have it tomorrow. With the group they have working on research now, you'll be lucky to have it in three days."

"See if you can rush them?"

"You afraid Mazzetti's gonna die?"

Frankie laughed. "He might—if I don't kill him first."

"Go home and help Kate plan this wedding. I have high expectations: a good band, good food, and a lot of booze. I don't go to many weddings, so you better do it right."

"You'll have to take that up with Kate; it's her department. My job is just to show up."

"Bullshit, Donovan. Those days are long gone. Now go home and get busy."

"Yes, ma'am," Frankie said. "See you tomorrow."

THE TRAVEL REPORTS

"That report in yet, Carol?"

"No, Donovan, that report is *not* in yet, but I'll check on it as soon as the clock strikes and lets me know it's a decent hour."

"Yea, well when it does strike, tell them they better have that goddamn report today. I'm tired of waiting."

"Frankie, it's only been two days," Carol said.

"I know how long it's been. I'm reminded every day because I don't have Professor Reed's killer yet."

"All right, I'll get on it. And you better get some coffee. You sound like you haven't had any."

CAROL PICKED up the phone and dialed.

"Research."

"Sandi, this is Carol over at Homicide. Do you have that report yet on the student's travel?"

"Almost."

"Well, you better get it done. Donovan was asking about it, and he's got a stick up his ass this morning."

"All right, I'll put everyone on it. We should have it done by noon."

JUST BEFORE NOON, an alert sounded on Carol's computer—an email had arrived. She checked and saw it was the report from Sandi. She printed it out and took it to Frankie.

"Here it is, Donovan. Hope this puts you in a better mood."

"Get the hell out of here," Frankie said. "And thanks."

"Is that what we've been waiting for?" Lou asked.

"Supposedly," Frankie said. "Let's take a peek and see what's at the bottom of the box."

Lou put his coffee cup on the desk and stared. "Was that a reference to Crackerjacks?"

"Did it make me look old?" Frankie asked.

"Not old—ancient," Lou said.

"Just look at the damn report," Frankie said.

When he finished scanning the report, Lou said, "Depending on how you look at things, this is either a good report or a bad one."

"What the hell does that mean?"

"The report says only eight of the students went out of the country during the time we asked about. Two went to France. Three to Germany. And three to Italy."

"What about the ones who went to Mexico? It's a likely place to smuggle drugs from."

Lou shook his head. "I don't buy it. Drugs are too easy to get on the streets. If somebody wanted drugs, they could pick them up within hours. Probably cheaper too. They bring them in by the truckload down in Texas. Hell, in California and Arizona, they build tunnels to cross the border with them. I'm betting it's one of these eight."

"Let's find out," Frankie said. "I think we should bring them all in and have a chat."

"Together or separately?" Lou asked.

"Separately. We need to see if we can crack them when they're alone."

"I'll have them here the day after tomorrow."

"Damn, Lou, you're ambitious."

"It's amazing what a few good uniformed officers can do. And if they can't do it, I'll sic Carol on them."

"And they said you were ready for retirement. I think you're aiming for the lieutenant's badge."

SHERRI MILLER WALKED into Frankie's office holding a folder filled with papers. "Got a minute, Donovan?"

"For you, of course. What have you got?"

"I've been thinking about those articles I showed you."

"And?"

"And some others could be of concern to certain people, but the two I showed you stick out."

"I know," Frankie said. "We already talked about that."

"The curious thing is they didn't get printed until *after* she got the note. I know we talked about that too and considering who the articles are about, one of those groups having inside contacts is not surprising."

"Go on."

"One of them names a handful of corrupt politicians who are dealing with the Russians, and two of them name corrupt officials in the pockets of the Mafia, specifically Dominic Mangini."

"Your point, Sherri?"

"My point is that maybe you can check this out with some of your contacts. I know—"

"You're asking me to talk to Dominic Mangini."

"And Manny Russo," she said.

"No other articles she wrote looked as if it might instigate this kind of response?"

"None," Sherri said. "I checked all of them several times."

"How far did you go back?"

"I only asked her for the past month. If it was something she wrote before that, I don't know why they'd wait so long."

Frankie held up the papers Sherri had given him. "But how can you figure these articles if they weren't even published?"

"Come on, Donovan. Don't try to test me; besides, we've been through this. If Dominic Mangini is doing this, finding out about something going on inside the papers isn't going to be an obstacle. He has people inside the police, which means he has people inside the papers too. He probably knew what Shawna was writing about before she did."

"What about the Russians?"

Sherri looked to Lou. "How did I know he'd dismiss Mangini so quickly?"

"It *could* be the Russians, but I don't think they have the connections inside like Mangini does."

"All right, here's what we'll do. I'll talk to Mangini. We'll either list him as a suspect or rule him out. If we rule him out, we know where to go."

Lou chuckled. "You might as well plan on going to see the Russians now, Miller. There's no way Donovan is going to come back and say Mangini is a suspect."

"Pay no attention to Mazzetti; besides, it could be that the threats are from somebody else. It doesn't have to be organized crime."

"You've got a point, Donovan. Tonight while I'm praying for my four-story brownstone on a corner in Brooklyn Heights, I'll ask for guidance on who we should be looking for."

A TRIP TO NEW YORK

I woke at the regular time, went for a run, and got to work before anyone. I needed to make sure everything was in place before I left.

After leaving a few notes for Moresco regarding the bid he might be working on, I jotted down Bug's number and left. Rosa was waiting with hot coffee when I got home.

"Morning, Dad. You ready?"

"I'm ready. How about you?"

"I can't wait. I've always wanted to go to New York. What's it like?"

"Like no other city," I said. "But you'll see. You have to experience it. Words don't do it justice."

IT TOOK us about three hours to get to the city, but before long, we were parked near Frankie's apartment.

"This is it? This is where he lives?" Rosa asked.

"This is it," I said. "And they're expecting us. I think Kate took off work today."

"Be on your best behavior," Angela said.

We went inside and were surprised to find not only Kate but Alex too. "Hey, Alex, I wasn't expecting you to be here."

He gave me a hug, then gave hugs to Angela and Rosa and said hi to Dante.

"C'mon, Rat. You should've known I'd be home; you didn't think I'd miss a chance at any of Mrs. Fusco's cooking."

Angela gave him a big squeeze. "Alex, if you call him Rat, you can at least call me Angela."

Kate frowned and looked sideways at Alex. "Mr. and Mrs. Fusco will do, Alex. Now go out and help Rosa with the bags."

Angela walked over and embraced Kate. "Kate, we've talked on the phone but never met. I'm Angela."

"Excuse the shocked expression, but I'm trying to figure out how Nicky got so lucky. You're gorgeous."

"You're going to make me blush, Kate. Frankie is the lucky one. And it's about time he settled down."

Kate laughed. "I'll have to agree with you on the 'settling down,' Angela. I've worked hard on it, but truth be known, I think it was Alex who tipped the scales. Frankie loves that boy."

Angela sat at the kitchen table. "I know he does. I saw the way they interacted when he came to Wilmington.

"You want something to drink?" Kate asked.

"Nothing for me. But if you can give me directions to a store, I want to pick up a few things for dinner."

"Nonsense," Kate said. "We'll go out somewhere."

Angela shook her head. "I'll hear nothing of it. We're your guests; besides, Alex is expecting us to make something, and Rosa would be disappointed if she didn't get to show off her skills. She's a really good cook. Not to mention that Dante is a fussy eater, and Rosa's cooking is almost all he'll eat."

"I've heard about her cooking," Kate said. "It's all Alex talked about when he came back from Wilmington. It set a high bar for me to meet."

"When do you want to go to the store?" Angela asked.

"No sense in waiting," Kate said. "Let's beat the traffic. Tell me what you need, and that'll decide which store we go to."

As they walked out the door, I could hear Angela telling her, "If you're okay with sandwiches, all we need are the ingredients for spaghetti sauce and some bologna."

As they walked down the hall, Kate asked, "Bologna? What the hell do you need that for?"

"It's for a quick and easy meal that we love—fried bologna sandwiches."

"Fried bologna? That sounds like a recipe from way down South."

"If you're talking southern Italy, it is. First, you make the sauce and let it simmer in the pan. Then you fry the bologna, mix it with the sauce, and add garlic and Romano cheese as needed. Let it simmer for a while, then put it on crispy rolls and eat it."

"Sounds good when you describe it," Kate said.

"It is good. Most people don't expect it to be, but I haven't met anyone yet who's been disappointed."

"That makes our trip easier," Kate said. "We can go to the deli down the street. They'll have everything we need."

Twenty minutes later, they were back at Frankie's house. Rosa was cooking the sauce, and Angela was cooking the bologna.

~

FRANKIE CAME HOME a few minutes later. He opened the door, sniffed the air and said, "Is that Mamma Rosa's fried bologna I smell?"

"Sure as shit is, Bugs," I said.

Frankie raced over. "Rat! I wasn't expecting you until tomorrow. When did you get in?"

"A couple of hours ago. I thought we'd surprise you."

"And surprise me you did. Have a seat. Want a beer?"

"I'll pass on the beer, but I'll take a glass of wine if you have it."

"Coming right up," Kate said. "Since Angela and Rosa are doing the cooking, the least I can do is pour the wine."

I sat on the sofa. "What's up, Bugs? What are you working on?"

"Got an odd case. A college professor's body washed up from the river. But that's not the odd part. He was shot, but he was also tortured—like they wanted to get some information he had."

"Got any idea what they wanted?"

"Not much," Frankie said. "We're checking into his students, and we've got one lead that he was using students to smuggle things into the country. But so far, we've gotten no usable hits on who those students may be."

"Got any suspects?"

"Besides an anonymous caller and a list of a few hundred kids, we've got eight kids who took trips to Europe during the past two years."

"Eight is a number you can work with," I said.

"Why? You got any ideas?"

"Not yet, but I'll think on it."

"Give it some thought," Frankie said. "In the meantime, I think I see the ladies serving dinner." He stood and headed toward the kitchen. "As far as I'm concerned, the professor's killer can wait."

"Everything can wait," Alex said. "When Angie… I mean Mrs. Fusco, puts dinner on the table, I'm eating."

"Smart move," Frankie said.

About halfway through the meal, Alex said, "I can't believe this is bologna. It tastes good."

"Add more Romano cheese if you need it," Rosa said. "Mom never lets me put enough cheese in it."

"How many times do I have to tell you, Rosa? Cheese is like salt. You put enough in when you're cooking to flavor it, but then let the person decide if they want more. They can always add more, but they can't take it away."

Rosa rolled her eyes and put a plate in front of Frankie. "I hope you like it, Uncle Frankie."

"I'm sure I will, Rosa. I haven't tasted anything of yours I didn't like."

"You need to get your list down to one suspect, maybe two," I said.

"No kidding, Detective Fusco. That's what I'm trying to do."

If you don't find a way using your normal interrogation methods, take a look at the bank accounts of all your suspects. Look for deposits that are above the normal, then see who traveled just prior to that."

"I don't think you understand, Nicky. A lot of these kids come from money, so big bank accounts are the norm."

"I understand, but the ones who come from money would likely be making deposits on a regular basis, not in big chunks."

"That would be a lot of legwork, and it would take a lot of warrants."

"Then find another way to get the information. I'm sure you know somebody who has contacts inside the banks. You don't need the information to use in courts, just to know who to go after."

"I don't know that many people."

"If you don't know the right people, I know who does."

Frankie took another bite of his sandwich, then stared. "You don't mean Dominic?"

I smiled. "Use whatever information you need to get the job done. If you don't like dealing with Dominic, use Manny. Either of them will be able to get the information you need."

Frankie shook his head. "I don't know, Nicky. I don't like it. I don't want to owe those guys favors; besides, Dominic may be involved with another case."

"One you're working?"

Frankie shook his head. "Not one I'm working, but one I'm close to."

"Then let me get the information. You can't have a problem with that."

"Let you get what?" Angela asked. "Nicky, I don't want you involved with anything—especially anything to do with Dominic Mangini. Mind your own business while we're on vacation."

"Relax, Angie, It would just be helping Bugs get some information. Nothing to worry about."

"I'm not concerned about *what* you're getting Bugs; it's *who* you're getting it from. You once told me that asking a favor from the guys at the smoke shop was dangerous. From what I've heard said about Dominic Mangini, he's a lot worse than they are."

I swallowed his last bite of sandwich, then looked at Angela. "Babe, just because a person has done a few bad things in life doesn't mean he's a bad person. Dominic has his good side. You just have to learn how to get on it."

Angela wiped her mouth with a napkin. "All right, Nicky, we'll talk later. This is not the time or place to discuss it."

Frankie looked at me and smiled. "Sounds like your course of action has been cut off."

"We'll see. Just slip me a list of who you need the info on. I'll take care of it."

A VISIT WITH AN OLD FRIEND

I got up early and was enjoying my coffee when Bugs stepped into the kitchen.

"Rat, what the hell are you doing up? You're supposed to be on vacation."

"I'm up early every day, Bugs. Need to go for my run, then I thought I'd see an old friend."

Bugs reached into his pocket and handed me a piece of paper. "Speaking of which, here's that list of names I was telling you about. There are eight of them. Any help you can get would be great."

I stuck the list in my pocket and smiled. "Don't worry. He won't know who it's for."

"Good. I gotta go to work. See you tonight."

I waited a few minutes while I finished my coffee, then left a note for Angie before leaving. After that, I headed for Dominic's house. It had been almost two years since I'd seen him. I hoped I was still welcome.

FORTY MINUTES LATER—AS I took the exit for the Bronx—I placed a reminder on my iPhone to pick up bagels for everyone. I had left a note saying I would, so I needed to deliver. Ten minutes after that, I was knocking on Dominic's door.

Dominic opened the door himself. "Niccolo Fusco. I haven't seen you in two years."

"Your memory is still sharp, Mr. Mangini." I opened my coat showing him I wasn't armed.

"No need for that. I don't frisk guests, even uninvited ones."

"I'll get right to the point, Mr. Mangini. I'm here to ask a favor."

"A favor. I like favors. I deal in them frequently."

"I was hoping this one could be a friendly favor, the kind you don't have to pay back."

"Friendly favor? I think I've heard of them, but I'm not accustomed to dealing with them."

"Come on, Dominic, it's just a little information."

"Information is a valuable thing, Niccolo. I think you know that. By the way, my manners are atrocious. Would you like some espresso?"

I smiled. "Of course, thank you. I have a suggestion. How about I tell you what I want, and when you do it, you can ask me a favor if you want. If you don't think it requires a favor, that'll be good."

Dominic called for his "assistant" to make espresso for two, then leaned back in his chair. "Ask what you will. I'm listening."

I started to reach for my list, then thought better. "I have a piece of paper in my pocket that I need to get. Is that all right?"

Dominic laughed. "Of course. Go ahead."

I pulled out the list and handed it to Dominic. "There are eight names on that list. I need to know which banks they use, and ideally, records of any deposits within the date range next to the names."

"So, this is a favor you ask for your detective friend?"

I was going to lie but thought better of it. "Yes, it is."

"Why didn't he ask me himself?"

"He was afraid to ask because he didn't want to owe you a favor."

"Yet you risk it? Why?"

"Because he and I are friends."

"That is perhaps the only acceptable answer. Go on, tell me what else you need."

"That's it. Just what I said."

Dominic stared. "So little?"

"It's not so little if you don't have the right connections."

"I guess not," Dominic said. "Regardless, consider it done, though it may take a few days. Leave me your cell number, and I'll call you when the information is ready."

"What's it gonna cost as far as favors go?"

Dominic smiled as he opened the door. "Let me see what it costs me to get what you need. I'll tell you afterward."

I picked up a dozen bagels on the way back to Bug's apartment and did a quick run before I went in in order to keep up appearances.

"Dad, where have you been?" Rosa asked. "You've been gone forever."

"I went running, then got these delicious bagels," I said and held out the bag.

"Those bagels better be good," Angie said. "You took so long to get them that I was ready to start cooking without you."

"How about we eat quickly, then head out to see some sites. I know Rosa has got a full list. Maybe we can scratch a few off; besides, I'd love for Dante to see New York at his age."

"Oh my God, I'm ready. I don't need to eat," Rosa said.

"Maybe *you* don't," Angela said, "but some of us do. Now get knives for the cream cheese and sit." Angie cleared her throat and shot me a glance, then gestured toward Alex.

"And if it's all right with Kate, Alex can join us."

"Really? I can be ready in five minutes," he said. Then he pushed his chair back from the table and raced to the bedroom.

"Are you sure?" Kate said. "This is supposed to be a vacation for you."

"We'd love to have him along," Angie said. "He and Rosa can keep each other busy while I watch Dante."

"Okay, but let me give you some money."

"Nonsense!" I said. "You're letting us stay here. That's more than enough payment."

AFTER BREAKFAST, we went to the regular tourist traps: Statue of Liberty, Ellis Island, Empire State Building, Wall Street, Brooklyn Bridge and a few others.

While the kids were eating lunch, Angie and I sat and talked. "This day may never be over," she said.

"At least we'll get these destinations out of the way. Afterward, we'll only have what you really want to see left to visit."

We ate lunch and went to Wall Street and the Empire State Building, then finished the day at Central Park. Rosa couldn't believe how small it was, and Alex still thought it was huge.

When Frankie got home, we moved to the far side of the room and sat. "Did you see him?" he asked.

"You should have what you need in a day or so. He said it would be no problem."

"Damn, I'd like to have his connections," Frankie said. "It would make life a lot easier."

"Isn't that the truth."

"Did he want much in return?"

"I don't know yet. He said he'd let me know when he got what we needed."

"Remember, Nicky. If it's too much, just refuse. I don't need the information that badly."

"What's the other thing you said Dominic may be involved with?"

Frankie looked toward the kitchen where Angela and Kate were talking, then he whispered. "A reporter friend of mine has been getting threatening letters because of something she wrote in the paper. Some of the articles were related to Dominic's businesses."

"Doesn't sound like Dominic," I said. "He'd do it differently."

"How so?"

"First off, there's been so much written about him that I doubt he'd think twice about one more article. Secondly, if he did act on it, he'd probably send someone to talk to her; he wouldn't send a letter."

"Maybe you're right," Frankie said. "Maybe I'm looking for an easy answer, but I should know better. The answers are seldom easy."

"If it was easy, they wouldn't need good people like you to find the bad guys."

Frankie laughed. "I haven't been finding that many bad guys lately. Just looking for them."

"That's all right," I said. "I'll be here to keep you on track."

"Screw you, Rat. If I'm guessing right, you'll have me looking on the wrong side of town with all the wrong clues."

"That depends on who you're looking for," I said, then joined in the laughter.

"Enough shop talk for tonight," Kate hollered from the kitchen. "Come out here and pay these beautiful women some attention."

Frankie jumped up. "Come on, Nicky. I don't think we can refuse that."

"Not if we want to live happily ever after," I said.

WHO'S SMUGGLING WHAT?

Frankie walked up the stairs, nodded to a uniformed officer passing by, and went into the coffee room.

"About time you got here, Donovan. I'm on my second cup already. If anybody's watching, they'd think you were the one ready to retire."

"If I have to put up with you much longer, I will be."

"Have a late night?" Lou asked.

"I got company visiting. Some people from the old neighborhood came up for the wedding."

Lou shifted in his chair. "Don't tell me it's your friend, the Rat."

"All right, I won't tell you; besides, if I remember right, you and Sherri owe him your lives."

"How long is he in town for?"

"About a week."

"A week? Is the wedding that soon?"

"You know it is, Lou. Kate sent out the invitations, and when we got an earlier date, she followed up with phone calls."

"Why'd you move the date up anyway?"

"The place we were holding the reception got a cancellation, so we grabbed it. We had wanted an earlier date anyway."

"And the church and everybody else was okay with that?"

"We gave them all plenty of notice. And with the money they're getting paid, they made accommodations."

"All right, enough wedding shit. How do you want to handle it with these kids? When do you want them in here?"

"I don't know yet. I'm waiting on some information."

"What kind of information?" Lou asked.

Frankie poured more coffee and sighed. "The kind you don't want to know about so just wait for me to tell you."

"Shit. I should've figured. 'The Rat' comes to town and things get turned sideways."

"It's just information, Lou. For Christ's sake."

"Yea, it always starts that way. But we've got laws for a reason."

Frankie got up and slammed the door. "We've got a dead professor, Lou. And he was tortured. If I have to bend a law or two to catch the scum who killed him, I'm okay with that."

"Your call, Frankie. I'm not going to be here long. As long as your decision doesn't interfere with my pension, I'm okay with any of it."

Three hours later, Nicky called.

"Dominic said he'd have what we need later today. I'm picking it up from his man before dinner."

"Thanks, Nicky," Frankie said, then went back to Lou. "Have them all brought in starting tomorrow morning."

"What did you get?" Lou asked.

"Don't know yet, but we got it. I'll know tonight."

I sat on a bench in Prospect Park, my hat tilted slightly to the side. I was reading a paper when a man approached.

"You waiting for someone?" he asked.

"Depends upon who's asking," I said.

"Dominic told me to meet someone here at five o'clock."

"It's only four o'clock," I said.

"Guess I'm early," he said.

"Did Dominic say what he'd need me to do for this?" I asked.

"Dominic said the only thing he wants is for you to ask your friend in Texas to keep an eye on someone."

"I can't promise what my friend will do," I said.

"Dominic didn't ask for that. He said for you to *ask* your friend. If he says 'yes,' everything is settled. If he says 'no,' it's settled as well."

"And that's it? Just ask him?"

"That's what Dominic said. He said you have good friends, and he is confident they will do what you ask."

"And if they don't?"

"Like I said, 'all is well.'"

"I'll agree to that," I said, and patted a spot next to me on the bench.

The man sat and handed me a USB drive. "Take this and forget who you got it from."

"I don't know who I got it from," I said.

"That's good," the man said, then stood and walked away.

Frankie was already home when I arrived with the kids and Angela.

"Have a fun day?" Frankie asked.

"We went everywhere," Alex said.

"Everywhere consists of a lot of places," Frankie said. "Why don't you wait for Kate to get here, then you can tell us about your day."

I sat on the sofa with Frankie and slipped him the drive.

"This is it?" he asked.

"I haven't looked, but that's what the man said."

"Thanks, Nicky. I needed this."

"You won't know until you look if it helps. Maybe it's nothing."

"I'm betting what I need is on here. I'll look later. I've got the suspects coming in tomorrow for questioning, so this is timely."

After Kate and the kids went to bed, Frankie put the USB drive into his computer. It had everything he needed and more. Not only did it have the bank where the kids had accounts, it showed deposit amounts and dates for the ranges requested as well as twelve months prior to those dates.

I sat next to Frankie at the kitchen table. "Does it have what you need?"

"And then some," Frankie said. "Four of the students had deposits while they were out of the country although two of those have similar deposits made every month."

Frankie took a sip of beer. "But these two—Jake Milinski and Paul Stutgard—hadn't had a deposit made in the six months preceding this one."

"Are they from wealthy families?" I asked.

"Not if I remember correctly," Frankie said. "So how's that figure? Where'd the money come from and how did it get deposited when they weren't here?"

I thought for a moment, then said, "Only two possibilities. They were either here and made the deposits, or they had someone do it for them. Since we know they were in Italy at the time, then someone must have made the deposits for them."

"It would be nice to *see* who made those deposits," Frankie said.

"Then we need to see who was so generous as to deposit such large amounts of money," I said.

"And how do you plan to do that?"

"I'm betting that we could access the video on the dates the deposits were made. Shouldn't be too much trouble."

"Frankie shook his head again. "I don't like it, Rat. I hate getting Dominic or Manny involved."

"Don't worry. They'll look to me for payment, not you."

"That still worries me," Frankie said.

"I can handle it, Bugs. Relax."

"All right, what do you need me to do?"

"Nothing. All I have to do is ask for the videos."

I moved to the other side of the room and dialed Dominic's number.

"What is it, Niccolo?"

"Mr. Mangini, I need another favor. I need videos to accompany the deposits that were made on two of those accounts you accessed."

"You should have asked for this all at once. Now it will cost me two favors."

"I'm sorry. I didn't know I'd need them when I asked before."

"I'll get the videos," Dominic said, "but you'll owe me another favor."

"I figured as much. What do you need?"

"I don't know yet," Dominic said. "I'll let you know when I do. But do I have your word on the favor?"

"I'm not going to kill anyone," I said. "Or hurt any innocent people."

"You won't have to. Do I have your word?"

"You've got it," I whispered.

"Then you'll have your videos. Probably tomorrow. I'll call you at this number. You'll meet the same man at the same place."

"Sounds good. And the earlier the better as far as the videos go. I'll wait for your call."

I poured a glass of wine and returned to the table where Frankie was. "You'll have your videos tomorrow," I said.

"At what price?" Frankie asked.

"Not your concern, Bugs. I'll call you when I get them."

WHO MADE THE DEPOSITS?

Frankie climbed the stairs two-at-a-time. As he walked into the coffee room, Lou was pouring a cup. "Lou, grab me one of those, will you?"

"You got it," Lou said.

"Were you able to schedule the kids the way I asked, saving Jake and Paul for last?"

"If you mean was I able to cater to your whims without knowing one goddamn thing about what's going on—yes. Now, you want to fill me in, or do I have to keep guessing?"

Frankie closed the door and lowered his voice. "I only kept you in the dark to protect you, Lou. You know that."

"I hear you, Donovan, but I'd rather know what the hell we're doing."

Frankie leaned forward. "I've got information that four of the eight kids had deposits made while they were in Europe. Two of them—Jake and Paul—were not normal deposits."

"What do you mean by that?"

"The other two had deposits of similar amounts made on a schedule. Jake and Paul didn't."

"What are we going to do?" Lou asked.

"I'm expecting video of whoever made those deposits before the end of the day. That's why I needed them brought in last. Once we see who deposited money for them, we may have something to pressure them with."

"Well, the first one will be here soon. Let's see how it goes."

Frankie drank two more cups of coffee as he prepared his questions. An hour later, the first student was brought in. Frankie and Lou let him sit in the interview room a few minutes, then walked in and sat.

"Randy Blicken," Frankie said while looking at a folder in front of him.

"What's this about, Detective? I don't appreciate being dragged down here for no reason."

"It's not for no reason. We're trying to find out what happened to Professor Reed."

"I don't know anything more than I knew when you came to the university, and that is nothing."

"You went out of the country two months ago. Where did you go and what for?" Lou asked.

Randy shot a look at Lou, then Frankie. "Yes, I did go out of the country a few months ago, but it's none of your business where I went or for what reason."

Lou whistled long and slow. "Pretty sensitive, Randy. You hiding something?"

Randy looked at Lou and smiled. "I'm sorry, Detective, did I offend you by asserting my rights as an American citizen? If I did, please accept my apologies, then let me the hell out of here. I'm through talking. Get a warrant if you have more questions." He got up and stormed out the door.

"That didn't go so well, did it?" Frankie asked.

"I hope that's not an indication of how the others will be," Lou said.

"I guess we'll find out soon enough," Frankie said.

The next several interviews were not antagonistic, but they weren't very helpful either. No one seemed to know what the professor had been into. If they did, they were good at covering it up.

Sasha Pravel was next on the list. After a few minutes of doodling, Frankie and Lou walked in.

"Sasha, I'm Detective Donovan, and this is Detective Mazzetti."

"I remember you from school," she said.

"Yes, we were there, but we didn't get much cooperation. Did you think of anything else that might help?"

"Actually, I did. On the way over here, I remembered that last year there was something in the paper about him. I remember because I told my mom that he was going to be my professor."

"What was in the paper?" Lou asked.

"I don't recall all of it. It was something to do with smuggling. But nothing ever came of it," she was quick to add. "I think he threatened to sue the paper or something, and they dropped it pretty quickly."

"What did they accuse him of smuggling?" Frankie asked.

Sasha shook her head. "I don't know if they said. If they did, I don't recall. I just remember thinking it was pretty cool."

"You've gone to Europe twice in the past year, Sasha. How do you pay for the trips?"

"My dad. He's rich. I think he sends me away so he can have time to himself."

"And your mother?" Lou asked.

"My mother left ages ago. I don't even know where she is. I've talked to her on the phone—when she calls—but I never know where she's calling from."

"That's a pretty odd relationship if you don't mind my saying," Frankie said.

"I know it is," Sasha said. "I think she is avoiding any contact with my dad. Their divorce was messy."

"You said you talked to your mom about the article, was it—"

"Over the phone? Yes."

"Okay," Frankie said. "You can go now, but if you think of anything else, let us know."

"I will. See ya."

"She was pleasant," Lou said. "I wish everyone was as cooperative."

"Me too," Frankie added. "What do you think about what she said about the article on the professor?"

"I think it couldn't have been much if the papers dropped it so quickly. Worth following up on though. I'll have someone look into it," Lou said as he jotted down notes.

One of the uniforms brought Paul in a moment later.

"Have a seat, Mr. Stutgard," Frankie said. "This won't take long."

"I hope not. I've got a lot of studying to do."

"You recently returned from a trip to Europe," Frankie said. "Why did you go there?"

Paul scrunched his eyebrows. "Because I wanted to see Europe. Doesn't everyone?"

"A lot of people want to see Europe," Lou said. "But not all people can afford it. How'd you pay for the trip?"

Paul turned and looked at Frankie. "How did you pay for that suit? You taking bribes?"

"You little shit," Frankie said, and moved toward him.

Lou grabbed Frankie's arm. "Easy going, Detective. Paul didn't mean anything. I'm sure that slipped out of his mouth."

"It didn't slip," Paul said to Lou. "If you can ask how I afforded a trip to Europe, I can ask how he afforded a suit that's a lot nicer than the ones I have."

"But we're asking the questions," Lou said.

"Only because I am allowing it. I came here on my own free will. I didn't have to come. If you arrest me, that's a different story. Am I under arrest?"

Lou looked to Frankie, then back to Paul. "No, you're not under arrest. You're free to go at any time."

Paul stood and pushed his chair back. "Good, then I'm going. Been nice visiting with you, Detectives. I hope to do it again sometime." Paul left and closed the door behind him.

"That son of a bitch is hiding something, Lou. I know it."

"But we're not going to find out what it is this way. And the only one left is Jake. Where the hell is this information you're supposed to get?"

Frankie looked at the clock. "I don't know. I'm calling him now."

He stepped to the side of the room and dialed Nicky's phone. "Rat, where the hell are you? Did you get it?"

"Just leaving the park. I can bring it to you if you want."

"Could you? That would be fantastic. I'll be waiting outside."

"I'm ten minutes away. See you soon."

"Lou, tell someone to stall Jake for about fifteen minutes. The information is on its way."

NICKY GAVE FRANKIE THE USB, and he went back inside and got Lou so they could look at it. On the drive were videos of the transactions for the deposits made while Jake and Paul were away.

Jake and Paul were shown making deposits, and the images were as clear as day.

"I thought you said they were in Europe," Lou said.

Frankie stared as if lost in thought. "They were in Europe. I reviewed the files before we started this morning."

"How could they have been in Europe if we're seeing them depositing money?"

"I don't know, Lou, but we need to get to the bottom of this."

Frankie and Lou walked to the interview room where Jake was waiting. "Why did you go to Europe for two weeks?" Lou asked.

"To visit," Jake said. "We wanted to see things."

"How did you afford it? You're not from a wealthy family."

Jake smiled. "I've been saving since I was a baby."

"Do you recall where you were on Tuesday, the ninth? That was the week after you left."

Jake was quick to answer. "That's easy. We were in Paris. I remember telling Paul that it had only been a week and already I was enamored with Paris."

Frankie smiled. "Paris is captivating, isn't it?"

"Absolutely," Jake said.

"Who made the deposit in your bank account while you were in Europe?" Lou asked.

Jake lowered his head. "I don't know," he said. "I don't remember."

"Maybe you'd remember if I told you it was you," Frankie said.

"What are you talking about?"

Frankie laid the USB drive on the table in front of Jake. "Perhaps if you look at this video and *see yourself* depositing money when you are listed as being in Europe it would refresh your memory."

"Let me make this simple for the dim-witted people in this room," Lou said. "We have video footage of you making a deposit on the day we inquired about, Tuesday, the ninth."

"The day you said you were in Paris," Frankie said. "How is it possible to be in Paris and New York at the same time?"

Jake looked from Frankie to Lou and then back again. "I must not remember things clearly. I think I'd like a lawyer."

"What do you want a lawyer for?" Lou asked.

"Because I want one. Now either arrest me, let me go, or get me a lawyer."

Frankie looked to Lou and said, "Detective, why don't you get the pictures of the professor to show to Jake."

Lou brought back the pictures of the professor's body, explicitly showing the torture he endured. "This is what happened to Reed," Lou said. "If you don't want the same thing happening to you, you better cancel that request for a lawyer and talk."

"I think I'll pass on the talking," Jake said. "Get me a lawyer or let me go."

"Go ahead. You can go," Frankie said. "But we're not going to protect you. That falls in your court now."

"I think I can handle it," Jake said, then he got up and left.

"That didn't go as planned," Lou said after Jake left.

"Nothing ever does," Frankie added. "Guess we'll have to do this another way."

BRAINSTORMING

Frankie came home while Alex was kicking my ass on a video game we were playing. "Looks like I've been saved," I said. "Your dad's home."

He laughed. "Saved is right, Rat. You were about to get your butt whipped again."

I tousled his hair. "Go beat Rosa. She's pretty good at those games, although she should be. She plays them enough."

Frankie walked to the stove and turned the burner on. "Want coffee, Rat?"

"Sure. How'd it go today?"

"Not as good as I hoped," Frankie said. "He lawyered up."

"And you've got nothing to charge him with?"

"Not a damn thing."

I thought for a moment, then said, "Let's think about this, Frankie. What the hell were those kids bringing in? And why would they go to Europe, then return and go right back?"

"Can't figure it out," Frankie said. "Lou and I have been stewing on it."

"If you hurry up with that coffee, maybe we can figure it out. There's got to be a reason."

"Got to be a reason for what?" Frankie asked.

"For returning to New York days after going to Europe, then going back to Europe. No sane person would do that. There *has* to be a reason."

Frankie poured the coffee and said, "All we have to do is figure out why."

About halfway though the coffee, I looked at Bugs and said, "I got it! Identities."

"What?"

"Identities. They're smuggling in identities. It's the only thing that fits unless they took a boat or something home."

"What do you mean?"

"We know they were in Europe. We know they were in New York making deposits while they were supposed to be in Europe. The travel records don't show them returning to the United States during their trip. The only way to explain that is that they came back to New York using a different name."

"Which explains the identities," Frankie said. "But why?"

"Money," I said. "There's big money in good untraceable identities."

"No way," Frankie said. "You can get them online for no more than a few bucks. All you have to do is know where to look."

I shook my head. "I'm not talking about *stolen* identities or a miscellaneous credit card. I'm talking about professional identities that a person could use to disappear with and not have to worry about it."

Frankie nodded. "You mean ones with a long track record: credit history, license—"

"Birth certificate, social security, electric bills being paid, everything. The right people would pay a fortune for that."

"How easy is it to smuggle them in?" Frankie asked.

"Smuggling in ID cards is easy if you only need one. You simply carry that one as your ID. You book your flight with it, pay for the ticket with it, and use the license and credit cards that you're smuggling as proof of who you are. Since you're traveling internationally, it's even natural to carry your social security card and passport, which would be part of the package."

Frankie nodded. "Makes sense. But I can't see sending kids to Europe to smuggle in one ID."

"Exactly. So the kids book a flight for say two weeks. Once they get to where they're going, they get a stack of identities and book a flight to the US. They smuggle in the cards, hang around for a few days, then go back to the country they just came from. One week later, they return home using their own ID."

"And it looks like a simple vacation," Frankie said.

"The best part is they've already had a trial run using the IDs, so they know they're good."

"And if they get caught smuggling the cards in, they'll be arrested while using their fake ID, so when they make bail, they can simply skip."

"Not quite so easy, but something like that. If they got caught, the cards would be confiscated. They might get away, but the identities they used to come back to New York with would be flagged. They'd have to find a way to get back to Europe so they could re-enter as themselves. And the kids would have to be clean, with no record, no fingerprints on file; otherwise, if they're caught and booked while using the fake IDs, it would show up."

"What do we do now? They have got to know we're onto them."

"Follow them," I said. "Check their purchases."

"What purchases? They're not gonna be dumb enough to go on a buying spree."

"No, but if they're smart, they're gonna want to keep those cards active and current, so they'll use them sporadically at logical places: corner stores, the mall, places like that. They won't pay the pizza-delivery man because the address where they live may not match the address on the card, but you should be able to nab them using false identities to buy things."

"You're saying I should follow them and check what card they use to purchase items."

"Exactly," I said. "Wait until they go into a store and buy something, then send someone in after they leave to see what identity they used to buy it."

Frankie took a long swig of beer, then set the can down. "You know, Rat, this has been a big help. I'd like to have this case finished before the wedding."

I smiled. "Bugs, that's what friends are for."

"I know that, Rat. But not many people do. Kate is my friend. Lou and Sherri are friends. But none of them understands what true friendship is."

"Not many people do, Bugs. Most people do you favors anticipating something in return. Not many people do them because you're a friend, expecting nothing. Remember what Mamma Rosa used to say: 'If you have one true friend in life, you're lucky.'"

"Then I guess we're both lucky, Rat. Now let me get to work so I can figure out how to catch these pricks."

Frankie worked until Kate, Angie, and the kids got home, then he and Nicky played board games until it was time for everyone to go to bed.

"Morning, Donovan," Lou said. "Get any bright ideas last night?"

"Actually, I did," Frankie said. "I figure this may be a case where the professor was having some of his students smuggle in false identities."

"False identities? What the hell for? You can get them for almost nothing, and if the hackers keep at it, they'll be like penny candy before long."

Frankie shook his head. "I'm not talking about those kind of identities. I mean good ones that have been nurtured, not stolen from someone else."

"What's somebody want one for?"

"We're talking witness-protection type identities but without the protection. In other words, someone could use these to disappear, and no one would ever find them unless it was by coincidence."

"If they're that good, they'd be worth a fortune," Lou said.

"That's what I'm thinking."

"How'd you think of this? Or was this Rat's idea?"

Frankie looked around him, then back to Lou. "Rat thought of it, but I have to agree. And he thought of a good way to get them," Frankie said, then he explained the idea to Lou. "We should start first thing in the morning. Follow them from their houses to school, then from school back home. We'll do this until we catch them buying something using a different name."

"What do we do when we catch them?"

"Put the pressure on and find out who else is involved."

"Sounds good," Lou said. "How about the autopsy? Kate find anything?"

"Nothing worthwhile. The nails used were standard, the shots in the head were .22 calibers. We've got people working on the tides to determine where he may have been dumped, but that's all it will tell us—where he was dumped. It won't tell us a damn thing about where he was killed."

"What you're saying is the body will give us nothing."

"I didn't say it, but that's pretty much the way it looks," Frankie said.

"What do we do while we wait? Any ideas on that?"

"Have we heard from Sherri?"

"I haven't," Lou said. "Give her a call and find out. If nothing else, I'd love to drool over Shawna again."

"Lou, you're sick. You know that?"

"I know, Donovan, but that's what makes me lovable."

Frankie dialed the phone.

"Miller."

"Sherri, it's Frankie. Anything new on Shawna's case?"

"Not much. Forensics analyzed the letter, but it was pretty standard stuff. They picked up on the author of the letter using 'we' instead of 'I,' so they're assuming it was a group or at least more than one person."

"Or a deliberate attempt to mislead us," Frankie added.

"Yeah, they mentioned that too. So it's either a group of people with no sense or a single person with brains. Narrows it down, huh?"

"What else?"

"No fingerprints or DNA. The postmark is Manhattan, so that doesn't narrow it down. The letter is printed, which makes handwriting analysis out of the question. And the paper the letter was written on as well as the envelope are run-of-the-mill stationery. We'll get nothing from them."

"In other words, the letter was useless?"

"Pretty much," Sherri said. "How about Mangini? You talk to him?"

Frankie sighed. "Not yet."

"What are you waiting for? Right now, he looks to be the best lead. You want me to do it?"

"No way. I'll do it."

"I'm not afraid to talk to him," Sherri said.

"You should be," Frankie said. "He's not a man to be taken lightly."

"We're talking to him today," Lou shouted.

Frankie shot Lou a glance and raised his eyebrows.

"I heard what she said. She talks loud. Besides, we've got nothing else to do."

"You heard the boss," Frankie said to Sherri. "I guess we're talking to Mangini today."

"Good, let me know how it goes."

~

HALF AN HOUR LATER, Frankie called Dominic Mangini. "Mr. Mangini, this is Detective Donovan. I have a few questions for you and wondered if we could meet."

"Detective Donovan. Of course, we could meet. Would you like to come to my house, or would you prefer a public location?"

"Probably the latter, sir."

"Fine, how about Cataldi's restaurant at noon. If you arrive before me, tell them you're there to meet me, and they'll seat you at my table."

Frankie hung up the phone and turned to Lou. "He wants to meet for lunch."

"I assume that means I'm not going?" Lou said.

"I'll handle this," Frankie said. "No sense in you coming along."

"Great, because I didn't want to eat good dago food. I'll just grab a hot dog from the corner."

"Christ's sake then, come on. You can go."

"You mean it? What's good? I've never eaten there."

Frankie and Lou went over the questions to ask and how to ask them while driving to lunch.

"What's the protocol here, Donovan. Does letting him pay for an expensive lunch constitute a bribe?"

"What the hell do you care? You're retiring soon. Order whatever the hell you want. Trust me; it'll be good. I've never had anything here that wasn't."

"Never had anything here that wasn't? How many damn times have you eaten here?"

"I don't know," Frankie said. "Maybe half a dozen."

"Half a dozen! And you said you weren't on the take. Son of a bitch!"

Frankie pulled in front of the restaurant and got out. "I'm here to meet Dominic Mangini," he said.

The man handed him a ticket and took his car. "I'll park it, sir. Go on in."

"Look at this, a fuckin' celebrity. You sure you told the truth about how many times you been here, Donovan?"

"Screw you, Lou. And remember your manners. I don't want to have to shoot anyone."

"More importantly, I don't want to be shot," Lou said and followed Frankie inside.

"I'm here to see Mr. Mangini," Frankie said to the hostess.

She smiled and extended her hand. "You must be Detective Donovan."

"And this is my guest, Detective Mazzetti," Frankie said.

"Follow me," she said. "I'll show you to your table. Mr. Mangini phoned a moment ago. He's on his way."

"I've always wanted to eat here," Lou said.

Frankie looked at him and smiled. "You've never eaten here?"

"Hey, Donovan. Remember who you're talking to. Not everyone is connected to the mob. And cops can't afford to eat here."

Frankie and Lou sat at the table and ordered coffee while they waited.

A few minutes later, Dominic came in. He had a bounce in his step and wore a smile on his face.

"Detective Donovan, how nice to see you." He glanced at Lou, extended his hand and said, "And this must be Luigi Mazetti."

"Have we met?" Lou asked.

Dominic laughed. "No, but I make it a point to be informed. I knew who Detective Donovan's partner was, and I made a presumption you were his partner."

"Well, you're right. Nice to meet you," Lou said.

"I doubt you meant that, Detective, but it was kind of you to say so. Now, please order whatever you want and enjoy the meal. We can discuss business afterward."

"I'd rather we get the business done with first," Frankie said.

Dominic put down the menu and stared. "And I would rather we didn't. By the way, I recommend the Veal Marsala; it's to die for."

The waitress came by a moment later. Frankie ordered the seafood ravioli, and Lou went with the Veal Marsala.

"Excellent choice," Dominic said when the waitress left.

"She didn't get your order," Lou said.

"She knows what I want. It's always the same."

"Veal Marsala?"

"Exactly."

"Good. Now I feel better," Lou said.

"I understand you're getting married, Detective," Dominic said to Frankie.

Surprise showed on Frankie's face. "How did you know about that? I don't remember you on the invitation list."

Dominic laughed. "No, I don't think it would be wise. And I didn't bring a gift because it could be judged as a bribe of some sort, so you'll have to accept my good wishes as compensation."

"Good wishes are fine. I'd expect nothing else."

The waitress brought the food a moment later, along with a bottle of wine. "No wine for me," Frankie said. "It's too early."

"Nonsense," Dominic said. "You can't eat a meal without a glass of wine," and he poured drinks for the three of them. "Detective Mazzetti has no objections."

"You won't find me objecting to a glass of Brunello no matter what time it is. I'd drink it with breakfast."

Dominic laughed. "A conviction I can appreciate, Detective."

They finished the meal in almost complete silence, then Dominic folded his napkin and placed it on the table. "All right, Detective, you can tell me what you want now. And by the way, you'll need a good reason for having met with me because undoubtedly, someone is watching."

"That meal was a good enough reason," Lou said. "I'd meet with you every day for that."

Dominic poured more wine for Lou. "It *is* good, isn't it? I would come more often if it wasn't so far away."

"Enough talk about food," Frankie said. "Let's get to the reason why I came."

Dominic turned slowly and looked at Frankie. "Why *did* you come, Detective?"

Frankie exhaled loudly. "A reporter friend of mine has been getting threatening letters, and they're serious enough to scare her."

"Threats about what?"

"Articles she's written. Whoever is threatening her wants her to stop writing the stories. The trouble is, we don't know what those stories are."

"What does it have to do with me? Where do I fit in?"

"One of those stories is about corruption in the construction business. Concrete, to be specific."

Dominic laughed. "And you think *I* may be the one threatening her? Detective, I'm surprised at you. I would never do such a thing."

"I'm not sure I buy that."

"Detective, I'm not in the business of making threats, and I certainly wouldn't make threats using letters. If I were to make a threat, I would send someone to deliver it face-to-face."

"So you're saying these threats are not coming from you?" Frankie asked.

"I thought I just said that, Detective."

"And you'd tell me if you did make the threats?"

"No, I'd simply evade the question. But I'm telling you straight; the threats are not from me. Why do I care if someone writes an article about me? The police and the FBI already presume all crimes committed in the city are a result of something I did. Some reporter writing an article won't make much of a difference."

"What about Manny?" Lou asked.

"I can't speak for Manny, but that's not his style either."

"Who else would it be? Have any ideas?" Frankie asked.

"Send me the list of articles this reporter wrote, and I'll look through them. By the way, Detective, did those bank videos help?"

Frankie blushed. "We're still working on them, but I think they'll help, yes. Thanks for the favor."

"That was not a favor for you; it was for your friend. Your favor will be me looking into these threats for you. Consider it a wedding gift."

"Mr. Mangini, I—"

"I said it would be a "gift" Detective, not a favor. You'll owe me nothing for it."

"In that case, I'll take any help you can provide."

"Fine," Dominic said and stood. "If we're done, I have places to be."

"We're done," Frankie said. "Thank you."

They walked past one of the Cataldi sisters on their way out. "Lorena, please see to it that Detective Donovan and his wife and son, and Detective Mazzetti and his wife, are treated to a meal anytime they want. Put them on my account."

"Of course, Signor Mangini. I'll let my sisters know."

"I can't accept that," Frankie said.

"Nonsense. It's done," Dominic said. "Eat the meal, or it will go to waste."

"If you don't want it, I'll take it," Lou said. "That veal was as good as Dominic said."

An attendant brought Frankie his car, and as he and Lou drove away, he said, "What do you think, Lou? You think he had anything to do with it?"

"I don't think so," Lou said. "I think it's like he said. If he wanted to threaten someone, it wouldn't be with a letter."

"That's not the Veal Marsala talking, is it?"

"It might be," Lou said. "Goddamn, that was good."

Frankie shook his head while driving. "I can't wait for you to retire. It's tough to be partnered with a cop who can be bribed with a meal."

"Not any old meal, Donovan. I'm not giving information up for a cheap meal, but that Veal Marsala was no damn hot dog."

"Lou just shut the hell up and figure out how we're going to nail the professor's kids."

TRACKING THE CREDIT CARDS

Frankie met Lou a few blocks from Jake's apartment. He was ready for something as mundane as a tail. Morreau had given Frankie another team, and they were positioned to follow Paul. Between the two of them, Frankie hoped to catch the kids using the fake identities.

It didn't take long. Jake stopped at a coffee shop a few miles from his place. Frankie waited for him to leave, then Lou went inside.

He flashed his badge to the person behind the counter. "Detective Mazzetti," he said. "I need to see the receipt for the young man who just left here."

"Why? Did he do something wrong?"

"Give me the damn receipt, or I'll haul your ass in too."

The cashier quickly opened the cash register and handed the receipt to Lou. He looked at it closely. "You're sure this was his? An espresso and a scone?"

The cashier nodded. "That was his. I'm positive."

"Okay, can you make me a copy of this, please. Then I'll be on my way."

"No problem. I'll do it now," he said, and walked into the back room.

He handed Lou the copy, then Lou said thanks and left. He got into the car with Frankie.

"Well?" Frankie asked.

"Jake didn't buy anything," Lou said. "But a guy named Felix Marsh did."

"That's what we needed," Frankie said, and put the car in gear. He raced until he caught sight of Jake's car, then slowed and settled in to follow him.

"What are you waiting for?" Lou asked.

"Just seeing if he goes anywhere interesting. Besides, if we arrest him at the university, it may get people talking. Maybe enough to cause some of them to act. Remember, we don't know if these two represent all the kids Reed used or just a few of them."

"And seeing us arrest Jake might spook people too."

"I'm not concerned about spooking them," Frankie said. "If my hunch is right, Jake will be a talker. And if he's a talker, we'll get the others."

"Then maybe we should have a patrol car pick him up? It would be more visible and attract more attention."

Frankie smiled. "Good thinking, Lou. Call it in."

Frankie and Lou followed Jake to the university. He parked, and when he got out of the car and headed toward school, Frankie told the uniformed officers to pick him up.

"Do it now," Frankie said. "And make sure a lot of people see it."

"You got it, Detective."

A patrol car approached Jake, then sirens blared, drawing plenty of attention. A crowd gathered while the officers frisked Jake, then cuffed him and put him in the back seat.

"That should be enough," Lou said. "Word will spread quickly."

Lou walked into the interrogation room with a smile on his face. "Good morning, Jake. How are you?"

Frankie walked in a few seconds later. "Good morning, Felix. How are you?"

"My name is Jake. Jake Milinski."

Frankie looked sideways to Lou. "Is it? Then who is Felix Marsh? You purchased some items at the coffee shop this morning and provided that identity."

Lou picked up some papers and read through them. "Yeah, and the identity looks real. I ran it through the database after we picked you up. Good credit, has been active for years, great driving record. And look, it even shows a purchase at the same coffee shop yesterday."

Frankie leaned forward and whispered, "You may want to know, Jake or Felix, that Lou went into the coffee shop this morning and verified it was you who purchased things using that ID."

"I want a lawyer," Jake said.

"Would that be Jake or Felix who wants a lawyer?" Lou asked.

"Maybe he wants two lawyers," Frankie said, one for each identity."

"Okay, what do you want?" Jake asked.

"We want to know about the IDs, and we want to know it all. We already know that the professor had you smuggling them in—you and Paul and others."

"And if I cooperate, I get off?"

"We'll see," Lou said. "What I'd be more concerned about if I were you is making sure you don't end up like Reed. Remember those pictures? Somebody put him through a lot of pain looking for answers. Don't think they won't do the same to you."

Jake swallowed, causing his Adam's apple to move. "Paul and I were doing this for Professor Reed. He paid for our trips to Europe, and he paid us money in addition—good money."

"Who else was doing it?" Frankie asked. "Or was it just you and Paul?"

"As far as I know, it was just us. It doesn't take much to smuggle in cards."

"How'd you do it?" Lou asked.

Jake smiled. "The professor had special shoes made for us with the heels hollowed out. We'd put the cards in there. And the heels were coated with a lead-based paint that prevented the X-Ray machines from discovering them."

"So, you'd go to Europe, bring the cards back, go back to Europe and return in a few days.," Lou said.

Jake looked surprised. "How did you know?"

"Don't worry about how we know, just tell me why you returned with the cards. Why not just bring them when you came back?"

"In case we got caught. We would bring them back using a fake ID, that way, if we got caught, we'd be out on bail in a flash, and then simply disappear. The only difficult part would be we couldn't take our scheduled flight back to Europe, so we'd either have to risk not going, or find another way to get there."

"You couldn't go back using the same ID; they'd be flagged," Lou said.

"And you couldn't use your own because you were already supposed to be in Europe," Frankie said. "That means you'd have to use another ID."

Jake nodded. "That was the plan if we got caught."

"But you never got caught?" Lou asked.

"No. Well, not really."

"What's that supposed to mean—not really. You either got caught, or you didn't."

Jake breathed deeply and raised his head in the air. "On the last trip, we were stopped at Customs and searched on our way back. The guy found the cards."

"And?" Lou asked.

"And instead of turning us in, he asked for money—ten grand."

"And you paid him?" Frankie asked.

"We gave him five the day he caught us, then returned with five more."

"And then he gave the cards back?" Lou asked.

Jake nodded.

"My guess is that he's tied in to whoever tortured the professor. And if he is, you can bet he copied the names on the cards before he gave them back to you. That makes you vulnerable." Frankie stared. "My suggestion is to tell us everything you know. You don't want to end up like Professor Reed."

Lou pulled his phone out and looked at it. "That's a text from Collins. He just picked up your buddy, Paul."

Frankie slid a pen and pad of paper to Jake. "Write down everything you know. We'll see if we can keep you out of prison. More importantly, we'll see if we can keep you alive."

Fifteen minutes later, Jake was still writing. Collins escorted Paul into the room. He took a seat next to Jake and looked at what he was writing. "I should have known you'd talk," he said. "I didn't want you in on it to begin with."

"I think you'll be thankful that he talked," Frankie said. "It might keep you alive."

Frankie pushed pen and paper in front of Paul. "Add something to it, or be prepared to face prison. There are no other choices."

"I'll read what Jake wrote when he's done, and if there's anything to add, I'll add it."

"No, you won't," Frankie said. "You'll start writing now, and if it doesn't match what Jake said, you'll be sharing a cell at Rikers with a not-so-friendly inmate."

"Trust me; you don't want that option," Lou said.

Paul picked up the pen and began to write. Twenty minutes later, Frankie and Lou were reviewing the statements.

"Anything else you can tell us about Daniel," Frankie asked.

Paul shook his head. "Just what I said, that he works in Customs and fits the description I wrote down."

"Is that it?" Jake asked. "Are we free to go?"

"You're free to go," Frankie said, "But if I were you, I'd find someplace else to stay. We don't know who is behind this yet, and we have no idea if they're onto you, but chances are that they know who you are and where you live. Go someplace safe if you have it, or stay here, or get a motel room, but don't use a credit card, not even a fake one. I'm guessing Daniel told them about you."

"I almost forgot," Paul said, and handed his phone to Frankie. "This might help."

"What's this?" Frankie asked.

Paul took the phone back and navigated to a video. "This is a video I took of us paying off Daniel. He doesn't know I took it, so it should come as a surprise."

"Send it to me," Frankie said.

"It's too large to email, but you can use the phone."

"No need to," Lou said. "If you hang around for a few minutes, I'll have the tech guys get it off the phone."

Lou returned and handed the phone to Paul. "All done," he said. "You did the smart thing by cooperating. Now get out of here and find someplace safe to stay while we wrap this up."

"Will do," Paul said.

"Thanks," Jake said.

"Think we did the right thing? Letting them go?" Frankie asked.

"Better than adding fuel to the fire at Rikers," Lou said. "They'd have been back-doored before the week was up. Besides, we can assign a team to watch them, and if we're lucky, we'll get whoever might be trying to find the cards."

"All right, sounds good to me. Now, let's figure out how to get this guy Daniel."

"Won't be hard. He's a pussy."

"A pussy? How the hell do you know that?" Frankie asked.

"He works in Customs, doesn't he? Everybody in Customs is a pussy."

Frankie shook his head. "Lou, is there anybody you don't have a pre-formed opinion of?"

"Not so far, but I'll let you know if that happens."

"When is it you're retiring?"

WELCOME TO AMERICA

$\mathcal{I}$ was sitting on the sofa loafing when Bugs got home. "Hey, Bugs, you're home early."

"I needed it. I'm looking forward to some of Angela's cooking."

"I'll deny it if you ever repeat it, but I'd be wishing for Rosa's cooking. She's gotten to be a better cook than Angie."

"Nicky, why are you whispering? No one is here."

I laughed. "Habit, I guess. If Angie heard me say that she'd be proud as hell of Rosa, then she'd kick my ass for saying what I did."

"Just remember that. I'm going to hold it over your head like the Sword of Damocles."

"I'm not worried. I've got plenty to hold over your head, and you know it."

Frankie grabbed a beer and plopped on the other end of the sofa. "What's Angie cooking? Do you know?"

"I think they're making meatball sandwiches. I *hope* they are."

"I'll go along with that," Frankie said.

"Rough day, Bugs?"

"No, a pretty good one, actually. We nabbed the students who were doing the smuggling, and they gave up a guy at Customs who found out about it and was shaking them down."

"What are you going to do about him?"

"Lou and I will talk to him, of course, but I haven't figured out yet how to bust him, although I do have a video taken by one of the students that shows him accepting a bribe."

"But you can't use it legally, right?"

Frankie shook his head. "No, I can't."

"Then let me use it," I said.

"What? What do you mean?"

"I mean let me talk to the Customs guy. I'll persuade him that he should cooperate with you."

"No way, Nicky. I can't do that."

"Why not? He won't be harmed."

"Because it's against the law. I can't let you do that."

"Do what? You have no idea what I have in mind."

"No matter what it is, I can't allow it."

"Because it's against the law?" I asked.

"Yeah. Because it's against the law. I *am* a cop, remember?"

"Was it against the law to kill the professor? And will it be against the law to kill the students?"

"The students aren't dead."

"Not yet," I said. "But they will be if you don't do something quickly."

"And you think you can stop that by simply talking to this guy?"

"Yeah, I do."

Frankie put his head in his hands. "Christ's sake, how do I get in these messes?"

"You get in these messes by trying to follow the strict letter of the law. Now give me the video and let me do my job."

"I've got to think," Frankie said.

"No you don't, Bugs. You've already made up your mind to do it. You simply want it to look like you struggled with the decision."

"You're an asshole, Rat. You know that?"

"I've heard that from better people than you, Bugs. Angie tells me that all the time."

The sounds of kids laughing came from outside the door. "Whatever your decision is, you better hurry."

"All right, but we'll have to transfer the video to your phone tonight using air drop or something. It's too big to email."

"I'll leave my phone on the table," I said. "If you get a chance, take it and make the transfer."

We ate a great dinner, then talked most of the night. In the morning, I told Angie I had a few errands to run, but then I went to look up Daniel at Customs. On the drive over, I called Dominic. "Mr. Mangini, this is Niccolo Fusco."

"And what can I do to help such a pain in the ass?"

"I wanted your permission to use your name to frighten someone."

"What?"

"Someone needs to listen to reason, and I think if I mention your name, he'll listen."

"If all it amounts to is mentioning my name, go ahead. And thank you for asking, Niccolo. You have respect. I like that."

"No problem, Mr. Mangini. Thanks again."

I walked in, found a man who looked to have some authority and said, "I need to see Daniel, please. It's important."

"I'm sorry, he's working. You could come back at noon."

"But I've got to see him now. His mother is sick, real sick, and…well, I need to see him."

"His mother? You should have said so right away. I'll get him now." As he was leaving, he called to another person standing nearby. "Roger, get someone to fill in for Daniel."

A few minutes later Daniel came rushing out with the man I spoke with.

"What is it? Is my mom okay?"

"I grabbed his arm. "You better come with me," I said.

"Who are you? Who sent you?" Daniel asked.

I handed him the phone with the video set to play. "Here, look at this while we walk."

Daniel pushed *play* on the video, and it didn't take long for him to realize what it was. He stopped walking and stared. "Who gave you this. What do you want?"

"Now we're getting to questions that matter," I said. I grabbed his arm and tugged. "Come with me, and I'll tell you what we want."

"We? Who's we?"

"Just follow me and act worried so people think you're concerned about your mother. I'll explain once we get to the car."

Daniel got into the passenger seat, turned quickly to me and said, "What the hell is this about?"

My name is Detective Carrahan. I should be the one asking *what the hell this is about?*"

"I don't know where you got that, but—"

"Bullshit, Daniel. You know exactly where I got it. Paul took the video when he paid you the rest of your money."

"I've got a lawyer, you know. He'll make sure that video is never seen in court."

I laughed. "I hope not. If it is seen, it'd be bad for both of us."

A look of surprise came to Daniel's face. "What do you mean? You're not arresting me?"

"Daniel, if I were arresting you, I'd have put you in cuffs ten minutes ago. I'm not interested in arresting you, and I'm not interested in the money you took. I want to know who you told about the cards."

"I didn't tell anybody."

"Daniel, don't lie to me. My boss doesn't like liars. And he doesn't tolerate failure. So I'm not going back empty-handed."

"Who do you work for?" Daniel asked.

"Nobody. I shouldn't have said anything."

"No, who? I need to know. Is it Viktor?"

I didn't know Viktor, but I made a presumption based on the name that he referred to the Russians. "No, I don't work for Viktor. Let's get on with it. Who did you tell about the cards?"

"What do you know about the cards?" Daniel asked.

I exhaled in a long, slow breath. "Daniel, I know everything. Paul and Jake worked for the professor, who worked for us. I need to know who you told because someone killed the professor, and my boss wants to find them before the cops do."

"I have to ask again who your boss is?"

"Forget it, Daniel. You wouldn't know him if I told you."

"Try me."

"All right, for God's sake. Dominic. Dominic Mangini."

Daniel gulped. "Dominic Mangini? How do you work for him if you're a cop?"

I laughed. "What do you mean? Dominic has dozens of us working for him. How do you think he's still walking the streets a free man?"

Nicky lifted his shirt up and revealed a gun. "Daniel, please don't make this difficult. Who did you tell about the cards? We know you told somebody because the professor died two days after you stopped Jake and Paul."

"I don't know...I—"

"Daniel, do yourself a favor and tell me. Don't make me take you to Dominic. You wouldn't like that."

"Viktor. His name is Viktor. And he's—"

"He's with the Russians?"

"Yeah, you know him?"

"Dominic knows everybody, Daniel. It's a good thing you told me. I'm sure they'll work it out. If I were you, I'd take off for the rest of the day and go in tomorrow and say that your mother is feeling better."

Daniel reached for the door handle. "Okay, thanks."

"And don't tell Viktor we spoke. Let Dominic handle that."

"You got it," Daniel said. "Thanks again."

On the way back to Frankie's apartment, I called him.

"Donovan."

"Bugs, you know somebody named Viktor? He's with—"

"The Russians. Yeah, I know him."

"He's the one you're looking for. Daniel gave him the information on Reed."

"You're a life-saver, Nicky. I should have listened to you when you said it wasn't Dominic."

"Yeah, Dominic can be a son of a bitch, but threats aren't his way."

"Now I have to figure out how to pin this on Viktor," Frankie said. "It's not going to be easy."

WELCOME TO BRIGHTON BEACH

Frankie took the stairs two-at-a-time, grabbed a few things from his desk, then stopped by the coffee room. "Come on, Lou. We need to get our asses moving."

"Moving? I just sat down for Christ's sake. Where are you off to in such a hurry?"

"We're going to Brighton Beach to see Viktor."

"Viktor Pavic?" Lou asked.

"The one and only," Frankie said. "We've got a lead that he may be involved in the professor's killing."

"A lead? From whom?"

"Don't worry about from whom. It's a solid lead."

"Just what I thought. Did you ever think that maybe Dominic wants Viktor out of the way? That maybe that's why we got this lead."

"Yeah, I thought of that, smart ass, but the lead isn't from Dominic. So get in the car and help me figure out how to get Viktor."

Frankie pulled out of the lot and onto the street.

"So you want me to figure out how to solve this case by the time we get to Brighton Beach?"

"That would be great if you could."

"I got a better idea," Lou said. "How about you figure it out while I smoke."

Frankie made good time getting to Brighton Beach. Once he got there, he parked the car near Little Kiev, a club frequented by the Russian mob, often known as the Bratva. If he hoped to find Viktor, this was the place to start looking.

"I'm guessing you did your homework, and this is where Viktor hangs out," Lou said.

"You're a damn good guesser."

Two men who looked more like mercenaries than bouncers stopped Frankie and Lou at the door. "Weapons?"

"I'm Detective Donovan, and this is Detective Mazzetti," Frankie said. "I need to see Viktor."

"You need an appointment to see Viktor," the man said.

Lou showed his badge. "Consider this an appointment. Now get Viktor, or I'll shut this place down."

The smaller of the two men sneered. "You won't do—"

"I'll get him," the other man said. "Wait here."

Thirty seconds later, Viktor came to the front. "How can I help you, detectives?"

"You can help me by telling me why you killed Professor Reed. Was it to get his fake IDs? Is that why you did it?"

Viktor stepped back. "Detective, I don't know what you're talking about. I don't even know this Professor Reed."

"Really? I'm guessing that when my men finish tearing this place apart, they'll find evidence. Traces of blood, hair, something that will show he was here. And my guess is that this was the *last* place he was."

"You have a vivid imagination, Detective, but I have no idea what you're talking about. I'm afraid you'll have to look elsewhere."

Frankie shook his head. "I don't think so, Viktor. And now that you know I'm onto you, you'll make a mistake, and I'll be watching."

"There will be nothing to see," Viktor said.

"We'll see about that," Frankie said. "I'm betting there will be a *lot* to see. And when I see it, I'm gonna put you away."

"You'll need a good pair of glasses," Viktor said.

"I don't need the glasses. I just got Daniel. You remember Daniel, your snitch in Customs. And don't even think about using the cards. I've got the names registered. The first time anyone tries using one of those cards, they'll be picked up."

Frankie noticed the twitch in Viktor's face and his scowl. "I don't know anyone in Customs, and I don't know about any cards."

"Really? Then let's keep it that way. I've got Daniel under surveillance. Any threats or moves to harm him will be noted. Think about that while you're sweating, Viktor."

Frankie headed toward the door, then turned and faced Viktor again. "And just so that you understand how things work, if anything happens to Daniel, you'll suffer the consequences. I'll dedicate my life to tearing down every business you're involved with. That's a promise."

Frankie and Lou left after that and headed to the car. When they were almost there, Lou said he had to go back, that he had forgotten his sunglasses.

LOU WALKED in and went straight to Viktor. "Viktor, just in case you had any stupid ideas about taking revenge on my partner, know this: I'm retiring in a month, so I don't give a shit. If anything happens to Frankie, I'll do more than tear your businesses down; I'll flat out kill you. Put a bullet between your eyes."

"You shouldn't make threats like that."

"As my partner Frankie is fond of saying, it's not a threat, it's a promise."

Lou got back into the car and buckled up.

"I don't see any glasses," Frankie said.

"I must have left them at home," Lou said. "I could've sworn I left them there."

Frankie nodded. "Lou, these guys are not people to mess around with."

"You started it," Lou said. "You're the one who threatened him."

"All right, that was stupid of me, but we don't have to continue being stupid."

"What do we do?"

"First thing is watch out for Daniel since I just put a target on his back."

"I thought that was nice of you. Especially since you didn't warn him."

"I've got his cell number," Frankie said. "We'll call him now." He picked up his phone and dialed. "Daniel, this is Detective Donovan. Yeah, hello to you too. Listen up. The reason I'm calling is to tell you that I told Viktor you ratted on him."

"You did what? What the fuck! He's gonna kill me."

"He might. That's why I'm calling. You got anywhere to go for a few weeks? If not, I can try to find you one."

A moment of silence followed, then, "I might have."

"It can't be relatives or friends. Nowhere that Viktor would look."

"I know. I've got somewhere in Jersey."

"Good," Frankie said. "Even Viktor won't look in Jersey. Give me a number to leave a message when it's safe."

Daniel gave Frankie a number, then hung up, saying he was leaving.

"Good," Frankie said. "Don't call *anyone*. And don't come back until you hear from me."

VIKTOR STORMED THROUGH THE CLUB, his fist pounding on tables. "I told you that bitch was trouble. "Now she needs to be taken care of. And no kid gloves. Get rid of her."

His man was almost out the door when Viktor called him back. "And put tails on that cop. I want to know what he's up to at all times."

FRANKIE FINISHED THE DAY, then went home to relax. Nicky returned moments later with Angela and the kids.

"Hey, Rat, have fun today?"

"Saw a lot of things, Bugs. I think Angela and the kids enjoyed it. How about you? Anything new?"

"I think we got a big break in the case. It looks as if it is definitely the Russians who are involved."

"Be careful, Bugs. They play nasty."

"Nasty or not, you don't get a pass on murder," Frankie said.

SIGHTS TO SEE

I woke up, went for a run, and returned before the others were out of bed. I enjoyed being up before anyone else; it gave me time to think about things.

Today I was thinking about Bugs and his current problems with the murder case. It was obvious that the professor had been tortured (by the Russians if Bugs had it right), and that probably meant the professor gave whatever information he had to them. Considering what we were dealing with—fake IDs—that meant the Russians would now be wanting to step in and handle the operation.

If Bugs wanted to get ahead of this, he'd need to find who was making the IDs before the Russians did, and that means he'd have to hurry.

Bugs was the next one out of bed. I told him my ideas over a cup of coffee. "That means you have to get those kids the professor was using to spill the beans before the Russians find the person who's making the IDs."

"All we know—and it's only presumption—is that the IDs came from France," Bugs said.

"You need to narrow it down better than that," I said.

"I'll talk to Jake and Paul again. They swore they knew nothing, but they *have to*."

Our conversation ended when Angie got up. Bugs fixed her coffee, and she sat next to us.

"Good morning," she said. "What are you guys talking about?"

"Not a damn thing," I said. "Just shooting the shit."

"Won't be long, Frankie. I still can't believe you're getting married, but I'm glad you are. I prefer Nicky's friends be married."

Frankie laughed. "Angela, if there's one thing you never have to worry about, it's Nicky running around on you. He adores you. Always has."

"And always will," I said as I squeezed her hand. "Those years I spent without you were the worst years of my life. It'll never happen again."

"It better not," Angela said and kissed me on the cheek. "Where are we going today? I hope it's someplace we can sit for a while. Yesterday wore me out."

"I thought we'd go to Prospect Park. That way, the kids can mess around while we plop our fat asses on a bench somewhere."

"Sounds good to me," Angie said. "At least the sitting part." She then reached over and playfully smacked the back of my head. "And if you mention 'fat ass' again, I'll withhold certain favors."

Bugs gulped the last few sips of his coffee and stood. "I gotta go. Lou will probably be waiting for me as it is; besides, I don't want Kate to hear Angie talk of withholding favors."

"No need to worry about that," I said. "They're born with that knowledge, and they know how to use it for threats, bribery, blackmail, and more."

"A guy can hope can't he?"

"Hope all you want, Bugs. But it won't work."

"All right," Bugs said. "I've got to go."

FRANKIE RACED to the station and ran up the stairs. He found Lou in the coffee room, as usual. "Am I missing something, Lou? Have you moved in here?"

Lou took another sip and nodded. "Yeah, Donovan. I fold up the cot every day before you get here."

Frankie laughed. "We should go back to the university and ask around to see if anyone spotted Viktor," he said.

"He wouldn't have gone there himself," Lou said. "He'd have had one of his men do it or two of his men. Did you see him at the club? He had people doing everything for him. I'd be surprised if he took his own shits."

"What you're saying is you don't think it will do any good to pass his picture around."

"I don't think so. I think we need a different approach."

"Like what? The techs studied the tides, and based on where Reed landed, he could have been dumped anywhere from Manhattan to Queens to the Bronx."

Lou snorted. "Lot of damn good that'll do us. Just means about five million people could have dumped him."

"Or more," Frankie said. "Don't forget the commuters."

Lou snapped his fingers. "Hey, wait a minute. What would you do if you had just gotten information on where a source for good identities was?"

"I don't know."

"You'd go get them," Lou said. "And we already know that the identities probably came from France."

Frankie sat up, an excited look on his face. "Damn, Lou. I think you're right. 'Rat' had the same idea, but I ignored him. Let's grab Jake and Paul and get a more specific location, then see if we can nab a Russian."

It only took two hours to find Jake and Paul. Frankie knocked on the door to Paul's apartment. When he answered, his eyes were wide and his mouth agape.

"Detective, how did you know where to find me?"

"Because you're stupid," Lou said. "It only took about an hour of asking around at school to figure out you'd be at your girlfriend's place."

"And it didn't take any pressure on your friends to get them to spit it out within about a minute. We never even showed a badge. Think about that—if we could find you that way, so could the people who killed the professor."

People? It was more than one?"

"We think it was the Russian mob," Lou said. "And trust me, you don't want anything to do with them."

"Shit! What are we gonna do?"

"The first thing is find some place safe to go, and I mean some place safe, not an apartment in your girlfriend's name. The second thing is even more important. You need to help us get these guys because no matter where you go, they'll find you eventually. Your best bet is if we can pin Reed's murder on them and put them away."

"What do you need?" Paul asked.

"We need to know who the supplier is," Frankie said.

"I told you, or I thought I told you. It's somebody from Paris. Actually, it's a small town about six hours from Paris—Agen—and we met her at a cafe by the name of L'Amandine."

Frankie and Lou questioned Paul for twenty or thirty more minutes, then walked with him to the car so he could get away safely.

"You're sure you'll be all right?" Frankie asked.

"I'm fine," Paul said. "And I'll get Jake to come with me."

Frankie and Lou returned to the station, where Frankie called the police in Agen, France and told them what he had. Fortunately, the captain spoke almost fluent English, making communicating with him easy.

"Detective, we have had a local under surveillance for some time now. She is suspected of dealing in such things."

"She? That fits. My informant said the person who met with him was a woman."

"What should I be looking out for? In addition to the normal things," the captain said.

"We believe a member of the Bratva is either already there or will be there soon. We think they are looking to take over the operation."

"I never did like the Russians," the captain said. "I'll make sure to keep a careful watch on her, and especially who she meets with."

"If you get them for anything, try looking for the cards in the heel of the shoe," Frankie said. "You might hit gold."

"Good to know," the captain said. "My thanks."

"Captain, do me a favor? If you get anything on this, call me. I want these guys. We're pretty sure they already killed one person. I don't want any more bodies."

"I have your number, Detective. Expect a call soon."

I walked out the front door of Frankie's apartment, Angela by my side and Rosa and Alex trailing behind. Dante was in my arms. I noticed a guy sitting behind the wheel of his car reading a paper. *That's odd*, I thought, and took note.

My time on the streets made me aware of things like that. It had become almost instinctive. Sometimes it was simply what it looked like—a guy reading the paper. At other times, it was something else. I didn't mention anything to Angie because I didn't want her to worry, but I'd make sure to pay attention throughout the day.

We piled into the car, Angie in the passenger seat and the kids in the back. "Where should we go?" I asked.

"Boat ride!" they yelled. "We want to go on a boat ride."

"Boat ride it is," I said. "There's one ride that will take us all the way around the city. You can see everything from there."

"Have you been on it, Dad?" Rosa asked.

"Years ago, I was. But it's been a long while."

"Kate took me on it last year," Alex said. "It's great."

"Looks like we're going on a boat ride," I said, and headed in that direction.

As I turned, I noticed the guy who had been reading the paper was following a few cars behind me. He wore a brown cap, slanted to the left, and he had on a pair of sunglasses. I now felt pretty certain that this was more than coincidence. What puzzled me was who the hell would be following me. Dominic knew I was in the city, and Manny wouldn't care. *So who does care?*

We took the boat ride. The guy who I now felt sure was following me stayed in the parking lot. After the boat ride, we went to one of the museums and then Prospect Park. I hadn't spotted him at the museum, but while trying to find a space at the park, I did. Now, it was beyond any form of coincidence as far as I was concerned. Someone was following me, but I had no idea why.

We finished out the day at the park, then headed back to Frankie's place. I never let the kids out of my sight, and I was sure Angela was with me at all times.

When Bugs got home, I waited until we were alone, then asked, "Any reason for anyone to be following me?"

He narrowed his eyes and stared. "None that I know of, but if you're asking, I presume you spotted a tail."

I nodded. "A pretty good one too. Mid-thirties and appeared to be stocky. Mind you, this is from spotting him in the car, so take the description as suspect."

"Black? White? Hispanic?" Bugs asked.

"Definitely white. Other than that, I have no idea. Why? You thinking of someone?"

"I doubt it, but…"

"But what?" I asked.

"Lou and I just started looking into a branch of the Bratva on that murder case. And those guys don't play nice."

"You looking into them would explain them tailing you, but not me."

"That's what I was thinking too," Bugs said. "Still, keep an eye out and let me know if you see anything else. In the meantime, Lou and I will try to watch for anyone following."

"All right, Bugs, but enough about it now. Angie's coming over, and I haven't told her about this."

"No shit!" Bugs said, faking a different conversation. "I can't believe he did that."

I smiled and leaned against the back of the sofa. "Well, he did. Right in front of them?"

TIME TO GO BACK TO WORK

Shawna finished her breakfast, took the dishes to the sink and rinsed them off, then grabbed her purse and left, making sure to lock the door. Locking the door had become of primary importance since her apartment had been broken into. Now, she didn't leave the door unlocked even if she was only going to the laundry room.

The subway entrance was only a block away, but she must have looked over her shoulder ten times while walking.

She got off at the stop for her work and made sure to mingle with the crowd as she rushed to the building. Once she was safely inside, she breathed a sigh of relief and immediately began feeling foolish for having been so worried.

Jackson tapped her on the shoulder while she waited for the elevator. "Shawna, what's up? I've been watching you, and you look nervous as hell."

"I'm sure it's nothing. I got all flustered over that break-in at the house —and the threats."

The elevator bell rang, and a small group entered. "Did you report it?" Jackson asked.

Shawna nodded. "Yeah, the police were out to investigate."

"I wouldn't worry about it. They'll find out who's doing this. In the meantime, be more cautious; in fact, I'll have someone take you home tonight, just to be safe."

Shawna laughed as she entered the elevator and turned to face the front. "No need for that. I'll be fine. It's my mother's tendency to worry coming out in me. Seems like I do the worrying when she's not around to do it for me."

"No harm in worrying," Jackson said. "Nobody's died from it that I know of. At least not directly."

At the end of the day, Jackson had his driver, Edward, take Shawna home. "He'll take you home tonight and pick you up in the morning. No arguments."

Edward took her home and let her out in front of the building. "I'll wait for you to signal me at your window once you're inside, and I'll be here to pick you up in the morning."

"No need for all that, I—"

"No arguing. Jackson's orders. I'll see you at seven."

Shawna entered the apartment, then gave the signal that all was okay. She made sure the door was locked, then put on a pot of coffee. She was behind on her work, so this was going to be a late night.

She spread her files out on the table, opened her laptop, poured a hot cup of coffee, then settled in to work. Not ten minutes later, the doorbell rang.

She went to the door, wondering who it could be and peeked through the hole. A man stood there with flowers.

"Yes?" she asked.

"Flowers," the man said. "Delivery for Shawna Pavic."

Shawna opened the door and reached for the flowers. "Who sent them?"

The delivery man pushed his way inside, then slammed the door and pointed a gun at her.

"What the hell do you think you're doing? Who are you?"

"*Who I am* is the person who told you to stop writing those articles. And I'm here to ensure you don't write them again." With that, he fired two shots to her chest and one more to her face. She slumped to the floor without a word.

The delivery man picked up the flowers, holding them in front of his face, and made his way back out, making sure he wasn't seen by any cameras.

When Shawna wasn't outside by 7:15, Edward went in and had them buzz her. No one answered, so he went up and rang the bell. When he still got no answer, he called Jackson, who immediately called the police.

Lou Mazzetti's phone rang while he was enjoying his second cup of coffee. "Mazetti," he said.

"Lou, this is Jergens over in Manhattan Homicide. I used to work with you in Brooklyn."

"Yeah, I remember, Jergens. Manhattan now, huh? Moved up to the lazy man's job."

Jergens laughed. "I wouldn't say it's that bad, Lou. It's not Brooklyn, but it's not Beverly Hills either."

"What's up, Jergens? What can I do for you?"

"No way to say it but straight out," Jergens said. "Shawna Pavic is dead."

"Dead? How?"

"Two shots in the chest and one in the head. At first glance, it looks like a professional job. Neighbors were home and heard nothing. I suspect it may have been a silencer because nothing indicates anything was used to muffle the shots. And it wasn't a break-in; she must have let the person in. And nothing was stolen except her laptop, which tells me it may be connected to the threats she was receiving."

"Shit! Did you call Donovan?"

"No. I remembered he had something going on with her, or at least he did when I was still there."

"That ended a while ago," Lou said. "But he kept in touch with her. I'll tell him. We're partners now."

"I know. I'd heard that which is why I called you."

"All right. Thanks, Jergens. Keep me up to date on this."

"Will do," Jergens said.

Lou called Sherri Miller. "You may want to get together anything you've got on Shawna Pavic."

"Why's that?"

"Somebody killed her last night in her home. Shot her three times."

"Damn," Sherri said. "Anybody tell Donovan?"

"Not yet," Lou said. "I'm waiting until he gets in."

BAD NEWS

Frankie climbed the stairs slowly. He was tired from being up half the night playing canasta and pinochle.

Lou met him at the top of the steps with coffee. "Here you go, Donovan. Just how you like it."

Frankie stared at the cup, then at Lou. "Is this a trick? Why are you being nice?"

"I'm a nice guy," Lou said.

"Since when?"

"Just take the goddamn coffee and follow me," Lou said.

Frankie followed Lou to the coffee room, where Lou closed the door and took a seat. Frankie sat across from him. "What's up, Lou? Something wrong?"

"Yeah, it's—"

"It's what? Did something happen to Marie?"

Lou shook his head. "Shawna Pavic is dead. Murdered last night."

Frankie stood quickly, bumping the table and spilling his coffee. "What? Where? What happened?"

"Take it easy, Donovan. Sit down."

"What happened, Lou?"

"Somebody shot her in her apartment. Two to the chest and one to the head. Jergens called me this morning. Remember Jergens? He was a rookie when he was here."

Frankie nodded. "Yeah, I remember him. He's in Manhattan now?"

"Yeah. He caught this case and recalled that you and Shawna dated. That's why he called. And before you ask, no, they don't know anything yet and have no leads. It's early, so don't go blaming people."

Frankie stared at the table. "You're right, Lou. Thanks for reminding me because that's what I'd have done. I was already thinking it."

"Don't I know it," Lou said. "You don't get to be an old prick like me without picking up some wisdom along the way."

Frankie pulled out his phone.

"Who you calling, Donovan?"

"I'm calling Miller. Why?"

Lou took the phone from Frankie and shook his head. "Because whether you intend to or not, you'll end up making her feel bad, as if she could have prevented it, and we both know she couldn't. So put the phone away; besides, I already filled her in without making her feel bad."

"You're right again, Lou. Damn, I hate saying that. When you talk to her again, ask her to get us copies of the articles Shawna wrote. I've seen them once, but I want to study them again. Whoever killed her is in there, and I'm gonna find the son of a bitch."

"And I'm gonna help you," Lou said, "but first we have to solve this other case, figure out who killed the professor."

"We already know who killed him—the Russians."

"Knowing and proving are different. We need to find a way to get enough evidence to prove it."

Two hours later, Frankie was reviewing the professor's case file when his computer alerted him that an email had arrived.

He opened the attachment, saw that it was the copies he'd requested, then hit *print* so he could take them home and read them.

Lou walked in just as Frankie was printing the papers.

"That what you were waiting for from Miller?"

Frankie nodded. "Yeah, all the articles she wrote in the past four weeks. Whoever killed her is bound to be in here."

"I'll go over them with you, if you want."

"Thanks anyway, Lou, but I'll do it tonight at home."

"Getting 'The Rat,' to help you?"

"Probably. He sometimes has good insight."

"Yeah, I can see that, but I don't think he'd pass the requirements to get into the department, so you'll have to keep him as an outside source."

Lou poured another cup of coffee.

"Just the same, Donovan, print copies for me too. I'll take a look after Marie goes to bed."

"Thanks, Lou. That'd be great. I'll take all the help I can get on this one."

Two hours later, as Frankie was reading one of Shawna's files, the detective from France called.

"We caught the woman meeting with one of the Bratva on tape, and we arrested them on suspicion, but we found nothing, not even in the shoes. I don't know if they suspected we'd be there, but whatever it was that alerted them, we have nothing. We can't hold them."

"Shit!" Frankie said.

"The good news is that the Russian is spooked. He took a flight home soon after we let him go. I suspect we ruined the operation, at least temporarily."

"If you accomplished that, it's something. Hell, it's a lot. Thanks. And thanks for keeping me in the loop."

"No problem, Detective. I will continue to do so. Have a good day."

Frankie filled Lou in on the call. "We didn't get much, but it's something," Frankie said. "I think we should gloat. Go see Viktor and tell him that this is just the beginning, that a lot more will come."

Frankie looked over and saw Lou working on his computer. "Lou, are you listening?"

"Yeah, I heard you, Donovan, but right now I'm shopping for a new bullseye. I don't think the one you're painting on yourself is big enough."

"Fuck you, Lou."

"That's what Viktor is going to do—fuck you. Or kill you. As you know already, the Bratva doesn't play around. Your Italian buddies like to pass around money; the Russians pass around bullets with no regard for who gets them."

"He wouldn't dare hurt a detective," Frankie said.

"I wouldn't bet my life on it. Hell, I wouldn't bet *your* life on it. Those people have no respect."

~

JERGENS CALLED when Frankie and Lou were talking strategy.

"What's up, Jergens? Got anything?" Lou asked.

"Maybe. We found a floral delivery van abandoned with the driver tied up in the back. He said some guy stole his van, tied him up, gagged him, and blindfolded him, then drove off. He never got a good look at the guy, but he said he thinks he had an Eastern European accent."

"What's a flower van got to do with anything?" Lou asked.

"We have video of a guy delivering flowers to her building around the time she was shot, and the thing is, he walked back out with the same flowers he walked in with, both times making sure the flowers covered his face from the cameras."

"Sounds professional," Lou said. "Combine that with the accent, it smells like Russians to me."

"That's what I was thinking."

"All right. Thanks, Jergens. I'll fill Donovan in, and we'll get back to you. We might have something to add to that."

"What?"

"I said we'll get back to you. There's nothing concrete yet."

"Make sure you do, Mazzetti. This cooperation door swings both ways, you know."

"Yeah, I know, Jergens. Remember who taught you how to wipe your ass."

Jergens laughed. "I remember. Some fuckin' old man who smoked too much. Call me when you get something."

Lou filled Frankie in on what Jergens said. Frankie pounded his fist on the desk. "Son of a bitch, if that prick had something to do with Shawna, I'll put a bullet in his head."

"Easy going, partner," Lou said. "How about we focus on any article Shawna wrote that has to do with the Bratva and see where it takes us. If it points to Viktor, we'll nail him."

Frankie gathered up his copies, put them into a folder, and laid them on his desk. "I'm going through all of them tonight, Lou. We'll have someone to go after tomorrow."

"That's great, Donovan. But for now, let's figure out what to do about this information from France."

A LOOK AT THE ARTICLES

Bugs got home early, and he had a concerned look on his face. Long ago I learned to recognize that look.

"What's up, Bugs? Something happen?"

He sat on the sofa and shook his head. "Nothing. Just a bad day."

"Bugs, there's no sense in lying. You've got the same look on your face as you did that time you lost your favorite knife."

Bugs laughed. "You're a shithead, Nicky. You know that?"

"Why? For making you laugh?"

"Maybe so," he said. "My friend Shawna was murdered."

"Who?"

"Shawna, the reporter who was getting the threats."

"Son of a bitch! And you think it was the person threatening her who did it?"

"We don't know yet, but that's the way I see it." Bugs pointed to a folder on the kitchen table. "I brought home the articles she'd written so I could study them, see if I can make anything of it."

"I'll help you, Bugs. I've got nothing else to do."

Bugs looked around. "Christ, that reminds me, where is everybody?"

"They went to the movies. Some show the kids wanted to see."

"Anything else on that suspected tail?" Bugs asked.

Nicky shook his head. "Not that I could tell, though they could have used someone better and I didn't notice. How about you?"

"I don't even know. I forgot to watch for it with all this shit going on."

"Any suspects on the murder?" Nicky asked.

"Maybe, but I'd rather not say. I don't want to taint your thinking before you read the articles."

"Then let's get started. No better time than when the ladies are gone."

They went to the kitchen. Nicky put on coffee while Bugs organized the files.

"These are the articles she wrote in the past month. I figure whoever did this is in here somewhere."

"All we've got to do is find him," Nicky said. "Can't be too hard."

Bugs pushed Nicky about half the stack. "Set aside anything that looks like it may have threatened people, then we'll read it again. We need to come up with a suspect list."

"Just start reading, Bugs. You might get halfway through by the time I'm done."

Forty minutes later, Nicky finished. He came up with a short list, only three articles. Bugs finished a few minutes later, and he had only flagged two articles.

"What have you got, Nicky?"

"Not much. The two you mentioned earlier: concrete and money laundering, and one dealing with rezoning of apartment buildings in Queens. How about you?"

"I didn't see much either: one article dealt with road construction, and another with licenses for vendor stands."

"Where do you want to go from here?" Nicky asked.

"Trade articles. You take the ones I went through, and I'll take yours. Let's see if we come up with anything else."

Thirty minutes later, Nicky had one more article and Bugs had none. "I can't believe you didn't put this aside, Bugs. It's about that professor's murder, the one you're working on."

Frankie nodded. "Yeah, I know, but every reporter in the city covered that. I can't see why someone would single her out for it."

"I guess so," Nicky said. "The problem is that the one that looks the most damaging is the article dealing with the concrete, but I still say Dominic wouldn't bother her about it. He definitely wouldn't kill her."

Bugs nodded. "I agree. He might get her fired, but he wouldn't kill her."

Bugs got up and grabbed a beer. "That still leaves us with the money-laundering article. I didn't tell you this before, but the one lead we have points to a man with an eastern European accent."

"And you think it's the Russians?" Nicky asked.

"I do, Nicky. And I'm gonna kill them."

"Before you kill them, we might want to make sure they're the ones who did it."

"I know they did it."

"I'm sorry, Bugs, but you don't *know*—you *think*. As one of Brooklyn's premier detectives, you should know the difference."

"I know the difference, Rat, but he deserves it whether he killed Shawna or not. I'll tell you what we need to do."

Nicky held up his finger. "What we need to do is get rid of this crap. I think I just heard the ladies come home."

Bugs grabbed the papers and put them back into the folder, which he set on the counter, then rejoined Nicky at the table.

A moment later the door opened, and Kate and Angela stepped inside followed by noisy youngsters.

"Did you guys have fun?" Nicky asked.

"It was great, Nicky. We'll have to go again when we get home. Dante loved it."

Kate leaned over and kissed Frankie on the cheek. "What's wrong? You look upset."

"Nothing, I—"

"I thought we were being honest with each other," Kate said.

Frankie grinned. "All right. I didn't want you to worry, so I didn't tell you, but Shawna's dead."

"What? How?"

"Somebody shot her. I'm guessing it was whoever was threatening her, but we don't have any leads yet."

"My God, that's terrible. I can't believe it."

"Who's this?" Angie asked.

"A reporter Bugs knows. Someone was threatening her for writing something in the paper, and it looks as if he killed her."

"That's terrible," Angie said, "and right before the wedding."

"I don't think she scheduled her death to accommodate Frankie's wedding, Angie."

Angie smacked Nicky. "You know what I mean." Angie turned to face Bugs. "What happened, Frankie? I mean if it's not too much to ask."

"No problem," Bugs said. "Someone shot her while she was in her apartment. There doesn't appear to have been forced entry, so we're guessing the person was admitted by Shawna."

"Why would she let someone in?"

"Who knows? Maybe they were disguised as a repairman or a delivery man. That's one of the things we need to find out. They have footage of a guy delivering flowers to the building, but they don't have cameras in the halls, so we don't know where he went yet."

"What do you mean 'we' need to find out?" Kate asked. "This isn't your case."

"I was speaking as a cop, not as if it were my case."

We played cards, played a game of scrabble, then the ladies went to bed. Bugs and I sat up chatting. "You want me to visit these Russians?" I asked.

"Nicky, what I want is for you to stay out of this. The last thing I need is someone questioning who the hell you are."

"Consider it done. We're going to Ellis Island tomorrow anyway."

"Ellis Island? What for?"

"Rosa wants to go. She said she wants to see where her ancestors came ashore. I told her there were plenty of more interesting places, but she'd have nothing of it."

"Sounds like you're going to Ellis Island," Frankie said.

"I will. Keep me up to speed, and don't do anything stupid."

"Goodnight, Rat."

THE CIRCLE FORMS

*L*ou Mazzetti woke to the smell of coffee. The coffee wasn't brewing yet, but his wife must have ground the beans, leaving that magnificent aroma to waft through the air. That smell—and the fact that he only had thirty days until he retired—made everything better.

Lou dressed and went to the office, parked his car, and went inside. As he climbed the steps, he thought about what he'd do after the next month, and then he put a cigarette in his mouth and smiled. It would piss Frankie off that he was smoking inside the building again, and not much gave Lou more pleasure than pissing Frankie off.

Donovan was at the top of the stairs, glaring. "Lou, put that goddamn cigarette out. I know you've already mentally retired, but you could at least follow the rules."

"I could, yeah, but there's no sense in starting now."

Lou walked past Donovan and into the coffee room. "You get anything last night?" he asked.

"Not really," Frankie said. "I still think it's the Russians, but I can't see where."

"Did you read the article she did on the professor?"

"Yeah, I read that, Lou. But every damn reporter in town did a piece on him. There was something new every day."

"I know that, but did you *really* read the article?"

"I just said I did."

"Then you must have missed the part where she linked to an article she wrote last year. It questioned the professor's involvement in a criminal operation suspected of smuggling false identities."

"What?" Frankie said, and got up and moved next to Lou. "How the hell did I miss that?"

"Because you're not old and wise like your partner."

"If she was talking about the professor's involvement with the identities, and the Russians now have the identities because they killed the professor, then…"

"Exactly," Lou said. "They wouldn't want the attention it would draw, and it might prompt them to do something about it."

"You think they'd do something that drastic?" Frankie asked.

"I think there's only one way to find out," Lou said. "Let's pay Viktor another visit."

Frankie and Lou made the drive to Brighton Beach in less than half an hour. As before, the club was crowded with bouncers at the door. They stripped Lou and Frankie of their guns, then admitted them.

More muscle-bound buffoons rushed to greet them. Frankie flashed his badge as they approached.

"Detectives Donovan and Mazzetti. We need to see Viktor."

"What for? Viktor's busy."

"I would say I'm here to arrest him," Frankie said. "but I don't want to have to shoot you when you try to stop me. Tell him I'm here to keep my promise. He'll know what I mean. And if you're thinking I can't shoot you because they took my gun—think again—I've got another."

The man stared at Frankie for maybe five seconds, then he called someone over. "Get Viktor. Tell him two cops are here to see him."

"Smart move," Frankie said.

The man sneered. "We'll see."

Viktor came in a moment later accompanied by two more of his bodyguards. "You're here again, Detective. What can I do for you? More questions about the professor?"

Frankie shook his head. "No questions at all, Viktor. I don't even want to know why you killed the reporter. I already know why. I'm here to tell you that I'm gonna make you pay for it by busting every operation I can find, and that's *before* I lock your ass up for murder."

Viktor laughed. "Really? Good luck then, but don't get carried away, Detective. Even detectives aren't bulletproof."

Frankie reached to grab Viktor, but one of his bodyguards stepped in the way. "You're not the only one who can make threats, Viktor. And just so you know, captains of the Bratva aren't bulletproof either."

Viktor scorned. "Did a New York detective just threaten me?"

"I don't know," Frankie said. "I repeated your words. Did you threaten a New York detective?"

"I don't think I did. I wouldn't do that," Viktor said.

"It's a good thing because there are a lot more cops in New York than there are members of the Bratva. I'd hate for it to come to an all-out war, but I'm willing to go that far if you want."

Viktor signaled the bartender to fix him a drink, and he offered one to Frankie and Lou.

"I wouldn't take one from you even if I wanted it," Frankie said.

"I think we started off badly," Viktor said. "Perhaps we—"

"You started things off badly by killing the professor," Frankie said. "But you really screwed up when you killed the reporter. I knew her. She was a good lady who was simply doing her job."

Frankie poked his finger at Viktor's chest. "You should have left well enough alone, Viktor. Now, I'm coming after you."

"Be careful what you hunt, Detective. You may catch it."

"I'll catch you, Viktor. I have no doubt of that." Frankie turned to leave. "That's all I've got today. I just wanted to stop by and tell you what to expect. I'm coming after you, and I'm bringing a shit-storm with me."

As they walked out the front door, Lou went back inside and spoke to Viktor. "You may not realize it, but you're fucked. Frankie *will* catch you, and if something happens to him, you're fucked anyway because I'll put at least one bullet in your head. You can count on it."

Viktor sneered again. "Get out of my club. You're not welcome here."

Lou rushed to catch up to Frankie. After he got in the car, Frankie asked, "What did you go back in for?"

"Nothing," Lou said. "So you didn't forget the same sunglasses that you forgot last time?"

Lou laughed. "No, had to take a piss, that's all."

"You're full of it, Lou. I know you. You wouldn't even piss in a place like that. You said something to Viktor. What?"

"Christ's sake, Donovan. Do you need to know everything? I told him I'd kill him if for some reason we couldn't arrest him. Okay?"

Frankie nodded. "Okay, that's reasonable. I might even help you."

"Good. I knew I could count on you. Now, tell me what your plan is for busting up his operation. Not like we haven't been trying."

"I'm gonna convince the lieu to put a special team together—people we know aren't on the take—then we're gonna bust every damn thing we can find that Viktor's involved with."

"Damn, Donovan. It almost sounds like you're out to piss him off."

"I am out to piss him off, and busting up his operations might do that," Frankie said. "I hope so because pissed-off people make mistakes."

"Sounds good to me," Lou said. "I've got nothing else to do for the next thirty days."

"That makes two people for our team. All we need now is a half a dozen more and the lieu's blessing."

"Then pick him up a cinnamon roll and a coffee on the way back. He won't refuse you then. He's like a ten-dollar street whore when it comes to cinnamon rolls."

THE CRACKDOWN BEGINS

Frankie dropped Lou off at the station, then drove home slowly, thinking of what to tell Kate and Nicky. If there was one thing he didn't want, it was Nicky getting involved with this. He felt certain that if Nicky got involved, people would be killed, and he was trying to avoid that.

"What's up, Bugs?" Nicky hollered as Frankie walked in the door.

"Same old shit," Frankie said. "Another day dealing with scum."

"It's a wonder it doesn't wear off on you," Nicky said. "I don't know if I could keep my cool."

"And *that* is why you're not a cop," Frankie said. He tried to stifle a laugh, but it didn't work. "Well, *that* and a few other reasons."

"You find out anything today?"

Frankie shook his head. "Nothing. But I'm working on it. It shouldn't be long."

"And you wouldn't lie, right? I mean, you wouldn't be working on something and not tell me, would you?"

Frankie looked at Nicky. "Hell no. If I need help, I'll tell you."

"I'll take your word for it, but I don't believe you."

"Where are Kate and Angela?"

"Angela met her, and they took the kids to some museum. They called a little while ago, and Kate said she's stopping to pick up dinner from someplace you *really* like."

"Damn, I know where she means, and wait until you taste their seafood ravioli. It's to die for."

"I'm glad because I told her to get me whatever you normally get."

"Good choice, Rat. You won't regret it."

AFTER STUFFING AT DINNER, Frankie made coffee for Nicky and himself.

"You weren't shitting about the seafood ravioli, Bugs. That was as good as Cataldi's, and that's saying something."

"What have you got planned for tomorrow, Nicky?"

Nicky sighed and whispered. "I think they have more museums on the itinerary, though I don't know why. I've been to enough museums to last a lifetime."

"Tell me about it," Frankie said. "Kate loves museums, and not for just taking visitors either. She drags my ass down there all the time."

"Get used to it, Bugs. If she's like that now, it'll probably only get worse. And you've only got a short time left to be single."

"Asshole! Don't remind me. It's only a few days."

"Worried?"

Bugs shook his head. "Not really. Kate and I get along well."

Nicky laughed. "Get used to saying 'I'm sorry' and you'll be fine."

"Screw you," Bugs said.

"We playing cards tonight?" Nicky asked.

"I don't think so. I've got to see the lieutenant early in the morning."

"About the Russians?"

"Don't even try it, Rat. It's about 'none of your business.' That's what it's about."

Nicky played board games with Kate and Angela while Frankie watched TV and Rosa and Alex watched music videos. In the morning, Frankie left before anyone else was up.

FRANKIE KNOCKED on the door to Lieutenant Morreau's office, then walked in and sat.

"What do you want, Donovan? I know it must be important or you wouldn't be here so early."

"I need your help, Lieu."

"You didn't have to tell me that—just seeing you at this time of day tells me that much."

"Remember that reporter that was killed? That was Shawna Pavic. I knew her. In fact, I used to date her."

Morreau put down his paperwork and looked at Frankie. "Go on."

"I think I know who did the killing, but I need some muscle to make him crack."

"Who are we talking about? And what kind of muscle?"

"Viktor Polenko, and before you ask, yes, the same Viktor Polenko who is connected to the Bratva."

"And the muscle?"

"I want a small team that I put together and use to bust up his operations."

"You know what this will do, don't you? It'll more than piss him off."

"I hope so. That's my intention. And that's why I need to pick the team myself. I need people who aren't afraid."

"Everyone is afraid to die, Donovan. Except maybe Mazzetti."

"Can you get me the okay?"

Morreau shifted in his seat. "Who do you want for the team?"

"I don't know yet. I know the types but not the names. I figure some old farts like Lou who don't give a shit and some young studs who think they're invincible."

"Got plenty of both kinds right in this precinct. I'll see what I can do and let you know."

"When?"

"Later today, for Christ's sake."

"All right, I'll get working on the list," Frankie said, then stood and left the office.

By one o'clock, Morreau had given him the okay, and by two o'clock Frankie had selected his team. Now he had to see if they wanted in. He asked Morreau to get them together in a private room so he could address them.

Frankie stood in front of the room. The six potential team members sat before him waiting.

"Nobody knows why they're here, and that's the way I want it. In fact, if you join this team, no one can know what it's about afterward. Not even your spouses."

"What is it about?" Ruiz asked.

Ruiz was a young stud from Narcotics. His brother had overdosed on heroin. "You'll know *if* and *when* you're chosen. First I want to tell you what you'd be in for."

"Spit it out," Franco said.

Frankie glanced at his sheet. Franco was another young stud, but he had just made the Major Case Squad.

"Hold onto your ass, Franco. I'll get to it when I'm ready."

"What's keeping you?" Morgan asked. "If we're gonna buy into this, we gotta know what it is."

Frankie didn't need to look at Morgan's record. He was an old fart like Lou. He'd been around for thirty years and had a reputation for being tough as nails.

"Sign me up. I don't give a shit what it is," Jasper said.

Frankie smiled. Jasper was an up-and-comer that had joined the department after growing up in the projects. He had a hard life, and his file said he chose assignments that didn't make it any easier.

"Whatever you plan on doing, get on with it," Ronan said.

Frankie cracked another smile. Ronan had a reputation as the toughest female in the department. She had made a name for herself in the Strategic Response Group. Frankie was surprised that she would even consider this assignment.

"Why should I join this team?" Marino asked.

Frankie stared. The way he asked the question pissed him off. "You shouldn't," Frankie said. "You can go now."

"What? Hey, I just asked."

"I know," Frankie said. "But I didn't like the way you asked, so you can go. Goodbye."

After Marino left, Frankie scanned the group. "Looks like there are just five of us now. If anyone else wants out, now's the time to say so. You'll get another chance after I tell you what you're in for, but if you have doubts, express them now."

The potential team members nodded, and Frankie continued. "A few days ago, a local reporter was killed for running stories. We have reason to believe it was Viktor Polenko from the Bratva."

A couple of the younger cops turned and looked at each other.

"Anybody have a problem with going after him?" Frankie asked.

"None," they all said at once.

"Good, because I intend to nail his ass to a cross," Frankie said.

"Sounds good to me," Jasper said.

Frankie held up his hands. "It may sound good, but this is going to be dangerous. Viktor is already suspected of killing a reporter, a professor from the university, and probably dozens more. I have no doubts that he'd just as quickly kill one of us."

"Then he'll have to kill all of us," Ronan said, and she sounded as if she meant it.

"All right, if you're in, here's how it's gonna work. As I said, no one can know, but I want to carry that to the extreme. That means you don't report to work here, and we don't meet anywhere. I'll call each member the night before and tell you where to go. We'll all meet there and get started."

"Get started on what?" Ruiz asked.

"We're going to bust up every operation of his that we can find. Hit him where it will hurt the most—in his pocket."

"If we know where his operations are, why haven't we busted them before?" Franco asked.

"Stick around long enough, and you'll learn, Franco. Viktor has too many men on his payroll. He's always been tipped off when a raid is going to happen. That's another reason I want this group to remain secret. We can't afford to give him warning."

"How's this going to help bust him for murder?" Morgan asked.

"We'll arrest enough of his men until one of them talks. It'll happen sooner or later."

"Count me in," Morgan said.

"Me too," they all said.

Frankie nodded. "All right. Expect a call from me tonight. I'll tell you where we're going to meet."

Frankie had told everyone to meet him at the southern entrance to Prospect Park at 7:30. He only had to wait about three minutes for them to arrive.

"Okay, first stop is a bookmaking operation. Get in your cars and follow me."

"That would be 'follow *us*,'" Lou said. "Sometimes Donovan forgets who his better half is."

"Mazzetti, I thought you were retiring," Morgan said.

"Not for another three weeks. With that in mind, your primary job is to keep me alive."

Frankie parked a block away, then he and Lou got out of the car, along with the rest of the team.

"Okay, here's how it's gonna work. Lou is going in as a gambler. He knows the password, and he looks like a gambler, so they won't suspect anything. He's wearing a wire, so once he sees the operation in progress, he'll let us know. When we get that signal, we go in." Frankie looked out over the team members. "Any questions?"

～

LOU WALKED up to the door, guarded by a large man with a gun tucked in his waistband. "First race go off yet at Aqueduct?"

"Password?"

"*Spot-check*," Lou said.

The guy glanced at his watch. "The race starts in ten minutes. You can make it if you hurry," he said, then opened the door so Lou could enter.

Lou walked in and saw a flurry of activity, including plenty of money changing hands. He found a quiet corner and spoke into his mic. "It's a go, Donovan."

A few minutes later, Frankie and his team burst in with guns drawn. Frankie had his badge prominently displayed. "NY Police department," Frankie said. "Stand against the back wall. Nobody's going anywhere."

Ronan stood by the door with her gun drawn, preventing anyone from leaving. Franco and Jasper moved the crowd in an orderly fashion to the back wall, and Ruiz and Morgan gathered evidence.

Within two hours, they had everyone processed, and the bookmaking operation shut down.

Frankie met the team in the parking lot outside the station. "Okay, guys, that one went well. Now let's get the others. Follow me."

The next stop was a prostitution ring operating out of a townhouse located in an upscale section of Brooklyn. It was a bonus for Viktor; he made money from the prostitution and also from the townhouse as it increased in value. And if he worked it right, he could also turn it into a money-laundering opportunity using one of his construction crews to "fix" the townhouse when it was ready to sell.

They arrested eight prostitutes and six customers, and they were able to seal the house so it couldn't be used again.

As Ronan led the last prostitute out the door, Mazzetti said, "Tell Viktor that Mazzetti and Donovan said hello."

Franco was leading out a customer wearing cuffs. Frankie grabbed hold of him. "And tell people you know that Donovan said this is only the beginning. Before we're done, Viktor will be sleeping and pissing in the same alley."

"Guess you're looking to stir up trouble," Ruiz said.

"That's the gist of it," Frankie said.

Afterward, they busted another bookmaking operation, but this one was a more lucrative one. Frankie got together with his team at the end of the day.

"We did a lot of good work today. We busted more of Viktor's operations in one day than the department did in the past year. If nothing else, we sent him a strong message."

"Looking forward to tomorrow," Jasper said.

"That reminds me," Frankie said, "Lou will be handling the team by himself tomorrow. I've got a funeral to go to, and on the weekend we won't be working. Not because of the weekend, but because I'm getting married."

"Married? Congratulations," Ruiz said.

"Thanks," Frankie said. "Lou will call you tonight with the location of where to meet. I'll see everyone the day after."

VIKTOR POUNDED his fist on the counter. "How did they even get into our places? Who let them in?"

Gregor sheepishly responded. "I think the cops had an insider, or they sent in an undercover cop. It doesn't make a difference, Viktor. They got in. That's all that matters."

Viktor pounded the counter again. "How did this happen? Why weren't we told about this? Where were our inside men?"

"I checked. No one knew anything about it. The word is that those two detectives are doing this on their own."

Peter stepped forward. "It's true. When we bailed out the whores, one of them said that the detective said to tell Viktor that Mazzetti and Donovan said hello."

"That son of a bitch!" Viktor said.

"That's not all," Peter said. "The one detective—Donovan—said you will be pissing and sleeping in the same alley."

Viktor narrowed his eyes. "I want those cops followed. Find out everything you can about them. Where they live, who they love. I want to know everything."

Gregor moved out of Viktor's way. "Viktor, you can't do anything to a cop. You'll lose protection if you do."

"Money buys anything," Viktor said. "All we have to do is increase the pay."

"I don't know," Gregor said.

"I *do* know," Viktor said. "Get it done."

FUNERAL FOR A FRIEND

Kate and Frankie left for the funeral right after breakfast. "You sure you don't mind watching Alex?" Frankie asked.

"Why would we mind watching him? He's been a pleasure to have with us," Angela said.

"We shouldn't be long," Kate said. "It's supposed to be a quick service."

As Frankie and Kate drove to the church, Frankie said, "I still can't believe she's gone. And for just doing her job."

"It happens to cops all the time," Kate said. "Maybe now you'll understand why I get so worried."

"No need to worry. It's not gonna happen to me."

"I'm sure Shawna said the same thing, and now look. Saying 'it's not gonna happen,' won't stop a bullet, Frankie."

"I know. Let's just get this over with."

"Is Lou coming?" Kate asked.

"No, he's working on something and couldn't take off."

"Who's handling Shawna's case?"

"Manhattan has it. A detective named Jergens. I used to work with him a few years ago."

"Good. I'm glad you're not involved."

After a brief church service, Frankie and Kate followed the procession to the cemetery. Halfway through, Kate nudged Frankie's arm. "Frankie, don't look but there's a man standing to our right who keeps staring at you. It's giving me the creeps."

Frankie made the sign of the cross, said a prayer, then turned to kiss Kate. When he did, he took the opportunity to look at the man. He was still staring, and when Frankie looked his way, the man formed his fingers like a gun and pointed at Frankie.

Frankie didn't react, and he didn't say anything to Kate. When the service finished, he took Kate by the arm and hurried her to the car.

On the way home, Kate said, "Who was that man?"

"What man?"

"Are we playing that game? You know damn right well what man I'm talking about—the one who threatened you."

"Threatened me? Nobody threatened me."

Kate pursed her lips. "If you want to die, that's no longer up to you alone. That used to be fine, but it isn't now. You asked me to marry you, so I have a say in what goes on. And you swore to be Alex's father and protector, so you have an obligation to him as well. In light of that, I'm telling you, you need to get help with this. Whatever you're doing is pissing somebody off."

Frankie placed his hand on Kate's arm. "Listen, Kate, I've got it under control. I didn't want to tell you, but Morreau approved a six-man team to work under me so we can resolve this."

"Resolve what?" Kate asked. "Who are you after?"

Frankie sighed. "Some Russians. It's nothing. I just—"

"Some Russians! The same Russians who killed Shawna? You know what you're doing, don't you? You're inviting them to kill you."

"No way, Kate. He wouldn't dare touch a detective; besides, I've got six of the toughest cops in the city on my team. We're going to nail this guy."

Kate shook her head. "I don't like it, Frankie. We're supposed to be getting married in a few days. I don't want to go to another funeral instead."

"There won't be any funerals, Kate. Trust me. I know you think I'll go to any lengths to get out of this marriage, but I won't go that far."

"That's good because I don't want to have to do an autopsy on you."

"Believe me. I don't want that either. By the way, I'm going to drop you off and check on Lou and the team, see how they're doing."

Kate shot a frowning glance at Frankie. "I thought today was a day off in respect of Shawna's funeral."

"It is, but Shawna would want me to do this, and I owe it to her."

"That's a pitiful excuse if I ever heard one, Mario F. Donovan."

"It may be pitiful, but it's true. I feel rotten about this. Shawna came to me with a problem, and I pushed it off on Sherri because I didn't trust myself to be professional."

"It's not your fault she's dead," Kate said.

"It might be. Who knows what would have happened if Lou and I had taken the case instead of Miller."

"Nonsense. The lieutenant may not have even let you take the case. He knew your history with Shawna."

Frankie nodded. "You might be right."

"Besides," Kate said, "You've trusted Miller with a lot more than this, and she's always done a good job."

"I guess so," Frankie said, "But I'm still going to check on Lou. I won't be long."

Kate sighed. "How did I know that?" She breathed deeply, then said, "Just drop me off in front of the apartment. Angela and I will take the kids somewhere."

Frankie slowed as he turned on the street to his house.

"Frankie, you should ask Nicky for help."

"What? No way. He's here for the wedding not to get killed. Besides, he's got his family with him."

"He could help," Kate said.

"Help how? By killing people? I don't need that kind of help, and I'm not asking him to do anything. End of discussion."

"But, Frankie—"

"No! And that's final."

Frankie pulled to the curb. "Have fun," he said. "I won't be long. I'm just checking in."

Frankie let Kate off, then called Lou. The team was on the third bust of the day. "We've been hitting them hard," Lou said. "I've got a feeling at least one Russian will be pissed."

"That's what we want, Lou. Where are you going next?"

"That club we suspect of money laundering. We'll be leaving here within ten minutes. Meet us over there."

Frankie and Lou walked into the club, followed by the rest of the team. They were met by two barrel-chested men who were obviously carrying guns.

"I'm sorry gentlemen, we're not open for business yet," one of them said.

"Lou showed his badge. "I hope you have permits for those guns."

The second man smiled. "Of course we do. I'll get them if you like."

"No need," Frankie said. "We're here for your books."

"What?"

"Your books," Lou said, handing him a warrant. "This is a piece of paper that says you have to turn over your books to us. We're then going to let our guys go through them before we come back to shut you down."

"I don't know what for," the guy said. "This is a legitimate operation."

"Yeah, and I'm twenty-nine," Lou said. "Now get the books."

Frankie stayed with Lou for a couple of hours, busting another book-making operation and a low-level drug dealer.

"That guy won't hurt him much," Lou said. "It looks like he barely moves enough product to feed and clothe himself."

"I know, but it's something. Every little bit puts more pressure on Viktor, and the more pressure we put on him the closer we are to getting him. He'll crack soon."

"I hope you're right," Lou said, "because his men seem to be getting closer to pulling their guns with every bust. They're on edge."

"I'm sure they are," Frankie said. "And I'm betting it's because Viktor is putting them on edge, which is what we want. If one of them draws a gun on us, we can arrest him and maybe get him to talk. If the charge is serious enough, he just might."

"Hey, Donovan, while you're dreaming, dream me up a good cup of coffee, will you? You know those Russians aren't going to talk—no matter what you charge them with."

"If I can charge them with something that produces enough time, they'll talk. Faced with the right amount of time, anyone will talk."

"It's great that you have those thoughts, Donovan, but it's not necessarily true."

"What do you mean by that?"

"It's like my father told me when I was a kid. An older boy was picking on me, and my father said, 'fight back. Don't let him push you around.'"

"What happened?" Frankie asked.

"I fought back and got my ass kicked. That's what happened," Lou said.

FRANKIE NEEDS HELP

After Frankie went to work, Kate rifled through the papers on his desk. She opened the top drawer on the left-hand side and took out his contacts book. As she was looking through it, a voice came from behind her.

"What do you need, Kate? Anything I can help you with?"

Startled, Kate spun quickly, embarrassment showing on her face. "Nicky! I didn't see you there. I…"

"If I can help you, tell me."

"It's nothing," Kate said and started for the kitchen. She stopped halfway there. "Nicky, it's *not* nothing. I think Frankie's in trouble, and I need Dominic Mangini's phone number. Do you have it?"

Nicky stared. "I've got it, but why do you want it? Dominic Mangini is not a man to trifle with."

"I know what I'm doing, Nicky. Do you have the number or not? I'll tell you all about it later."

Nicky nodded slowly. "Okay. I'll give it to you, but be careful when dealing with Dominic. And don't promise him anything. Nothing."

"I won't."

"Does Bugs know you're doing this?" Nicky asked.

Kate shook her head. "No, and please don't tell him."

"All right, Kate. I'll trust you on this. Here's the number." Nicky wrote it out on a piece of paper and handed it to her.

She grabbed it and went to the bedroom. "Thank you, Nicky."

Five minutes later, the phone rang in Dominic's house.

"Pronto."

"Mr. Mangini, my name is Kate Burns. I'm a medical examiner, and I'm Detective Donovan's fiancé.'"

"I'm listening."

"I'd like an appointment so that we could talk."

"I'm flattered, Ms. Burns. If you are going to invite me to the wedding, let me save you the cost of sending an invitation. I'm afraid I cannot attend. I don't think Detective Donovan would approve either. If it's for any other reason, let me also save you trouble and time. I can't help. I'm a busy man."

"I thought you were his friend," Kate said.

"I don't dislike Detective Donovan, but there has never been an occasion when I have called him *friend.* I also can't imagine there would be an occasion in the future. Detective Donovan and I operate on different sides of the law."

"I know that, Mr. Mangini. Frankie's in trouble. The Russian mob is after him. They've already killed a reporter, and now they've threatened him."

"The Russians? What did Detective Donovan do to deserve their displeasure?"

"It's a long story, but to get back at them for killing the woman, he busted up some of their operations."

"I'm saddened to hear that, but Detective Donovan knew what he was doing. He knows that to invoke the displeasure of organized crime is dangerous. He should have thought harder about it."

"Are you saying you won't help me?"

"I don't see how I can," Dominic said. "The Russians are not under my command."

"But you could talk to them."

"Why should they listen? It wouldn't benefit them."

"Then do something so that it would benefit them. Tell them you'd owe them a favor."

Dominic laughed. "Ms. Burns, it is sweet of you to think that I'm so powerful or that one of my favors carries so much weight, but it doesn't. Perhaps among my fellow Italians it would but not the Russians. There would have to be something more solid."

"I can't believe you'd let him die."

"There is nothing I can do about it. I'm sorry. I hope that Detective Donovan gets through this. I truly do."

Nicky had almost finished coffee when Kate walked into the kitchen. "Kate, did you make the call?"

"I did. I don't have a lot of time because I'm supposed to be at work, but I wanted to talk with you."

"Talk to me? Is everything all right? What did Dominic say?"

Kate walked to the stove and poured a cup of coffee. "Yes and no.

Everything is all right for now, but it won't be for long. Dominic said he couldn't help."

"Whoa! Back up, Kate. What won't be okay for long? You're getting married in a few days. Don't tell me you're having second thoughts."

Kate tried to laugh. "Nothing like that. It's this thing with Shawna. She—"

"I thought she died."

"That's just it. She was murdered for writing things about the Russian mob, and now Frankie's going after them. At Shawna's funeral, I saw a guy threaten him."

Nicky sat up straighter. "And he was a Russian? One of the Bratva?"

"I don't know who he was, but he pointed his finger at Frankie as if he held a gun. It was plain as day. I told Dominic this, and he said he couldn't help Frankie. Can *you* help him?"

"Kate, you know I'd do anything for Bugs, but this isn't as simple as dealing with some lunatic on a killing spree. This is the Russian mob. They're not nice people."

"I could say that about a lot of people," Kate said.

"Yeah, I guess you could. But these people have power. political power."

"Then you'll have to find someone with just as much political power. Someone who's not afraid of what they can do."

"And who the hell would that be?" Nicky asked.

Kate hesitated. "Without mentioning names, I think you know who I mean."

"Yeah, I know who you mean. But didn't you say you just spoke with him, and he refused to help? Besides, dealing with Dominic may be as much trouble for me as dealing with the Russians. The situation is not as bad as it was before, but I could be buying into more trouble with him than trying to take care of things myself."

"Maybe if you go to him, Nicky. Tell him it's to help Frankie. I don't know what the relationship is, but Dominic Mangini likes Frankie."

"Kate, I told you. This is not a nice man. Dominic Mangini once told me not to step foot in New York again, or he'd have me killed. He eased up on that before I left last time—and things don't seem bad now—but who knows with Dominic."

Nicky sipped his coffee, then stared at the wall, thinking.

"Nicky, are you still with me?" Kate asked.

"I'm here, Kate. Just thinking."

"If you can't go to him, I'll go. I can't imagine he'd refuse me in person. He doesn't scare me."

"He should scare you. If you think what I did to my enemies was brutal, you haven't seen anything. And Dominic is not always a reasonable man."

"Nicky, I don't care what I have to do. This is Frankie's life we're talking about, the man I'm about to marry."

"I hear you, Kate. I'll figure things out and do what I can. But I need some time, and I'll have to think of something to tell Angie as a reason why I'm not going sightseeing with her. I'll also need to convince Dominic Mangini that it's in his best interest to let me go about business with the Russians undisturbed."

And I'm going to need help, Nicky thought, but he didn't tell Kate that.

"I'll call him again," Kate said.

"That's not a good idea, Kate. It won't be easy to convince Dominic to go along with this. He may not love the Russians, but they play for the same side. Dominic Mangini is a tough man. Once his mind is made up, it's difficult to change it, so I'd prefer that he hears me out first.

You may have tainted his thoughts with your earlier call. If so, we'll have to deal with that."

"Whatever you think is best, Nicky. I appreciate it. I may…"

"No need to say it, Kate. I know that I'm not your favorite person, but I'd do anything for Bugs. Don't worry. I'll get it done. I can't have you be a widow before you're married."

Kate leaned forward and kissed Nicky on the cheek. "Thank you, Nicky. I owe you for this."

Nicky smiled. "Be careful of who you dish out favors to. I may call it in." I turned to go rest on the sofa, then said, "And don't tell Frankie about this. He wouldn't approve."

Now all I need is a plan, Nicky thought.

LOU BECOMES A TARGET

"That's the fourth place we've busted today, Donovan. If we keep going like this, Viktor will run out of operations."

"That's what we want," Frankie said. "I intend to hit every spot we know about and some we don't know yet."

"It's a shame we can't get a better handle on his drug business. Busting a few street-corner dealers isn't going to do much damage."

"It won't do much, but it will do some. Anything helps."

"Speaking of *help,* why don't you go the hell home so we can get some work done. You're not needed, Donovan. When are you gonna learn that?"

Frankie laughed and headed for his car. "All right, you piece-of-shit dago. See you tomorrow."

Lou completed his paperwork, waited a few more minutes for traffic to die down, then he called his wife and told her he was on his way home.

He parked across the street from his building, then made his way through the small army of kids who were playing in front of the building. He climbed the steps and walked to his apartment door, pulling his keys out before he got there.

He inserted the key, and as he turned the lock, he heard a noise behind him. He turned to look, and a man shot him in the face, then shot him twice more.

~

"You hear that?" Darvel asked.

"Sounded like a gun," Tucker said.

A man ran out of the building. He raced past the kids, hopped into a waiting car and sped off.

Darvel ran into the building, saw Lou on the floor and ran back out. "Tucker! Call the cops. That detective is dead. That guy must have killed him."

~

Frankie was eating dinner when his phone rang.

"For God's sake," Kate said. "Is that work? Turn the ringer off. New York will survive one more day without you."

"Hello?" Frankie said.

"Detective Donovan. This is Franco from the team."

"Yeah, Franco. What's up?"

"It's Lou, sir. He's dead."

Frankie jumped up from the table. "What? When? How? Are you sure?"

"They just called it in. He was shot three times while trying to enter his apartment. It sounds like they were waiting for him."

"Are you sure he's dead? I just left him."

"Yes, sir. They pronounced it about ten minutes ago. I'm sorry, sir. I thought you'd want to know."

"You did the right thing, Franco. Where is he? Where'd they take him?"

"I don't know. I'll find out and text you the address."

Frankie hung up and looked to Kate. "That was Franco. Lou's dead."

"What?" Kate said. "How?"

"Someone shot him. Some fucker shot him three times when he was going into his house. His goddamn house!"

Kate rushed over and threw her arms around Frankie. "I'm sorry, Frankie. I'm so sorry. I know how much he meant to you."

Nicky got up and placed his arm on Frankie's shoulder. "I'm sorry, Bugs."

Tears formed in Frankie's eyes. "I can't believe it. I can't goddamn believe it. I was just with him two hours ago."

Kate led Frankie to the sofa and had him sit. "Try to calm down, Frankie. I'll fix some coffee."

Frankie stood, shaking his head. "I should go to the hospital. Marie will be alone."

"I forgot about Marie," Kate said. "Which hospital did they take him to? I'll drive you."

"I don't know yet. Franco's texting me."

"Wherever it is, I'll drive. You're in no shape to be behind the wheel."

"We'll take care of things here," Angela said. "Don't worry about that."

An alert sounded on Frankie's phone. "New York Presbyterian, in Park Slope."

"Will Marie be there?" Kate asked.

"I'm sure she will. It's not far from his house."

Frankie left with Kate moments later. After they were gone, Angie suggested to Rosa that she take Alex and Dante into the bedroom and play games. Once the door closed, she sat next to me.

"You want to tell me what's going on now?"

"Nothing. Why?"

"Nothing? You've been on edge for days, and when we were out the other day, you were continually looking over your shoulder. Then you told me earlier that you 'had something to do tomorrow,' which I know is a load of crap."

I looked into her eyes and held her hands. "I was going to lie to you, but I won't. Bugs is in trouble, and it's the kind of trouble that could spill over to you and the kids."

"The kids? What do you mean?"

"The group he's messing with is made up of bad people. It's the Russian mob. I'm sure they're the ones who killed Shawna, and I'm betting they're the ones who killed Lou. On top of that, I think we were followed the other day, and I'm not sure who it was, but I'm guessing that it was them."

Angela sat up straight. "Nicky, if that's the case, we need to get out of here and take the kids home."

I shook my head. "No way I'm missing Bugs' wedding, and I'm not leaving him to face the Russians alone."

"You could be killed! You said they already killed two people."

"I said they *probably* were the ones who did it; besides, I'm not as easy to kill as a young reporter or an old detective. And we have an advantage—they don't know who I am."

Angie pulled away from me. "That's it? You against the whole Russian mob, and your advantage is that they don't know who you are? Grow up, Nicky. You're not a kid anymore."

I grabbed hold of her hands and held her. "I know I'm not a kid, Angie. And I'm not scared. I'm not afraid to go to prison, and I'm not afraid to die. The only thing I'm scared of is losing you and the kids. But I'm not going to let that happen. I'm getting help."

"Help? Who's going to help you fight the Russians? They're not—"

I nodded. "Yeah, I'm asking Dominic for help. And I'll do whatever it takes to get that help."

Angie began crying. "Nicky, I can't believe we're going through this. I can't believe it's happening. You promised me this part of your life was over, that we'd be a normal family."

"And we will be a normal family. I just have to help Bugs with this one thing."

Angela took a deep breath. "You have to promise me that when this is over, there will be nothing else. No excuses for getting involved with anything. I don't even want you going to the smoke shop."

I smiled. "Deal," I said. "But one more thing. I'm concerned about the guy I saw who may have been watching us. I'm going to ask Bugs to assign someone to watch you."

"Good. That will make me feel safer anyway."

Kate let Frankie off at the entrance to the hospital and went to park the car. He rushed inside, stopping to inquire about where to find Marie.

He got off the elevator and headed toward the room where Lou was being held. As he turned the first corner, he heard Marie sobbing. He quickened his pace, and when Marie saw him, she rushed to meet him.

"Frankie! Oh, my God, he's gone. He's gone, Frankie. We were going to travel, do things. He was retiring next month."

Frankie held her tightly, patting her back. "I know, Marie. I know. I can't believe it. I just saw him a few hours ago."

Marie's crying intensified. "I *heard* it, Frankie. I heard his keys in the door, then I heard gunshots. I ran to the door and when I opened it… Oh, my God, there was so much blood. It was everywhere."

"Did you see anyone? Did Lou say anything?"

Marie shook her head as she wiped her nose. "No, whoever it was, had gone, and I didn't see anyone. They must have run out quickly."

"Don't worry," Frankie said. "We'll get who did this. In the meantime, do you have anyone who could stay with you? Don't you have a sister upstate?"

Marie sobbed. "I already called her. She's driving down. But I'll be okay, Frankie. You just get the son of a bitch who did this. And be careful. Don't let anything happen to yourself."

"I won't. Now if you don't mind, I want to say goodbye to Lou. Is that okay?"

"Of course. He's down there," Marie said and pointed down the hall.

Kate came around the corner just as Frankie was finishing his talk with Marie. She sat with her while Frankie went to see Lou.

No one was in the room with Lou when Frankie walked in. Lou lay there like a statue. Tears formed in Frankie's eyes again as he held onto Lou's cold hand.

"You old dago shit, why'd this have to happen to you? I'm sorry I got you into this, Lou. It was my fault, and you paid the price for it. Goddamn, I'm sorry."

Frankie squeezed Lou's hand, then stepped back. It didn't feel right being so cold. "We had a lot of good times together. Solved a lot of cases. I'm sure going to miss you. No matter who they put with me, they won't stack up."

Frankie looked toward the door, then leaned down and kissed Lou's forehead. "You were the best, buddy."

Frankie stayed another few minutes, then turned to leave. With his hand on the doorknob, he looked at Lou one more time. "And don't worry about who did this. I'm gonna find them, and I'm gonna kill them. There will be no getting off. No mercy. Count on it."

Frankie heard footsteps coming his way as he walked down the hall. He looked up and saw Miller. She ran to him and threw her arms around him.

"I just heard," she said. "Is it true?"

Frankie still had tears in his eyes. He nodded. "I just left him."

"Who did it? Do you know?"

"I'm pretty sure I know. I'll find out."

"I want in," Sherri said.

Frankie shook his head. "It's too dangerous. You shouldn't get involved."

"I know it's dangerous," Miller said. "But I don't care. Lou was a good guy. He may have been a prejudiced old ass to some, but I liked him, and I'm going to help you get the son of a bitch who did this."

Frankie stared for a long time. "It could get us killed. The men who I think are doing this have already killed one cop. Two more won't make a difference to them. I think it's the Russian mob."

"Let them try," Miller said.

Frankie walked outside, then turned and looked at Miller. "One more thing. Nicky is with me on this. If that's a problem for you, let me know now."

Miller shook her head. "No problem for me. I saw what he's capable of when he was here a couple of years ago. A guy had a knife to my throat, and Nicky put a bullet in his eye before you could blink. He saved my ass. I got no problem working with your friend, and if this Russian is as bad as you say, we may need Nicky."

"All right, you're in, but you'll need an okay from your boss. Also, some of what we do may be stretching the boundaries of the law."

"This is for Lou," Sherri said. "I'm in."

A FAVOR FOR INFORMATION

I woke to the sweet aroma of coffee and the sweeter sound of Angela humming.

After putting pants on, I walked to the kitchen. "You seem chipper this morning?"

Angie finished pouring her coffee, then grabbed a cup for me. "I assume you want some?"

"Of course. Thanks. What are you planning today?"

"By the way you phrased that question, I'll make another assumption—that you won't be joining us?"

"You're right. Remember I mentioned I'd need help? I'm going to see about getting it."

"Did you ask Frankie about the protection?"

"He'll have a man here by nine o'clock. Actually two men."

I waited until Angie left with the kids, then I headed out to see Dominic. I had thought about it all night and had come to the same conclusion that I mentioned to Angie the night before—that I'd do whatever it took to get Dominic's help.

I knocked on Dominic's door and within seconds the "waiter who wasn't a waiter" answered, the gun in his waistband producing an obvious bulge. "I'm here to see Dominic," I said.

He didn't respond, simply opened the door wider and stepped aside, all the while keeping his hand close to the gun.

I held up my hands as I entered. "I'm not carrying."

"Not even in your hat?" a voice from the other room asked. *"Buon giorno*, Niccolo." He smiled, and when he did, it appeared genuine. I was glad to see that. I didn't need to fight the Russians and him.

"Fabrizio! *Buon giorno.* Good to see you. And to answer your question, no I have no gun in my hat. I left the gun in the car, trusting my fate to the good graces of Mr. Mangini."

"You were right to do so," Dominic said as he walked toward us. "Seeing you trust me, makes me trust you more."

I smiled. Dominic was nattily dressed, as always, and he still looked fit and trim. "Thank you, Mr. Mangini."

"Niccolo, I think we can stop the Mr. Mangini; it's simply 'Dominic.'" Dominic draped his arm over my shoulder and led me to the living room. "Salvatore," he said. "Refreshments for our guest, please."

Since it was still morning, I knew refreshments meant espresso. "Thanks, Dominic. I could use some."

"Have a seat and tell me why you're here."

I sat on the chair and tried to think of how to say what I needed. I had the entire drive here to come up with something and now I was at a loss for words. Finally, I decided to blurt it out. "I need help, Dominic. My friend, Frankie Donovan is in trouble."

"What kind of trouble does Detective Donovan find himself in?"

"I think you know why he needs help. He was helping a reporter friend—the one you got me information on—and the Russian mob killed her. Now they've killed Frankie's partner, and I'm afraid they're coming after him as well. I've spotted men tailing me when I left Frankie's house."

"And what do you expect me to do about it?"

Salvatore brought the espresso in. I leaned back and took a sip. "I had everything planned before I came here, Dominic, but now that you ask, I don't know. The situation has escalated beyond 'reasonable.' That went out the window when they killed Frankie's partner."

"What do I have to offer the Russians if not relief from the police busting their operations?"

I hadn't realized what I was going to do until Dominic asked. "Tell them that they need to quit or they risk having their drug operations busted up. And we both know that's where the majority of their money comes from."

"And how would Detective Donovan know about their drug operations?"

"Because you're going to tell me."

Dominic set his cup of espresso on the table. "Really? Why would I do that?"

"Because I'll owe you a favor if you do. *Any* favor."

Dominic smiled. "*Any* favor? You know what kind of favor I'll want."

"I know, but Frankie's life is worth it."

"Let me try talking to them first," Dominic said. "Perhaps there will be no need for all of this. Finish your espresso, then I will make some calls."

"I don't have much time," I said. "More importantly, I don't think Frankie has much time."

"I'll have your answer by tomorrow."

I stood, recognizing that I was being dismissed. "Thanks, Dominic. I appreciate it."

"Some day you will have to tell me the story of how you and Detective Donovan became such good friends."

"Some day I will," I said and walked to the door.

After Nicky left, Dominic picked up the phone and dialed. The phone rang several times before a man with a gruff voice answered.

"Da."

"I need to speak with Viktor," Dominic said.

"Who's talking?"

"This is Dominic Mangini. Now get me Viktor, please."

A moment later, another person got on the line. "Dominic?"

"Si, Viktor. Long time."

"What's the occasion?"

"Not a happy one, I'm afraid. My sources tell me that your businesses are suffering from a crackdown by police."

"True, but it's only been a few days. It will go away."

"That depends, Viktor. My sources tell me this is retaliation for what your people did to a reporter. Now those same sources whisper that a detective has been killed."

"And what if those sources are right? They'll forget about him soon. He was ready to retire."

"That's just the kind of person they won't forget, Viktor. Other cops will look at him and think—that could be me, so close to retirement. When cops start thinking of things that could happen to them, it scares them. And when they become scared, they act out against that fear."

"It's done now."

"It may be done, Viktor, but we haven't finished feeling the heat. We need to give them a scapegoat, and we need to provide assurances that this won't happen again."

"Why are you so interested in this, Dominic? They aren't busting up your operations."

"Not yet. But I've been in this business a long time. Once the people get excited by the police busting up criminal activities, they want more of it. And when the people become excited, that carries over to the cops. Before you know it, the cops forget where all their extra money comes from, and they act irrationally. I don't want it to come to that, Viktor. I like things the way they are."

"Why the hell should I provide assurances? Why should I do anything?"

"So that we can prosper. If we want to continue our activities, we need to have police cooperation. I thought you understood this."

"I understand one thing, Dominic. Someone was getting in my way, and I had that person removed, like I will anyone who gets in my way. I'm sorry if your business suffers as a result, but you'll have to live with it. I do. If you can't weather the storm, perhaps you should get a better boat."

"I'm surprised you would speak to an associate like that," Dominic said.

"Your people had a great run in this country for a long time, Dominic. Now it's our turn. I have never interfered with your business, and I haven't asked for favors. I expect the same courtesy from you. When you've had your turf wars and bloodied the streets, did I say anything? When your people shot innocent tourists in the restaurant, did I say anything? When a councilman who opposed one of your building plans was "accidentally" killed while jogging, did I say anything? The answer to all of those questions is *no*. I expect no less respect from you."

"This is different," Dominic said.

"Respect is respect. Nothing is different."

"I'll give you a week to get things in order, Viktor. I expect this to be resolved by then."

"Or what?"

"You should not ask. If you have to ask what will happen, you are weaker than I thought."

"And you're dumber than I thought. The Italians began losing power as soon as we moved in. You are but a remnant of what you once were."

"Remnants can be formidable, Viktor. You should be careful."

"Is that a threat?"

"Nonsense, Viktor. I never make threats, only promises. I must go now so enjoy your day, but remember what I said—one week."

Viktor didn't seem fazed. "There are a lot of promises in life, Dominic. You have to make sure you can keep them."

Dominic laughed. "I *always* keep my promises, Viktor. *Always.*"

UNWANTED VISITORS

After leaving Dominic's house, I had mixed emotions. He hadn't said he wouldn't help me, but he didn't commit his support either.

Going on logic, he should support Viktor and not Frankie, but Dominic was difficult to predict. He didn't necessarily decide based on what were his best interests.

I drove through the city wondering what he'd do and eager for the decision. As I drew closer to Frankie's house, I thought of other ways to accomplish what we needed done—in case we didn't get Dominic's help—but the only one I came up with was killing Viktor, and I preferred not doing that.

I parked the car and went inside. Angela and Kate were in the kitchen talking, and the kids were in the bedroom playing video games.

"Hey, everybody," I said.

Angie pecked me on the cheek and said, "Dante and Alex were asking for you. You should go play with them."

"I will, even though I'll get my ass kicked." I grabbed a bottle of water, then went to join the kids.

I was in the middle of fighting some kind of alien when Alex said he was going for a drink.

"Anybody want anything? he asked.

He left the door slightly ajar when he exited. While he was gone, I heard a knock on the door, then I heard Kate say, 'What can I do for you?'"

I put my finger to my lips and walked slowly to the door. Two men pushed their way in.

The bigger one said, "You can try not to scream when I fuck you." Then he grabbed Kate and threw her on the sofa. Alex ran and hit him, but it didn't faze the guy.

I opened the bedroom door. It creaked, and the men looked my way.

One of them laughed. "I guess she won't mind me getting some. It looks like she's giving it out already."

I stood in the doorway, smiling. "I would ask you to leave, but I don't want you to."

One of the men looked to the other. "You don't *want* us to? Not that it matters, but why not? And who cares? Because when we're done fucking her, we'll kill you and take the kid."

"How will you do that with bullets in your head?"

The larger man reached for his gun. He didn't make it halfway. I pulled a gun from behind my back and shot both of them twice. The first guy I got twice in the chest. The second one I got in the chest and face.

Kate screamed and grabbed Alex, hugging him. I walked to the men, kicked them with my foot, then felt for a pulse. Both were dead. "Kate, we need to leave quickly. I'll call Bugs and tell him what happened."

"Leave? Where are we going? Where *can* we go?"

"I'll figure it out when we're gone. Let's go. They've probably got more men outside."

Rosa ran out of the bedroom. "Dad, are you all right?" she asked.

"I'm fine. Just get moving. Grab hold of Dante and come with us."

We exited the apartment, and hadn't gone ten feet when two men got out of a parked car. I pointed my gun at them. "Get back in your car or die. Your choice."

They got in quickly, and I held them there while Angie and Kate got the car. "Give me the keys," I said.

The driver handed me the keys, and I put them in my pocket, then I got into the driver's seat of my rental car. "Everybody ready?" I asked and took off.

Rosa was in the back with Kate and the kids. "Dad, what's wrong? What happened back there?"

"I'll explain later. Just let me think."

We were only about a block away when I dialed Bugs.

"Rat, what's up?"

"Don't go home."

"What the hell does that mean? Did something happen? What's going on?"

"There is no other way to say it, Bugs; there are two dead men in your apartment. Probably Russians."

"What? Are you shitting me? Are Kate and Alex all right?"

"Yeah, everyone's fine. I've got them with me. Meet me at Manny's house. You remember where he lives?"

"Manny's house? Are you crazy? What the hell are you going there for?"

"Because he owes me, and the last place the Russians would look to find a cop is at a gangster's house."

"All right," Frankie said. "I'll be over there shortly. I need to send a crew to my house first. How the hell am I gonna explain dead men in my apartment?"

"Don't explain it. Play dumb. You're the cop. Figure it out. Tell them you had a visitor from out of town, and the Russians came after you. He shot them. With what they did to Lou, you shouldn't catch too much shit. If you do, you'll have to handle it."

"All right. I'll figure it out. See you later at Manny's. And be safe."

It only took me about fifteen minutes to get to Manny's. We got out of the car, walked to his house, and knocked on the door. Manny opened it a few seconds later.

"Nicky! Christ's sake, what are you doing here?"

"I need a place for these people to stay, Manny. This is my wife and kids and Bug's wife and kid. The Russians tried getting them, and they already killed Bug's partner."

Manny opened the door wide. "Mazetti? They killed Mazetti?"

"Yeah, when he was going into his house."

"Son of a bitch! Didn't even have the decency to do it away from family. Goddamn Russians."

"Can you put us up for a few days, until we get someplace else?"

"Hey, Nicky. You can stay as long as you want. My place is yours. And you'll be safe here. I'll make sure of that."

Manny led us to the kitchen and immediately boiled water for espresso. While he was making it, he dialed someone on his phone.

"Giorgio, this is Manny. Get a few guys over to my house. Tell them to plan on staying for a few days."

A moment later, Manny brought a cup of espresso and set it in front of me, then he slapped himself on the forehead. "Look at me. I didn't even ask if you beautiful ladies wanted anything. You want espresso? Biscotti?"

Kate waved her hand and shook her head. "We're fine, thanks."

"And look at me," I said. "I forgot to introduce you. Kate and Angela, this is Manny. Manny, those are my kids—Rosa and Dante—and the one on the left is Bug's kid—Alex."

"Great to meet all of ya. And don't worry. You're safe here. Nobody will touch you." Manny leaned close to me and whispered, "Nicky, I'm gonna make a few more calls. Get some more people over here. Be right back."

I smiled. "No problem, Manny."

After Manny left, Kate leaned forward. "Frankie *knows* him?"

I smiled. "Yeah, Bugs knows Manny. And don't worry about anything now. He was right. We're safe here."

Rosa looked around for Manny, then stared at me, whispering. "Dad, is he a gangster?"

I bent down and whispered back, "Yes, he is."

"How do you know him?"

"Keep all your questions until we get home. This is not the time to answer them. For now, just do as I say or as Manny says."

Manny was gone for about twenty minutes, then he walked back into the kitchen. "Look what the cat dragged in," he said.

Bugs was behind him. He grabbed Kate and hugged her, then did the same with Alex. "Are you guys all right?"

Kate was nodding when Alex said, "You should have seen the Rat. He shot both of those guys before they even drew their guns."

Bugs patted his back while nodding. "All right. Let's not talk about that now."

Alex looked at Manny, then he looked at Bugs. "You *know* him, Dad?"

Manny laughed, and when he did, his belly shook. "Yeah, kid, your dad knows me. But you be quiet about it because he's not supposed to be hanging around with me."

"Yes, sir," Alex said.

Manny almost choked on his biscotti. "Sir? You hear that shit, Bugs? He called me *sir*. I don't think I ever had anybody call me *sir*."

Bugs laughed. "Don't let it go to your head, Manny. Alex just has respect for *older* people. And yes, I'll take a cup of coffee, please?"

"Comin' right up. I forgot to ask."

Manny brought Frankie his espresso and set it on the table.

"Manny, I appreciate what you're doing for me, but this doesn't mean I owe you anything."

"No shit, Bugs. I wouldn't be like that. This isn't a favor. This is family stuff. Stay as long as you need to."

Frankie slapped Manny on the back. "Thanks. It's not a 'get-out-of-jail-free card,' but you may have bought a 'look the other way.'"

"Whatever you want, Bugs. If you want to drop a dime in the bucket, go ahead. I'll take it, but I ain't askin' for nothing. I wouldn't do that."

"I know you wouldn't, Manny. You're all right."

"Despite what they say, huh?" Manny laughed when he said it, causing his belly to bounce again.

Manny got a phone call and left the room to take it. Alex tugged on Frankie's arm. "I like him. He's funny."

Frankie looked at Alex. "It's okay to like him, as long as you don't want to be like him."

"Why? Is he a bad guy?"

Frankie struggled with how to answer. "It's not that he's a bad guy, but sometimes he does things that are bad. There's a difference."

"I know," Alex said. "It's like my friend, Shane. He's a nice guy, but he curses a lot and gets in fights."

Frankie smiled. "Yeah, Manny's kind of like that, but maybe a little worse."

Manny walked back into the kitchen and handed the phone to me. "It's Dominic. He wants to talk to you."

I took the phone from Manny. "Dominic?"

"You've got a deal. I spoke to Viktor, and though the time isn't up yet, I don't think he'll go along. I'm moving forward as if he won't."

"How did you know I was at Manny's house?"

"I didn't know. I called to speak with Manny, and he told me you were there."

"When will I hear from you again?"

"Tomorrow at noon. Meet me at Cataldi's. I'll have a surprise."

THE PLAN BEGINS

$\mathcal{M}$y phone rang around 8:00, while I was still having my coffee. Startled, I grabbed it quickly. "Hello?"

"Niccolo, we need to meet about a half hour earlier—say 11:30. I have an appointment to go to afterward."

"That's fine. I'll be there early. See you then."

I messed around with the kids all morning, played catch with Alex and word games with Rosa, then built blocks with Dante. About 10:30, I prepared to leave. "Manny, I've got to go see someone. Everything okay here?"

Manny brushed his hand in the air. "It's fine. I got three guys here already, and more are comin'. I'll keep the kids busy; you do what you gotta do."

At 11:15, I pulled in front of Cataldi's. They parked the car, and I walked in. One of the Cataldi girls greeted me with a smile. I didn't remember her name, but she remembered mine from when I used to come here with Tony and Bugs.

"Mr. Fusco. Wait one moment, and I'll show you to Mr. Mangini's table."

I followed her to a table in the corner. Dominic was already there as was Fabrizio, and it looked as if three of Dominic's bodyguards occupied the adjacent table.

Dominic's bodyguards stood until he waved them down. I remained standing until he invited me to sit.

"Sit down, Niccolo. Have a seat. Look at the menu and order what you like."

"What did you do to rate a permanent table?"

"I bought it," Dominic said. "I wanted to make sure it was available when I wanted it."

"I didn't know you could do that," I said.

"Neither did Signor Cataldi, but we came to an arrangement that satisfied both our needs."

I turned and nodded to Fabrizio. "You keep eating here, and you'll get fat," I said.

He laughed. "I don't think so."

I turned back to Dominic. "You said the talks with Viktor didn't go well?"

"He was as difficult as I presumed. He refused to recognize the situation as one that needed to be dealt with quickly. I gave him one week, but I don't think he'll agree. You should prepare to act on your own."

I took a long sip from an espresso that the waiter had brought. "I don't know if I can do it myself. I was looking for help."

Dominic chewed on a biscotto. "My suggestion is for you not to do it. Viktor and his people are dangerous."

"Any other suggestions?" I asked.

Dominic seemed to think for a long while. Long enough for me to finish my cup of espresso. "How important is this to you?"

"Frankie is my best friend."

"Is that important enough for you to owe me a favor if I help?"

Dominic's question was anticipated, and I felt I had the answer, but I wanted to go over it again. The last thing I wanted was to owe Dominic a favor. I thought for a long moment. Ordered another espresso and thought some more.

Dominic stood. "I know you haven't forgotten my question, but I'll excuse myself to attend to needs in the men's room. When I return, we can finish our conversation."

While Dominic was gone, I thought hard about what he asked. If I agreed to do him a favor, it wouldn't be like running to the corner store and picking up a pack of cigarettes. It would almost certainly involve killing someone, and it probably wouldn't be an easy kill. Most of the people Dominic killed deserved to die. I knew that, but I had vowed not to kill anymore. I had already broken that vow several times, but I didn't plan on there being any more instances.

On the other hand, if I didn't do something, Frankie was almost surely a dead man. Kate would be a widow before she was married, and Alex would be without a father once again. I squeezed my fist and pressed it against the table.

Why did God make decisions so difficult?

It was times like this when I wished I had Sister Thomas to consult with. As much as she was sometimes a pain in the ass, she usually had good insight.

Dominic returned, taking his seat and using his napkin to wipe the corner of his mouth. "Have you decided?" he asked.

"What kind of help would I receive in return for this favor?"

"Fabrizio."

That shocked me. Fabrizio was Dominic's best hit man. If he was willing to risk Fabrizio, the favor he'd ask would probably be worse than I expected. On the other hand, I couldn't ask for more. Fabrizio was said to be better than any three hit men. I nodded my head. "Done."

Dominic didn't flinch. "I thought you would," he said. "Just so that we're clear. If I do this favor for you, you will owe me a favor of my choosing, and you will be bound to do as I ask."

"I know how the game works, Dominic. I don't like doing this, but I agree for Frankie."

Dominic looked as if he was getting ready to leave. "I'm guessing you don't care what happens to Viktor?"

"Not at all," Dominic said. "In fact, if he disappears, it may make my life easier." He smiled, then wagged his finger at me. "But don't think Viktor's disappearance would clear your debt."

"I understand," I said.

"Fine, just so that we understand each other."

Dominic gulped the last of his espresso, then started for the door. "You can stay, Fabrizio. I'm sure you and Niccolo have things to discuss."

I sat at the table after Dominic left, wondering what I had gotten myself into. Who he'd have me kill? My guess was that it would be multiple kills. Sure as shit it wouldn't be something easy.

Goddamnit, Frankie. Why did you have to push things with the Russians? Why did you get me involved?

Fabrizio ordered a glass of wine and dessert. I ordered another espresso.

"Dominic said it might be … tricky." Fabrizio said.

"Tricky isn't the word I would have used, but it won't be easy, and it will be dangerous. The man we're going after is one of the top guys in the Russian mob."

"How difficult can it be?" Fabrizio asked. "They're only Russians."

"What do you think we should do, Fabrizio?"

"You're the boss. I do what you say."

"I don't work like that. We're both putting our lives on the line, and you know the city better than I do now, so I want your input."

Fabrizio nodded. "If it were me, I'd go see him. Look him in the eye, and let him know what he's up against."

"You mean two crazy dagos with a death wish."

"That's about it," Fabrizio said.

"I don't know about walking into his place like that. He might decide to kill us there."

"I don't intend to go in. He might recognize me as Dominic's man, and I can't have that. But I do have a plan."

Fabrizio leaned forward and whispered the details. "I just need an address," he said. "I'll get it from Dominic while we drive over."

"Sounds good," I said. "Let's go."

Fabrizio got the address we needed while I drove to Viktor's club. Once we arrived, I parked about a block away and walked to the club. Fabrizio waited in the car.

Two men greeted me at the entrance. Their guns showed as obvious bulges under their coats. "We're closed," one said.

"I'm here to see Viktor."

"Nobody here by that name."

I smiled. "I happen to know there is, and if I were you, I'd get him. It's about his bookmaking operations being busted up."

Two minutes later, they led me inside and walked me to a table near the back. A tall man with dark hair sat facing me.

"You want to see me?"

"Are you Viktor?"

"Yes. Who are you?"

"May I sit?"

When he nodded, I sat opposite him, then glanced at the two men hovering above me. Viktor gestured to the table next to them, and they sat.

"My name is Nicky Fusco. Some people know me by my nickname—Nicky the Rat."

I saw the recognition in his eyes. "I'm familiar with that name from years ago. You were the one who used to work for Martelli."

"That's me."

"What do you want? Did Dominic send you?"

"No. I don't work for Dominic. I came because I'm friends with Frankie Donovan, the partner of the detective you killed."

"I don't know what you're talking about."

"And I suppose you know nothing about the men who visited Detective Donovan's apartment yesterday?"

Viktor nodded. "So it was you they ran into. Now I understand. I wondered how the cop would have taken them out."

"I'm not saying anything."

"What do you want? Your friend is causing me a lot of trouble."

"I can help put a stop to that. You stop everything you're doing, and I can get the cops to lay off your businesses for six months. By then, they'll have forgotten about it."

Viktor shook his head. "Not interested."

"You should think about it," I said.

Viktor stared for twenty or thirty seconds. "And why shouldn't I just kill you now and get it over with? What's stopping me?"

"May I reach into my pocket?" I asked.

Viktor looked to his men, who gave a thumbs up, meaning I'd been searched, then he said, "Go ahead."

I pulled out the slip of paper Fabrizio had given me on the way over. "Recognize that address?"

He sat erect, and his eyes widened. "That's my house!"

"That's right. I have several men sitting on it. If anything happens to me, or if I don't check in within fifteen minutes, your wife and two sons are dead."

"You're a dead man," Viktor said.

"That's fine. I've lived my life. Have your sons?"

He crumbled the paper and squeezed. "Get the fuck out of here. My answer is no. Tell the detective that I'm going to kill him and his family. And now, I'll include you and your family."

I lost my smile and stood. "That was a grave mistake, Viktor. You threatened my family and I can't allow that. Now, I'll make you a promise—I'm going to kill you. You won't know when or where, but I will kill you." I turned to leave. "Have a nice day."

THE WORLD TURNS ON INFORMATION

I dropped Fabrizio off to get his car, then I drove back to Manny's place. To my surprise, Bugs was already there. He should have been at work.

I found him in the living room. "Bugs, what the hell are you doing here? Why aren't you at work?"

"I'm not working while the kids are in danger."

"Danger? Hell, they're safer here than they would be at the precinct, and you know it."

"That aside, where the hell have you been?"

"I had something to do."

"Something my ass. I'm guessing that something had to do with Viktor."

"And what if it did? I'm not letting you get in any deeper."

"Any deeper? These pieces of shit killed Shawna. Now they've killed Lou. And you expect me to stand on the sidelines?" Bugs shook his head emphatically. "It's not gonna happen. I'm going to get that son of a bitch, and I'm going to put a bullet in his head."

I grabbed Bugs by the arm and shook him. "Listen up. I know how you feel, but you can't kill someone just because you're pissed off—no matter how pissed off you are."

"What's stopping me?"

"I am. I'm not going to let you ruin your life. More importantly, I'm not going to let you ruin Kate's life or and Alex's life."

"Lou was my partner. He was my friend. I owe it to him to find out who did this."

"You know who did this. And you owe it to Lou not to get killed. So sit back, and let me handle this."

Bugs chuckled. "And what makes you think you can handle the Russians better than I can?"

"Because I have help."

"Who?"

"Fabrizio is working with me."

"Fabrizio? Dominic Mangini's man?"

"One and the same."

"What the hell are you doing working with him? What kind of deal did you make with the devil that Dominic allowed it to happen?"

"Don't worry about the little things. Worry about protecting your family. I'll take care of the rest."

Bugs glared at me. "Not going to happen, Nicky. I'm not letting you get involved. These guys are dangerous. They shoot first and ask questions later. They've already killed a New York City detective and most likely, a reporter. They won't hesitate to kill some idiot from Wilmington."

"I know that. But I don't intend to wait on the corner for them to come up and shoot me. I think I know how to handle myself."

"I know you do with regular people, but these aren't regular people. They're all killers, and they don't give a shit who they kill."

"I guess that means I'll have to cancel my guided tour with the Girl Scouts. I wouldn't want them to be in the line of fire."

"Fuck you, Nicky."

I laughed. "That's my buddy. Resorting to those two-dollar words again."

Bugs leaned toward me and punched my arm. "If I wasn't worried about Angela, I'd kick your ass," he said.

"You're probably worried about Angela kicking your ass, and that's after I do it. Then it would be Rosa's turn." I laughed. "Hell, by the time I leave here, Alex and Dante will be kicking your ass."

Bugs leaned back on the couch and laughed. "All right, enough bullshit. What's your plan? We need to be careful with these people."

I turned to face him. "I was counting on you for some of that. I'm sure Fabrizio and I could come up with some ideas, but I'd like to have as many options as possible."

"Let's go over them. What have you got so far?"

I shook my head. "Not now. We need to bring Fabrizio in on this."

"No way," Bugs said. "I can't be seen with him."

"Then we'll go somewhere you won't be seen. But this is his ass on the line too. He needs to have a say in things."

WE MET at a small diner on the outskirts of Brooklyn—a busy place, with a lot of noisy patrons. Fabrizio sat next to me in the booth, and Bugs sat across from us.

"Fabrizio, you know Detective Donovan. He knows what we're doing, so feel free to speak around him. And so you don't get confused, I usually call him 'Bugs.'"

Fabrizio nodded, but I could tell he remained skeptical.

"Viktor has made this a personal matter," Bugs said. "He's not acting rationally, so we need to do the same."

"What do you mean?" I asked.

"Ordinarily, putting pressure on the money end of things would elicit a response. They would stop doing whatever caused the pressure to start with. But that's not happening. Viktor is treating this like someone killed his brother; so we need to do the same."

"Kill his brother?" Fabrizio asked.

"No, kill him," Frankie said. "If we're going to stop this, we need to take Viktor out."

"It's not going to be easy," I said. "Have you seen the number of body-guards he has?"

"I've never known you to be afraid of a few bodyguards," Frankie said.

"You're right. A few I don't worry about, but Viktor must have twelve or more. There may have been a few I didn't see also. It won't be easy. Remember, my goal is for Fabrizio and me to come out of this alive. And to take care of Viktor, of course."

Fabrizio sipped on his espresso. "This is terrible. I've tasted better at an Irishman's house."

Bugs looked at him oddly, then at me. "You put him up to that, didn't you? I should have known."

"So what should we do?" I asked. "Any ideas?"

"Dominic used to say you move a mountain one shovelful at a time."

"What the hell does this have to do with our situation?" Frankie asked.

Fabrizio finished chewing, then said, "If Viktor has twelve body-guards, we take them out one at a time. Soon, he will have no bodyguards."

"He'll just replace them," I said. "If we take out one, he'll find another."

"He can't continue to replace men like he could weapons. Pretty soon, word will get around."

"You've got a point," Bugs said, "But it's a point I can't sit here and listen to. Instead of killing, I think you need to spread the word that working for Viktor is dangerous and that it's no longer profitable. Let whispers get out that working for Viktor is a prison sentence. Make people think about it."

"And the whole time, keep up the police pressure and reinforce that message." I scooped some eggs onto my fork and said, "If we're successful, we'll have Viktor's own people applying pressure on him."

"Maybe the combination will work," Fabrizio said.

Bugs threw a ten-dollar bill on the table as he stood. "I've got to get going. You guys figure out what you need, and I'll do what I can."

"One more thing, Bugs. I know you won't tell anyone where you are, but unless I'm way off base, Viktor's going to try to get to you again. To do that, he may have someone from the inside try to get the information."

"Don't worry. He won't get anything," Bugs said.

"I know that, but I want him to get something. If anyone approaches you, tell them you're staying at the Chelsea Savoy down on 23rd Street. They wouldn't expect you to be there, so it might ring true."

"What good is that gonna do?" Bugs asked.

"Because Fabrizio will be staying there."

Fabrizio smiled and nodded. Bugs shook his head, then walked out.

Fabrizio waited for Bugs to leave, then looked at me. "Do you agree with what I said? About killing his bodyguards?"

"I don't disagree. Besides, Viktor must be worried. If a man has so many bodyguards, he's worried."

"He has reason to worry," Fabrizio said. "No one likes him. Many people fear him, but no one likes him."

"I've heard the same thing said about Dominic—that he is feared."

Fabrizio smiled. "But there is a difference. Dominic may be feared, but he is also loved. Anyone who is loyal to Dominic knows this."

"I understand what you're saying, Fabrizio, but I prefer not killing Viktor or his bodyguards. If we hit him where it hurts the most— drugs—we might put enough pressure on him to make it work. Drug trafficking and gambling are the Russian mob's largest money makers."

Fabrizio nodded. "Then we need to make the people who push his drugs—and the people who buy his drugs—afraid to deal with him."

"That's not going to be easy," I said.

"Nothing is easy," Fabrizio said. "But it can be done."

"How?"

"We start by intercepting his drug shipment," Fabrizio said.

"How do we do that if we don't know where it's coming in," I said.

"Dominic could find out," Fabrizio said.

"I'm assuming drugs are his biggest moneymaker," I said.

Fabrizio nodded. "Gambling brings in good money, but drugs are by far the biggest. Sex slaves may be second."

"How does he bring them in?" I asked.

"Mostly by boat. Viktor has good connections with shipments from

Eastern Europe, even China. If Dominic can find out when a big ship-ment is coming in, we'll have what we need."

"This one's on you, Fabrizio."

"I'll ask Dominic for information."

"To sweeten the pot, tell Dominic that we'll give him some of the drugs."

"What about the money?" Fabrizio asked.

"You can have that," I said.

Fabrizio shook his head. "No, Niccolo. I wouldn't betray Dominic. We'll give him the money too."

"All right, let's see what happens. Maybe we should split it between Dominic and Manny. Call me when you hear something."

WHERE ARE THE DRUGS?

anny's phone rang, and he answered right away.

"Manny, questo é Domenico."

"Dominic! What the hell are you doing? Where you been? I haven't talked to you in ages."

"Manny, it's been two days."

"What the hell—two days, ages. What's the difference?"

"I've been minding my own business, Manny. Staying close to home. How about you?"

"Stayin' out of trouble. Or tryin' to. What's up?"

"I need a favor. I'm having trouble with Viktor, and I thought you could help."

"I'm assuming this trouble has something to do with Nicky. If that's the case, I'd be happy to help, but I don't know what I can do. I ain't got no dealings with Viktor."

"I know you don't, but from what I hear, one of your people deals drugs with one of his."

"What? You shittin' me? I'll kick his ass. Who is it?"

"I wouldn't worry about disciplining him at this moment, Manny. I need this person and his drug contact."

"Okay, I'll let it slide for now. Who is it? And what do you need?"

"It's your man Freddy, and he's dealing with a Russian named Pavel."

"Freddy! That mother fucker. I treat him good."

"I'm sure you do, Manny, but t's not about how well you treat people. Drugs make them too much money. They can't resist it. I imagine he's making more from drugs than all his other operations combined."

"Okay, Dom. Tell me what you need."

"Viktor is causing trouble, the kind of trouble that could bring a lot of pressure on us."

"What kind of pressure?"

"You heard about the Brooklyn cop being shot, Donovan's partner?"

"Yeah, I heard—Mazzetti, right? And that was Viktor?"

"It was. And from what I gather, he's after Donovan too. We can't let that happen."

"Hey, Dominic, I like Donovan, but this is Viktor's business. I wouldn't put up with him telling me who I could hit and who I couldn't."

"I don't care who he takes out, Manny—usually. But when it's someone whose death will have the cops sniffing my ass for months to come, then I do care. I care a lot. And you know how this works. Once the cops start busting up operations, the people get excited, believing that something can be done and that fuels the cops even more. Before you know it, they're doing things that they shouldn't be doing."

"Like busting up our operations," Manny said.

"Exactly."

"So talk to Viktor and explain it."

"I did. But he's not a man who listens to reason."

"Okay, I'll see what Freddy can find out and get back to you."

"I knew I could count on you, Manny. You're a good friend."

"Anything for you, Dom. You know that."

* * *

Freddy knocked on Manny's door and waited.

"Freddy, come on in," Manny said.

"What's up, boss? Why'd you call me over here?"

"Because I need help with something."

Freddy smiled. "Anything. What do you need?"

"I need to know when and where Viktor's next big shipment of heroin is coming in?

Freddy's smile disappeared. "Heroin? I don't know. How the hell would I know?"

"Because you sell the junk, and your supplier works for Viktor. His name's Pavel. Does that ring a bell, Freddy?"

Freddy shifted his gaze to the right side of the room, then the left, as if he were planning an escape. Manny might have suspected something if that wasn't the way Freddy always looked.

"Well?" Manny asked.

"Sorry, Manny. I was thinking."

"Thinking of what kind of lie you could tell? Because if you think a lie will work, it won't. You ever hear of Nicky the Rat?"

Freddy grinned. "Sure, everybody's heard of the Rat. He damn near wiped out Tito's crew a few years back."

"I was Tito's underboss back then. I knew Nicky. He's in town, and he's the one who wants this information, so if it's not up to speed, Nicky's the one who's gonna come looking for you. If I were you, I'd make sure the information is good."

Freddy returned to looking scared. "You got it, boss. I'll get you the information by tomorrow."

"Tomorrow or the next day. Either one is fine. Just make sure the information is right."

"Okay, Manny. You got it. Tell 'The Rat' I'm working on it. I should have it tomorrow."

* * *

Freddy sat in the booth at a small diner near Brighton Beach. His coffee cup ratted against the saucer every time he picked it up. He'd only been waiting five minutes, but it felt like it had been an hour.

A man wearing a leather coat walked in and scanned the surroundings. He had a small scar on the right side of his neck, and he was carrying a briefcase. His gaze settled on Freddy, and recognition lit his eyes. He walked over and took a seat, setting his briefcase down next to him. He ordered eggs, bacon, and toast to go with his coffee.

"Pavel, thanks for meeting. I ran short on product. When can I expect some more?"

"Don't worry. It will be soon," Pavel said. "Your customers getting eager?"

Freddy picked up his coffee cup, and the saucer shook.

Pavel looked around the diner. "You nervous about something,

Freddy?"

"No, but did you ever try to tell a junkie that it'll be soon? When they need a fix, they need it right then, not soon. They don't buy that soon shit. Hell, I might get cut just for telling them that."

"That's what guns are for," Pavel said, "so people don't cut you."

The waiter brought Pavel's meal and set it on the table. Freddy continued after he left.

"I can't go shooting my customers," Freddy said. "If I do that, the junkies start shopping with other dealers. And if the junkies move to other dealers, I've lost customers, because junkies ain't the most loyal customers."

Pavel slopped up his egg yolks with toast, then took a sip of coffee. "I should have something Friday night."

"Friday night! That's three days. I don't have enough for three days" Freddy said. "You gotta get me some stuff till the new shit comes in."

"What do you need?" Pavel asked.

"Two days worth, about 150 grams."

"That's a lot of shit."

"I know it's a lot of shit, but that's what I need. I got a lot of people wanting it."

"It'll cost you twenty-five large."

"I know what it'll cost. I got it with me. You got the product?"

"Give me the money. When we're done eating, I'll get up and leave, but my briefcase will be left under the table. The product will be in there."

"How do I know it's all there?"

"Because you know me. There are 160 grams in there. You'll be getting ten grams for nothing."

Freddy pulled an envelope from his jacket, pulled out a few bills, then handed it to Pavel. "Here's the cash. Take your time eating, then we'll leave about five minutes apart."

"Where do you want to meet on Friday?" Pavel asked.

"Where is the shipment coming in?" Freddy asked.

"Don't worry about that."

"If you're flying it in, be careful; from what I hear, they've beefed up security at all customs. You know how the cops have gone nuts about busting places up."

"No worries."

"All right, how about 9:00 at the park where we met before?"

"Nine's too early. How about 11:00?"

"I can do 11:00; that's probably even better. See ya then."

"And don't forget to bring the money—two-hundred large."

"Have I ever forgotten?" Freddy asked.

"Just saying."

"No need to say. Did I say 'And don't forget to bring the shit?'"

"Just bring the fuckin' money," Pavel said.

"Yeah, and you just bring the fuckin' dope."

Pavel slugged down the last of his coffee, then stood to leave.

Freddy waited until he left the diner, then reached under the table and grabbed the briefcase. A few minutes later, he followed Pavel out the door. Once inside his car, Freddy checked the contents; it was all there.

Freddy made the necessary stops, then he drove to Manny's house. The last thing he wanted was to disappoint Nicky 'The Rat.' He didn't feel good about betraying Viktor, but as bad as Viktor was rumored to be, Nicky 'The Rat' was far worse.

Freddy knocked on Manny's door and went in when it opened.

"Glad to see you've got some sense," Manny said. "You get what we need?"

"I think so, yeah."

"Get on with it, then. I'm waiting," Manny said.

"From what he said, and the way he acted, I'd say it's coming in on Friday, and it'll be on a ship, not a plane. And my guess is it's not coming in until nine or ten."

"You sure it's a ship?" Manny asked.

"No, I'm not sure, but he said it wasn't a plane, so I'm assuming it's a ship because we know he gets his drugs from China or Eastern Europe. Unless the drugs are coming across the fucking ocean on a train, I'll go with ship."

"But you don't know which pier?"

Freddy shook his head. "Not a clue. I don't even know if it is a pier, but if I had to guess, I'd say so. I couldn't risk asking more questions; Pavel would have suspected something."

"Do we know where they've brought stuff in before?"

Freddy shook his head again. "I don't, but Slappy might; he's worked with them for years."

Manny clipped the end of a cigar and lit it. "What the fuck you waitin' for? Get Slappy over here."

Freddy made a call on his cell, then poured another cup of espresso.

"Nothin's gonna happen to Slappy, right?"

"We ain't killed you yet," Manny said. "Yet."

TIME TO GET MARRIED

Frankie reached over, grabbed Kate's hand and pulled her to him, causing her to fall onto his lap. "One more day. That's all you've got left as Kate Burns."

Kate kissed him and smiled. "And I couldn't be happier. I was getting tired of being plain-old Kate Burns. Kate Donovan sounds better."

"You better like it because you're going to have that name for a long time."

"A damn long time," Kate said. "Just remember that." Kate leaned back and grew serious. "Are you sure everything will be okay?"

"I've got it covered," Frankie said. "Not only will there be about a dozen cops attending the wedding as guests, but another half a dozen volunteered to patrol the area."

Manny walked in at the tail end of the conversation. "Besides all that, I'll have about ten of my guys on the perimeter. Most of them know Viktor's men, so they won't get through."

Frankie shook his head. "I told you that wasn't necessary, Manny."

"I know what you told me, but I'm not lettin' anything happen to your bride to be. What are you gonna do—arrest me for protecting you?"

Kate smiled. "That's sweet, Manny. Even if Frankie doesn't appreciate the gesture, I do. Thank you."

"Don't worry about it," Manny said. "Just save me a piece of wedding cake."

VIKTOR SAT at the center table, a glass of vodka before him. Every few seconds, he'd pick up the glass and take a sip.

"Must be something wrong for you to be drinking so early," Vlad said as he approached.

Viktor glanced up and nodded. "A lot wrong. That fucking cop is still raiding all my places, and we haven't gotten to him yet. The one time we tried, we ended up with two dead men."

"I assume you have his apartment staked out?"

"Two teams. Two fucking teams. And they've got nothing. They say he isn't there. He must have gone to a safe house. I want you to find it. Use our men inside the department."

Viktor slugged the rest of his drink, then set the glass on the table while nodding. "That's what we need to do. Get it done."

FRANKIE WALKED into work feeling great. This was his last day as a single man. Despite being on edge about the situation with Viktor, he was excited to start a new life with Kate. She was the first woman he felt truly comfortable with, able to say whatever was on his mind.

"What the hell are you doing in here?" Sherri Miller asked as she passed by. "I thought Kate would have you on your knees scrubbing floors by now."

"I've still got one more day," Frankie said. "And there will be no scrubbing floors for me; that's a woman's job."

Sherri laughed. "With that attitude, I predict this marriage may last a full week."

"That's not enough time for the floor to get dirty," Frankie said.

"That's all right. I'm confident you'll find somewhere else to screw up."

Frankie laughed. "See you tomorrow, Miller. I've got floors to scrub."

Someone grabbed Frankie's arm as he was going up the stairs. He turned to see Richie Manciewicz, whom he hadn't seen in two years. He had a small gift in his hand. "Richie! What the hell are you doing over here? I thought you moved to Queens."

"I did, but I heard you were getting hitched, and I dropped by to give you a present. I stopped at the apartment several nights, but no one answered. What'd you do—move?"

Frankie's senses went on alert. Here it was—the query into where he was staying, just like Nicky said. "No, just been out doing shit for the wedding."

"Don't gimme that," Richie said. "I know better. You staying at her place, or what?"

Frankie thought about how to answer. He could keep avoiding him, but he may as well see if Richie was involved. "To tell you the truth, Richie, I'm down at the Savoy for a few days by the Brooklyn Bridge. I've been having issues with the Russians."

"You shitting me? That bad?"

Frankie nodded. "Yeah. I don't know if you heard, but they got Lou. Killed him."

"What the fuck! Lou? No, I hadn't heard." He placed an arm on Frankie's shoulder and handed him the present. "Shit, I'm sorry to hear that, Frankie. Here, take this, and best of luck in the marriage."

"Thanks," Frankie said. "See ya around."

Frankie watched Richie walk out the front door, then he pulled his phone out as he climbed the stairs. "Nicky, it happened just like you said."

"What happened?"

"One of the guys I used to work with showed up out of the blue and said he'd been by my place to drop off a present. He wanted to know where I was staying."

"And you told him?"

"Yeah, like you said. I told him I was at the Savoy."

"Good job, Bugs. I'll call Fabrizio, and we'll be waiting."

"What do you mean 'we'll be waiting'? You can't go there. I'll send some people over."

"Bugs, stay out of this. Your guys will mess it up, and I don't want this to go on any longer. Besides, I'm not leaving Fabrizio to face this alone. Viktor will send more than one guy."

"Like I said, I'll get some people over there."

"What will they do? Lock up Viktor's men for showing up at the hotel? No, Bugs. We're doing this my way. Whoever Viktor sends over won't be coming back."

"Nicky—"

"Bugs, I'm hanging up now. I've got things to do."

Nicky packed a few things and walked toward the door.

"Where you goin'?" Manny asked.

"To the hotel. I think it's going down tonight."

"Hang on. You can't do this shit by yourself."

Nicky said, "I'm not alone."

"You got help? Who?"

"Fabrizio is at the hotel."

"Dominic's Fabrizio?"

I nodded.

"Forget I asked," Manny said. "I guess you don't need my help."

"Thanks anyway, Manny, but more people will get in our way."

"I got that, but I'll tell you what I'll do. I'll send a couple of guys to hang out in the parking lot and call you when they spot Viktor's men."

"That's good, Manny. That will help. Just tell them to make sure they're not spotted."

"You got it," Manny said. "They'll be fucking ghosts."

~

* * *

Vlad walked to Viktor's table. "He's at the Savoy by the Brooklyn Bridge."

"We're sure about this?"

"Got it from the inside. I didn't see him go there, but he told our guy."

"Good. Send three men with a message and do it tonight."

"What kind of message?" Vlad asked.

"The kind that doesn't need an answer," Viktor said. "I need this problem to go away."

"Consider it done," Vlad said, then he left the room.

NICKY KNOCKED on the door and said, "Fabrizio, it's me. Open up."

Fabrizio opened the door while he tucked his gun back into his waistband. "What are you doing here?"

"Bugs got a hit. I think it's going down tonight."

"How many do you think he'll send?"

"I don't know. If I had to guess, three or four. The last time, he sent two, and he found them dead. My guess is he'll pick better men and more of them."

"Want to play some cards while we wait?" Fabrizio asked.

THE TRAP IS SPRUNG

Fabrizio and I prepared for our guests and discussed not only how to greet them but what to do afterward.

I convinced one of the room-service guys to let me use a uniform and cart for the night, and it only cost me fifty dollars. While I did that, Fabrizio scoped the place out so we could plan a strategy. Ordinarily, that was a job I would do, but I trusted his judgment.

"What do we do with the guns when we're done?" he asked. "I know you like to get rid of yours."

I nodded. "You take care of yours however you want; I'll ditch mine on the way back to Manny's. Which reminds me—you got a place to stay tonight?"

He nodded. "One of Dominic's men lives close by. I called him and said I might be over."

I pulled the curtains aside and peeked outside. "It's still light. We've probably got a few hours."

"Might as well play cards then. I've got a *scopa* deck and a pinochle deck," Fabrizio said.

"Why not both," I said. "I'll beat you in either of them."

"*Oddio*! In that case, fifty dollars a game and twenty a bump seems to be reasonable for pinochle. I'll take it easy on you in *scopa* and go only ten a game."

We played *scopa*, a popular Italian card game for about an hour, then we switched to pinochle. Fabrizio was ahead in *scopa*, and we had won the same amount of games in pinochle, but he was in front in the money column, as I had more bumps.

I had just won the bid for the "kitty" and was about to name trump when my phone rang. "Hello?"

"It's Slappy. I work for Manny. Viktor's men just showed up. They're coming in now."

"How many?"

"Three, and I know one of them. He's good."

"Okay, Slappy. Thanks."

I hung up and pulled my gun to check it. I was already dressed in the room-service uniform. "Time to go, Fabrizio."

We walked into the hall. Fabrizio turned right, and I went left, pushing the cart. I got to the end of the hall and took another left.

I pretended to be delivering to a room when I heard their footsteps. I didn't look up. They turned down the hall toward the room, and I followed, making sure the plates on the cart rattled.

When I turned the corner, plates rattling, they looked my way. Fabrizio stepped out of the room where the ice machine sat, and he shot one of the men in the back of the head.

Fabrizio's gun was silenced, but a silenced gun still makes noise. The other men spun around when the gun went off, their hands moving for their guns.

When they turned, I pulled my gun out and shot both of them in the back on the head, then Fabrizio shot each of them in the chest.

I put my gun away quickly. "Let's get them inside before anyone sees."

We dragged the bodies into the room, made sure the place was clean, then headed out one-at-a-time.

"I'll see you tomorrow," Fabrizio said as he got into his car.

"Not tomorrow," I said. "Frankie's getting married."

"Then I'll see you afterward," he said. "Call me when you get back to Manny's."

I took a detour on my way back to Manny's place so I could get rid of the gun. Most people keep their guns, but I always got rid of mine. Besides, Dominic had given me two clean guns when we started this. I could afford to.

I opened Manny's front door quietly and tiptoed to the kitchen. Manny was seated at the table.

"Rat! Glad to see you made it. How'd things go?"

"Viktor has three fewer men," I said.

"And Fabrizio? He okay?"

"He's fine. He's a pleasure to work with."

"Work with?" Manny laughed. "Yeah, that's one way of puttin' it. I still can't believe Viktor tried it. That convinces me more than ever that we gotta be alert tomorrow."

"The wedding will be loaded with cops."

"Yeah, but cops can't stop a bullet once it's fired. I'm puttin' my men on all sides of the church about a block away. If anyone spots one of Viktor's men, we'll start shooting, so if you hear gunshots, get Bugs on the ground."

"Got it," I said, then I stared. "Manny, why are you doing this? You and Bugs aren't friends, and you're on different sides of the law."

Manny bit into a biscotto and shrugged. "I like Bugs. There are plenty of people in hell that I like, and there are people in heaven that I don't. You can't choose who you like."

"I guess not," I said and walked to the stove. "You want some espresso, Manny?"

"Sure. Why not. Put enough in the pot for Giorgio too. He'll be right back."

While Manny, Giorgio, and I drank espresso, Bugs came down the stairs. "Rat, you okay? Is everything all right?"

"Everything is fine, Bugs. Sit down."

"What happened? Anybody show up?"

"My night was uneventful," I said. "Fabrizio and I played *scopa* and pinochle, and that son of a bitch won about fifty dollars from me. Other than that, not much went on."

"So no shoot-out? Viktor's men didn't show up?"

"Bugs, stop worrying. I'm sure when you check the papers tomorrow, that there will be no reports of a shoot-out. You can sleep easy tonight and worry about getting married."

"And that's all you have to worry about," Manny said. "I'll have you covered tomorrow."

Bugs sighed. "Just keep them out of sight, Manny. All I need is for some reporter to recognize your men, and it will be all over the headlines.

Gangsters attend detective's wedding.

"Better than having them read your obituary," Manny said, and Giorgio chuckled.

"All right, I'm hitting the sack," Bugs said. "I've got a big day tomorrow."

Bugs was on his way up the steps when I asked Manny. "What time is it?"

"Look at your goddamn phone," he said.

"Shit, I forgot. I've had this thing for years, and I still don't think of that."

I looked at the time on my phone, then said, "I need to call a guy. Be right back."

I went to the front porch and dialed Johnny Moresco's number.

Johnny answered after three rings. "It must be Nicky Fusco."

"You figure that out by yourself, or did you look at the phone's caller ID?"

"Fuck you, Nicky. I didn't need to look at the caller ID. Nobody else would call this late."

"Don't give me that shit, Johnny. You were up later than this when you were six-years old."

Moresco laughed. "You might be right. So what's up? How's it going up in the big city?"

"Going fine. How are things down there? Any troubles? Any problems?"

"No problems, but we might have a good opportunity."

"What?"

You know that new school project? The one out on Delaware Avenue?"

"Yeah, I know it. I've been dying to bid on that. It could mean a lot of work."

"Well, bids are going in. They just called for them, and they'll still be open when you get back."

"Good. I'm looking forward to that. If you get a chance, let them know I'll be submitting one shortly after I return."

"You want me to find out what you're up against?"

"What do you mean?"

"I know the foreman on the job. I can ask what the other bids are. He'll tell me because he owes me one."

I thought for only a second. "Thanks anyway, but no. I'm in this for the long haul. I want to do it right. Either I win the bid or I don't, but I don't want to cheat someone else out of it."

"You're a good man, Nicky. Fuckin' crazy but a good man."

I laughed. "When you said that, you sounded just like your father. Patsy too. I can still hear Patsy saying those same words."

"You couldn't have heard my dad say it too often because he didn't like many people."

I laughed. "I know. Your dad was the opposite of your uncle Patsy. Patsy "the Whale" loved everybody."

"That he did, Nicky. I still miss him, especially at family gatherings. He used to make everybody laugh. I'll never forget the time he dressed up like a whale for one of my birthdays. My friends cracked up."

"All right, listen up," I said. "I've got to get going, but thanks for the update and thanks for taking care of things. I owe you big time."

"You don't owe me shit, Nicky. Just be safe. I don't know what you're doing, but be safe."

I hung up from Johnny, said goodnight to Manny and Giorgio, then sneaked into the bedroom so I didn't wake Angela.

She woke anyway. "Where were you?" she asked.

"I was talking to Johnny Moresco. Everything is going great. Hearing him say that made me feel better."

"That's fantastic," Angela said. "Now get to sleep."

I NOW PRONOUNCE YOU MAN
AND WIFE

Frankie awoke before six, nervous about the wedding, but at the same time, eager to get it over with. He was nervous because despite the precautions he took—and the liberties Manny was taking—he still worried that Viktor may try something. And he was eager because he wanted to go on his honeymoon and spend private time with Kate.

Nicky and Angela had agreed to take Alex back to Wilmington while Frankie and Kate were gone, and that was fine with Frankie. It was one of the few places he felt Alex would be safe.

"All set?" Kate asked as she entered the kitchen.

She startled Frankie. He hadn't heard her come downstairs. "Damn, I didn't hear you," he said. "But yeah, I'm set. Are you?"

"You bet, Mr. Donovan. And it's too late to chicken out now, so don't even think about it."

Frankie pulled her close and kissed. "I wouldn't dare. I'm looking forward to this honeymoon."

"You're not worried about trouble with Viktor?" Kate asked.

"By the time you get back, the trouble with Viktor will be a thing of the past," Nicky said as he walked toward the stove.

Frankie laughed. "Somehow, I believe that, and I don't know if I should feel good about it or not."

"You should feel good."

"Is that your prescription, Dr. Fusco?"

"No, but I'll tell you what is. Get married, go on your honeymoon, then have wild church-approved sex for an entire week. After that, you're allowed to come home."

Kate laughed. "Nicky, I wish I had gotten to know you earlier."

"Plenty of time for that," Nicky said. "You and Bugs need to stay a few days when you come to pick up Alex."

"I'd like that," Kate said. "I haven't even met Frankie's family yet."

"Meeting my family is not anything to look forward to," Frankie said. "But you can judge for yourself after today."

Frankie and Kate ate a big breakfast—prepared by Manny—then changed and got ready to go to church.

MANNY TUGGED on Frankie's arm as he was leaving. "You know the drill, right? If you hear shots, get Kate on the floor, preferably behind a pew."

"I'll have guys there, Manny."

"I know, but who's to say they're not on Viktor's payroll. I'll have my men surrounding the place. I *know* my men are loyal. So go get married and don't worry about it. I got you covered."

Frankie laughed. "Okay, Manny. Thanks. I owe you for this."

Manny slapped Frankie on the back. "You don't owe me shit. Now get goin' before you're late."

Frankie and Kate got to the church early and stood outside greeting guests. They stayed as long as they could before stepping inside to prepare for the ceremony.

ALEX RODE to the church with Nicky and his family. "I can't believe they're finally getting married," Alex said.

"You're part of the reason," Angela said. "They want to provide a good home for you."

Alex beamed. "You think so?"

"I *know* so," Angela said. "Kate told me when we were shopping. And she said it was Frankie's idea."

"Really? I can't believe that."

"Nothing hard to believe," Nicky said. "Bugs told me he thinks of you as his son, so it's only natural to want you to have a mother too."

"Man, that's cool. Thanks for telling me, Mrs. Fusco. You too, Rat—I mean Mr. Fusco."

Nicky laughed. "*Rat* is fine, Alex. Pay no attention to what Bugs says, at least not now."

NICKY AND ANGELA arrived at the church after Frankie and Kate had gone inside. He noticed a few of Manny's men as he parked, and on the way inside, he spotted Fabrizio. He didn't know he'd be at the wedding.

Fabrizio nodded to Nicky as he walked by. With all the protection

Bugs had today, Nicky didn't think Fabrizio was needed, but it made him feel better knowing Fabrizio was there.

Throughout the ceremony, the priest talked, but Nicky wasn't listening. He kept alert for the sound of gunshots. He was prepared to make a dive and take Kate and Frankie down if necessary, and being the best man, he was close enough to do it.

On one of his occasional glances toward the door, he noticed Alex's broad grin and sparkling eyes. That was one happy young man.

When the priest pronounced them man and wife, Nicky felt relieved. Now, all they had to do was get home safely. He walked out first, checking to make sure things looked good. When he went outside, he saw Manny's men plus Fabrizio. A warm feeling washed over him. Viktor would have to be a lunatic to try anything at the church.

The newlyweds came out a moment later to much celebration, then they got in the car and drove to a small reception held in a Knights of Columbus hall. That didn't last long, and afterward, they drove back to Manny's house.

I walked inside, gave Kate a kiss on the cheek and said, "Congratulations, Mrs. Donovan."

"Nicky, I can't thank you enough for making this go smoothly."

"You just did," I said.

Happiness was evident in her looks and in everything she did: her smile, the light in her eyes, and the exuberance in her voice. "And don't worry about a thing while you're gone. Angie and Rosa will spoil Alex and probably fatten him up. He'll need it though because Dante will wear the weight off him with his insistence on playing."

"You're sure this isn't too much for you and Angela?"

I smiled. "Kate, taking care of Bugs would be too much. Taking care of Alex will be a joy. Now hush up and go have fun in San Francisco."

Kate went upstairs and packed, then she and Frankie left a few moments later. I was enjoying a glass of wine when my phone rang.

"Hello?"

"Niccolo. It's Fabrizio."

"Fabrizio? Is everything okay?"

"Fine, but we should get together to plan what to do."

"Plan what?"

"The drugs, Niccolo. Remember—the drug shipment comes in tomorrow. Today is Thursday."

"Oh shit, I forgot. I'm not used to Thursday weddings."

"I can come over to Manny's if you want."

"That would be good, but give me an hour or two, so I can spend time with Angie and the kids."

"Okay. See you then."

I meandered over to Angie, who was chatting with one of Manny's guys.

"Who was that you were talking to?" she asked.

"Just some guy I know."

"Some guy? Or some guy who works for Dominic Mangini?"

I looked at her and grinned. "You don't miss a trick, do you?"

"I can't afford to let my guard down. You're worse than watching the kids. Now tell me what's going on."

I stepped closer and whispered, "What's going on is that you and the kids will go back home tomorrow, and I'll follow in a few days. I've got things to finish up."

"*Things?* Like what?"

"Don't worry about *what*, Angela. If I told you, you'd worry, so I'm not telling you."

"Nicky, I—"

I kissed her lips. "End of discussion. I'll see you in a few days."

"How are you getting home if I drive?"

"Bugs and Kate are lending me a car. When they come to pick up Alex, they can drive it back."

"It's nice to know you've thought this out without asking me."

"Sorry, babe, but I know how you worry about everything, and I didn't want to upset you. I'll be fine. I promise."

"What about—"

"I told you the other night. I already talked to Moresco. He said things are fine—better than fine."

"You're not just saying that?"

"No way. If there was a problem with the business, I'd be home now."

Angela stood on her toes and kissed me. "Be safe. And come home soon."

I laughed. "You're the one I need to caution. You've got three kids to watch."

Angie started for the stairs. "I'm going up to pack. And I expect breakfast to be served at seven."

I made a mock bow. "Your will, my lady."

AFTER ANGIE WENT TO BED, I asked Manny if he had a room that offered privacy so that Fabrizio and I could talk. He showed me to a sitting room that served as a library.

"Manny, I didn't know you read so much."

"I don't," he said. "I collect books because I like the way they look on a shelf; besides, it makes me look smart. But if you see anything you like, take it. I'll get another."

"All right, Manny. Tell Fabrizio where I am when he gets here."

❦

Vlad approached Viktor slowly. He knew how volatile Viktor could be when he received bad information.

"You're walking slowly," Viktor said. "That means you've got bad news. What is it?"

"The men you sent to the church weren't successful. They said the cop was protected."

"I didn't ask for excuses," Viktor said.

"There weren't just cops," Vlad said. "They said Manny had a bunch of his men there. Maybe a dozen of them."

"Manny? What were his men doing there? Is that cop on the take?"

"I don't know," Vlad said. "I heard Manny's operations were getting busted up too, so that doesn't make sense."

"This is disturbing. Leave me alone and let me call Manny."

Viktor called Manny even though it was getting late. "Yeah," Manny said.

"Manny, it's Viktor. What were you doing at the cop's wedding?"

"Viktor. I heard some of your men were there. You could've knocked me over with a straw. I didn't know it was gonna be a cop getting married. Father Bill called last week and asked me to guard a wedding as a favor. That's what I did. You should have told me you had an interest in this."

"What? You know the priest?"

"Yeah, he baptized damn near everybody I know, so when he asks me for a favor, I usually do it. Why? You need something?"

"No, I'm fine," Viktor said. "I was just surprised, that's all. I'll make other plans."

"Okay, Viktor. See ya later."

"Yeah, goodnight, Manny."

LET'S GET THE DRUGS

I had papers spread on the table when Fabrizio walked in. "You're just in time, Fabrizio. We need to come up with a plan so tomorrow goes well."

"I've been thinking about it all day, Niccolo. And on the way here, Dominic verified Slappy's information about which pier Viktor will likely be using."

"I like hearing that," I said. "I hated relying on Slappy's information only. Not that I don't trust him, but I trust Dominic more."

"Now that we know the pier, all we need is a plan to take the drugs," Fabrizio said.

"Yeah, and I'm sure taking the drugs won't be as easy as it sounds. If the shipment is as big as Freddy thinks, Viktor will have five or six guys there to meet it."

"That's five or six well-armed men who will be alert and on edge," Fabrizio said. "We need an advantage—something to distract them, take them out of their game."

Manny walked in and shut the door behind him. "Hey, just so you know. If you need help, you can have two of my men for five large each."

I looked to Fabrizio, who nodded.

"Sounds like a plan, Manny. Who do you have in mind?"

"Giorgio will do it and so will Slappy. But they don't want to be seen by the Russians."

"You don't have to worry about that," Fabrizio said. "Are they good with a rifle?"

"Giorgio is good, and Slappy is even better. Don't let Slappy fool you. He's a crack shot. Got balls too."

"Tell them they're in," I said. "We could use the help."

I waited until Manny left, then turned to Fabrizio. "That solves some of our problem, but not all of it. I don't mind Viktor's men getting hurt, but I don't want us taking a bullet."

"Think of a distraction," Fabrizio said. "All we need is a few seconds."

"I'm getting more coffee," I said. "You want any?"

"If it's espresso, yes."

"Want any grappa in it?"

Fabrizio nodded. "*Un po, grazie.*"

Ten minutes later, I returned with the espresso. As we sipped from our cups, I recalled what Johnny Moresco had said about Patsy, and how he had dressed up like a whale, then I remembered how Doggs and Knuckles had robbed the competing card game on Lincoln Street by going in dressed up as cops. It was then that it hit me. "Cops!" I said.

"What about cops?" Fabrizio asked.

"We go dressed as cops. It will give us the edge we need. Viktor's men won't draw on cops, or at least, they'll hesitate."

Fabrizio smiled. "And while they're hesitating, we move in and take control."

"We'll need badges," I said.

"And uniforms," Fabrizio said. "The uniforms will be what gives them pause."

"Shit! We need them by tomorrow night. Where are we going to get them that quickly?"

Fabrizio thought for few seconds. "Manny could do it," he said. "Ask him."

I invited Manny to join us, and when he came in, I asked, "Manny, can you get us some police uniforms and badges by tomorrow night? We'll need at least two and preferably four."

"Jesus Christ, Nicky, I don't know. I'll have to check."

"They don't have to be perfect," Fabrizio said. "It will be dark, so anything that looks decent will do."

Manny nodded. "I can do decent," he said. "Decent's no problem. Just don't try to get into the policemen's ball wearing them."

"What do you need from us?" I asked.

"Measurements," Manny said. "Pants and shirt sizes from you and Fabrizio. I'll get them from Giorgio and Slappy."

"We need to check this pier out tomorrow morning," I said. "I don't want to go in there blind tomorrow night."

"I know the pier well," Fabrizio said. "We should definitely check it, but if I remember, it almost always has shipping containers there that would make great places to hide."

"We might have to wait a couple of hours," I said. "We're not positive what time the shipment comes in."

"That won't be a problem. There's plenty of room. We could even bring chairs to sit on."

"What about Giorgio and Slappy?"

Fabrizio looked as if he were thinking. "We'll check tomorrow, but there should be places for them to set up facing the water. That way, if they need to take a shot, we won't be in the way."

"Can you map it out for me?" I asked.

Fabrizio grabbed a pencil and paper and drew a picture of the pier, complete with containers, cranes, and more. "There are plenty of places to wait, but we'll see tomorrow."

"Okay, good. I've got to see Angie off in the morning, but I can be ready before nine. What time you want to do this?"

"I'll be here at nine," Fabrizio said. "If anything needs to be adjusted, we'll have plenty of time to do it."

I saw Angie and the kids off after breakfast, then got ready to leave with Fabrizio. He showed up a little before nine, and we drove to Red Hook.

The pier was as he said it would be, and we quickly confirmed where everyone would be stationed based on the previous night's strategy.

"What time you think we should get here?" Fabrizio asked.

"I think if we're in place by seven, we'll have plenty of time to spare. I'm guessing the shipment won't get here until eight or nine."

"All right," Fabrizio said. "I'll get to Manny's by five, then we'll get the uniforms on and be here by seven."

"Sounds good," I said. "See you then."

I went back to Manny's, made sure Giorgio and Slappy were ready and filled them in on the plans.

THE SHIPMENT IS ON TIME

Fabrizio came by just before five, and we dressed in our uniforms. Giorgio's was a tight fit, but it wasn't bad. He looked like a cop who may have gained a little weight.

"If anyone needs to relieve themselves, do it now. There will be no leaving your position once we're in place. And don't forget to turn your damn phone ringers off, and turn off the sound for texts and anything else."

"Remember, Nicky, I'm staying out of sight. Slappy and I both are."

I nodded. "I know the drill, Giorgio. Just make sure your shots are good when you make them. And make sure Fabrizio and I are out of the damn way."

"What's the signal again?" Slappy asked.

"The signal is that one of *us* will shoot one of *them*. When we do, open fire on the rest. We don't know how they'll be positioned, but let's presume that Fabrizio and I will take the guys closest to us, which means you and Giorgio take the guys on the outside. Decide between yourselves who takes left and who takes right."

"Got it," Slappy said.

By a little after seven we were in place, tucked away where we wanted to be with good views of the pier and good cover. Giorgio and Slappy were armed with rifles that had silencers, as were our guns. Silencers wouldn't actually *silence* the guns, but they would reduce the noise quite a bit, and more importantly, silencers would make it more difficult for people to determine where the gunshots were coming from—assuming you were outside.

Around nine o'clock I heard a car pull up. It was a blue van and was sitting low to the ground, so it must have had more than a couple of people in it. I tapped Fabrizio on the arm and nodded. He sent a text message to Giorgio giving him a heads up.

Within ten minutes, a boat came in, surprising me. I thought it would be coming in on a passenger ship or a cargo ship.

Viktor's men got out of the van and walked toward the dock. There were six of them. Two of the men carried bags that probably held the money they'd use to pay for the drugs.

Three more men got off the boat. "You ready?" I whispered to Fabrizio.

He nodded, and we stood and walked quietly toward the men. When we were about forty feet away, I drew my gun and yelled as loud as possible. "Police. Nobody move."

"For a few seconds, no one moved, then one of Viktor's men went for his gun. Fabrizio shot him before his hand touched metal. A second guy was ducking and reaching to draw. I took him out with two shots to the chest.

From there on, it was open warfare, with Fabrizio and I both firing, and Giorgio and Sloppy cutting down the men on the perimeter.

Two of the men from the boat made a run to get aboard, but either

Giorgio or Slappy stopped them cold, dropping them before they could get off the dock.

It was over in about thirty seconds, and there were only two of Viktor's men alive. One was lying on the ground, face down and hands over his head. The other had his head buried between his knees.

"Don't shoot," he repeated over and over.

"Get the money and have our other associates get the dope," I said to Fabrizio. Then I knelt next to the guy on the ground. "Here's what's going to happen. I'm going to let you live, but I want you to take a message to Viktor. Tell him that this is for the detective he killed. Tell him that it's not over either, that we're going to stop every shipment he tries to bring in. By the time we're done, he won't be able to sell a joint in this city, and any of his men that tries to deal will die. *Every* single one."

Fabrizio came back to stand beside me. I tapped the guy on the ground with my foot. "Don't look up, just listen," I said and nodded to Fabrizio.

"Shoot the other one in the knee."

Fabrizio stepped toward him and fired one shot. The man rolled to the ground, screaming. "Shut-up or the next bullet will be in your mouth."

"You're crazy," the guy in front of me said. "You can't do this. You're cops."

"We just did," I said. "And we plan on continuing to do it. Tell Viktor he isn't paying enough respect to the right people. You can't kill one of ours and get away with it, or we'll take it all."

I tapped him with my foot again. "And if I were you, I'd find something else to do. If I see you next time, you'll be one of the bodies left behind." I smiled. "And yes, there *will* be a next time."

The guy nodded and started to raise his head.

"Keep your head down," I said. If you see my face, I'll have to cut your eyes out."

The guy pressed his face to the ground and said nothing.

"I'm going to put a bag over your head so you can't see us. Wait five minutes after we leave, then you can go. If you go before then, I'll find you and kill you. Got that?"

"Got it," he said in a quivering voice.

Slappy brought the car around while Fabrizio checked the other bodies. One of them was alive, so Fabrizio finished the job. Giorgio waited for Slappy, then they went aboard and got the drugs.

Once we had the drugs and the money, we loaded it up and took off, driving back to Manny's house.

Manny was still awake when we got there; in fact, he had half a dozen guys there.

"Everything go okay?" he asked as I walked in.

"Like clockwork," I said. "And we've got a present for you."

"What are you talking about?"

I handed a large duffel bag to him. This is half the dope. Dominic is getting the other half. Fabrizio and I took a small amount for further disruption."

"Shit, Nicky, you don't have to do this."

"I know I don't *have* to, but you deserve it for helping so much. I have one request though, make sure no kids get the drugs." I then handed him twenty thousand dollars. "Here's ten each for Slappy and Giorgio."

"The deal was for five," Manny said.

"I know, but they did a good job. It's worth ten."

"We're going to need some of this money, but I don't know how much. When we're done, you and Dominic can split the rest."

Manny grabbed me and kissed my cheek. "Nicky, you're a saint."

"I can think of a few people who would argue that," I said.

Fabrizio tapped me on the shoulder. "I'm taking Dominic his cut. I'll call tomorrow."

Manny slapped me on the back. "Come on into the kitchen. I'll make some espresso."

As we waited for the water to boil, Manny said, "You know, you should keep that money, or at least split it up with Fabrizio."

I shook my head. "I don't need it."

"Bullshit. Everybody needs money. And you earned it. You put your ass on the line. You deserve to get something for it."

Manny got me thinking. It would be nice to have some extra money to take Angie somewhere, or maybe buy Rosa a car. "I'll think about it, Manny."

THE DRUGS ARE GONE

Anton fidgeted with a pencil and chewed his fingernails while he waited. Pavel sat in a chair by the door, bandages on his knee where Fabrizio had shot him. Two other men stood closer to the door.

He bit the end of the pencil, then crushed out his third cigarette in fifteen minutes. He sat still for a minute, then gulped down another drink. When the door opened, he jumped.

"Ah, my favorite earner," Viktor said. "What brings you so early? I thought you were out late last night."

Anton shifted in his seat and took out another cigarette to light.

Viktor gazed at the ashtray, nearly filled with ashes and butts, then at the bottle of vodka with several glasses gone from it. "You need vodka and so many cigarettes this early in the morning? Something must have happened. Maybe you better tell me."

Anton leaned forward. "It wasn't my fault, Viktor. I swear it."

"What wasn't your fault?"

"They took the drugs. All of them."

"What?" Viktor stood and kicked the chair. "Who took the drugs? When? How? Why wasn't I called?"

Anton shivered and moved his hands to cover his face, though no one threatened him yet. "The cops. The cops raided the place. They were waiting for us like they knew we were coming."

"And they took everything?"

"They took it all," Anton said. "They said it was payback for the cop we killed. And they said from now on, they'll be taking everything we bring in."

Viktor paced. "How did they find out the shipment was coming in? And how did they know where?"

"I don't know," Anton said.

"Who knew it was coming in? Who did you tell?" Viktor asked.

"I didn't tell nobody. Nobody knew but me and Pavel." He pointed to Pavel when he said it. "These cops were crazy. They killed everyone else, then they shot Pavel in the knee after we gave up."

"You surrendered my drugs and money?" Viktor asked.

"Yeah. There was nothing else we could do."

Viktor pulled out a gun and pointed it at Anton. "That's what I thought," he said and pulled the trigger. The bullet hit Anton in the face, knocking him off the chair and onto the floor. Viktor walked over and stood above him, then fired two more shots into his head. The sound of someone dragging his foot across the floor made Viktor turn. It was Pavel heading for the door, but with his knee in that condition, there was no hurry on Viktor's part.

Viktor fired twice, bringing Pavel down. He walked over and put another bullet in his head. Then he turned to the men standing beside him. "Clean this up. Make sure nobody finds the bodies."

Viktor sat in his favorite chair at his favorite table. "Vlad, get everyone here. We need to do something about this cop."

Viktor smoked and drank while he waited. Within an hour, his men trickled in. He had only called for the sub-bosses; they would have to be the ones to pass orders along.

"We've got a problem," Viktor said. "The cops took our drugs last night, and they took the money too. I'm going to check with our men on the inside, but my guess is that it wasn't even reported. That means we're dealing with crooked cops."

"Did they get the whole shipment?" Andrick asked.

"The whole goddamn thing," Viktor said. "And they killed all the men."

"All of them?" the man sitting to the right of Andrick asked.

"Not all of them. Anton and Pavel made it out alive. It seemed too much of a coincidence that those two were the only ones who knew where and when the shipment was coming in, so I killed them."

Several of the men flinched. "Don't worry. I don't intend to kill you— unless you lose a shipment," he said and laughed.

The men laughed with him, but it didn't seem natural.

"Maybe we should try to fix things with this cop," Andrick said. "With all the heat they're putting on us, it makes it tough to get things done. Even tougher to make money."

Vlad's phone rang. "Da?" He listened for a moment, then walked over, whispered to Viktor, and handed him a phone.

Viktor stepped away from the table to talk, then returned wearing a smile. "As I thought, the cops were renegades. I just verified with one of our inside men; there was no report of a drug bust last night. If this had been a sanctioned operation, the cops would already be bragging about it."

"What's the difference?" Andrick said. "Sanctioned or not, the cops have more men than we do. We can't declare war on them."

"Not on them, no. But we can declare war on *one* cop. And we will."

Vlad stepped forward. "Viktor, that's what got us into trouble in the first place, killing that cop. Why not sit back for a while and let them cool down. They'll forget it soon enough."

"Sit back? And let him steal from us? Take our money and drugs? Bust up our prostitution and gambling?" Viktor threw his glass across the room. "No fucking way. Not while I'm alive will some pissant cop do that to me."

"What do you plan on doing?" Vlad asked. "If you kill another cop, it will only put more pressure on us."

"I'm not going to kill him," Viktor said. "I'll think of something. We have a few days. Our man on the inside said he's away on his honeymoon. That's all right. I'm a patient man."

FRANKIE AND KATE were walking through the redwoods when his phone rang. He reached for it, but Kate grabbed his hand. "Don't," she said. "We're on our honeymoon. Whoever it is and whatever their problem is, can wait until we get back."

"But it might be—"

Kate reached up and kissed his lips. "It can wait," she whispered.

Frankie put his arms around her. "That's why I married you. You're too smart."

"It has nothing to do with my gorgeous body and stunning sex appeal."

"Well, that too," Frankie said and laughed, then he took Kate by the hand and continued to stroll through the trees.

Frankie's phone rang three more times while he and Kate were out, but each time—though he had an urge to answer it—Kate convinced him to let it go.

When they returned to the hotel, Kate took a shower. While she did, Frankie listened to his voicemail. They were all from the lieutenant. He looked at the time, realized it was too late, then searched for Morreau's cell number and dialed.

"Morreau."

"Lieutenant, it's Donovan. You called?"

"Yeah, I called. I called four goddamn times."

"I was busy," Frankie said. "This is my goddamn honeymoon, you know."

"There is talk all around that we busted up a big shipment of drugs being delivered to the Russians last night. You know anything about this?"

"How the hell would I know anything? I'm in San Francisco."

"I know where you are. But being in San Francisco doesn't mean you don't know anything. Do you?"

"Let me make this clear, Lieutenant. I had nothing to do with it, and I don't know who did. Is *that* clear enough?"

"It's clear," Moreau said. "I don't know if I believe you, but it's clear."

"Guess what, Lieu? I don't *care* if you believe me. See you next week."

"If I'm still here, I'll see you. If not, have a nice life."

"What do you mean—if you're still there? Why wouldn't you be?"

"Because the chief is crawling up my ass wanting to know what's going on. He's getting heat from the mayor, and he's putting that heat right on me. And guess why? Because of one Irish detective, that's why."

"What's that supposed to mean?"

"It means that you started this vendetta."

"Bullshit, they—"

"Yeah, I know. The Russian killed Mazetti, or so you say, but until we get proof, we can't do anything. At least, we're not supposed to do anything."

"And what about the fact that Viktor happens to be running illegal operations? Doesn't that have bearing on this?"

"I'm through arguing, Donovan. Just finish up your honeymoon and get your ass back here. I want whoever's doing this stopped. We can't have people impersonating cops and executing people."

"I say we find the son of a bitch and give him a medal."

"I know what you say, but that's not how the law works. Goodnight."

Kate came out of the bathroom with a towel wrapped around her, and nothing else. "Hello, Mr. Donovan. Got any plans for this evening?"

Frankie patted a spot on the bed beside him. "I should say no and make mad passionate love to you, but I won't." He took her hands and looked her in the eyes. "I've got troubles at home. It would be good if I went back early."

"What? We're on our honeymoon."

"I know," Frankie said. "I'll make it up to you, but this is important. Really important."

"And our honeymoon is not important?"

"It is," Frankie said. "It's very important, but this is life or death."

"What's the matter?"

"Somebody's impersonating cops. They're stealing Viktor's drugs and killing his men."

"And?"

"And I think it's Nicky."

"What? Why would he do that?"

"Because he thinks he's helping me."

Kate sighed. "Okay, we'll go. But I don't want your 'making it up to me' to be a roll in the hay."

Frankie kissed her and laughed. "You got it. It'll be something special. You're the best."

Kate stood and let her towel fall off. "Remember that."

PAVEL NEVER SHOWED

Freddy knocked lightly on Manny's front door. It was early, and he didn't want to wake anyone, but he had to see Manny. When no one answered after a minute, he knocked again but louder.

Manny opened the door, a scowl planted on his face. "Freddy, what the fuck do you want? I ain't even had my espresso yet."

"Sorry," Freddy said as he squeezed inside.

"Yeah, come the fuck in," Manny said, then smacked him on the back of the head.

Manny walked to the kitchen and began to prepare his espresso. "Since you're here, you want some espresso?" he asked.

"Yeah, thanks," Freddy said.

"So what's up? Why are you here so early?"

"I went to meet Pavel, and he never showed."

"Yeah?"

"I called his wife too. She hasn't heard from him."

Manny plopped a plate on the table containing few biscotti. "You can have two," he said. "The rest are for me. And wait for the espresso to be done. I don't like lookin' at crumbs before I eat."

"You make crumbs all the time."

"Yeah, but they're my crumbs. Now go on with your story."

"I'm thinking something happened to him."

Manny laughed and leaned against the stove. "Goddamn, Freddy, you're brilliant. I told you Nicky Fusco was interested in this. What I didn't tell you was that Dominic Mangini was also interested. You think Pavel is gonna come out of this alive if those two have something to do with it? You're lucky you're not missing too. You should go to church and say your prayers because somebody was lookin' out for you."

Manny poured two cups of espresso and carried them to the table. He handed one to Freddy and placed the other in front of his seat. "Freddy, this is way above your thinking range. This is Dominic having trouble with Viktor, and he's got Nicky helping him. If you try gettin' involved or even try to figure out what's goin' on, you'll probably get killed. My advice is to stay out of it. Don't ask questions of anyone."

"But I gave Pavel money up front. What about that?"

"It's gone, Freddy. Think of it as shit you flushed down the toilet; in fact, you'd have a better chance of recovering that shit. Safer too."

Freddy sipped on his espresso and took a bite of a biscotto. "So you're saying that money is gone?"

"I'm saying you shouldn't even mention it, Freddy. It would be dangerous."

"What's wrong with asking?"

"Dominic's what's wrong. You never know what he'll do. He may give you your money and say 'I'm sorry for your trouble,' or he may put a bullet in each of your eyes, or he may tell Nicky to go for a walk with you and trust me, as bad as Dominic is, going for a walk with Nicky would be worse. If you want to roll the dice, go ahead. If it were me, I wouldn't, 'cause the odds are, Dominic wouldn't choose door number one."

"And there's nothing we can do about it? It's a lot of money. I mean, Christ's sake, he's only a man. We could hold a meeting with him, and if it doesn't go well, put a bullet in him."

Manny laughed. "If you weren't so stupid, I'd put a bullet in you myself, but I feel pity for the mentally handicapped." Manny took a bite of the biscotto, careful not to spill crumbs. "I wouldn't even think about crossing Dominic. Dominic's got a guy working for him who could put a bullet in you before you reach for your gun, and Nicky could put a bullet in you while you're still thinking about it."

Freddy snorted. "I'm pretty handy with a gun."

Manny chuckled. "You ever hear the whole story of Nicky the Rat?"

Freddy's face went white. "I heard some."

"You ever hear of Johnny Muck?"

Freddy smiled. "Best hit-man ever."

"Not quite," Manny said. "If he had been the best hit-man ever, he'd still be alive. Nicky caught him and made sure he wasn't breathing when he left. In fact, he killed him in such a gruesome way that some of the cops at the scene got sick, and these were seasoned detectives."

"He's the one who got Muck?"

"That's him," Manny said. "I've seen what he can do. He's like a fuckin' ghost, and he's fast and quick, and he's fearless. I wouldn't take on Nicky with five guys like Johnny Muck at my side."

Freddy pushed his espresso cup to the side and stood. "Shit, Manny. Forget the money. Sorry I said anything."

Manny stood next to Freddy and patted him on the back. "Don't worry but do forget about it. Consider it over."

"You got it," Freddy said, and walked out the front door.

A moment after he left, Giorgio entered the kitchen. "Morning, Manny. How's it going?"

"Pretty good, but you're gonna have to make Freddy disappear. And make sure he's not found."

Giorgio poured his espresso and sat next to Manny. "When you want it done?"

"Today," Manny said. "Let him see his wife and kids, then take him for a ride."

"Manny, you sure about this? Maybe Nicky needs him for something still? Freddy knows a lot about Viktor's organization. It wouldn't hurt to ask."

Manny's instinctive response was to smack Giorgio, but he stopped and thought about it. "All right. We'll do it your way. I'll ask Nicky first. And I might as well get Freddy back here in case Nicky has questions."

Manny dialed the phone. "Freddy. Turn around and come back. I got some questions about Viktor's crews."

"I don't know his crews. I only know a few people."

"Maybe the people I want to know about are one of those 'few' Now get your ass back here."

Manny caught me as I was coming down the stairs.

"Nicky, I got Freddy here. You need to know anything before he goes?"

"Why would I need to know anything?"

"Freddy's the one who helped us with the shipment; he knows Viktor's crews better than any of us, especially the dealers."

"In that case, yeah, I do need to talk with him." I headed toward the kitchen. "But I need coffee first."

We went to the kitchen, and Manny gestured for Freddy to sit at the kitchen table. "Freddy, this is Nicky Fusco. He has some questions for you."

Freddy damn near jumped to get in a chair. "Nicky Fusco? What do you want? I didn't do nothin'."

"I didn't say you did, Freddy. But I need some information, and Manny thinks you can help."

Freddy seemed to calm down a little. "Sure. Sure. What do you need?"

"I need to know where Viktor's men would be peddling dope. All of them, and I need to know where to find his junkie customers."

Freddy seemed to become nervous again. He turned and looked at Manny. "Manny, you know I can't say nothin'. Viktor would kill me if he found out."

I smiled and took hold of one of Freddy's hands. "I wouldn't worry so much about Viktor if I were you."

Manny laughed. "He's got that right, Freddy. Remember the old proverb. Don't be afraid of the wolf when you're in the lion's den."

Freddy looked my way again. "Okay, but if I tell you, you gotta make sure it don't get out."

I nodded and handed Freddy a pad of paper and a pen. "Write it down, Freddy. And include any names you know and any other specifics, like where a junkie hangs out or what time of day they usually score."

"I don't know the names. Pavel was the only one I knew."

"I don't mean dealer names. I mean junkies. By the time I'm done, Viktor's not going to have a drug business, let alone a lucrative one."

"What are you doin' this for? I know Viktor's got to have some supply left, but he's bound to be running low after you took his drugs."

"I told you, I don't want him just running low; I want him out of business. I intend to take the supply and the demand from Viktor."

"That's gonna piss him off," Freddy said.

I put my hand on his shoulder. "You'd do better if you worried about pissing me off."

Freddy scribbled a few more lines, then handed the notepad to me. "Here it is. That's all I know."

"You're sure that's it?" Manny asked.

"Freddy nodded. "That's all. I swear."

I took the pad, and as I walked toward the room Fabrizio and I had used, I saw Manny nod to Giorgio. I knew what that meant.

I detoured to walk close to Manny and whispered when I passed. "Let him go, Manny. He did his job."

"You sure about that?"

"I'm sure."

THE PLAN TO SUBVERT VIKTOR

Fabrizio came by just as Freddy was leaving. "Did Freddy come early, or is he just leaving?"

"He came early, but now he's leaving," I said. "He helped us with dealer and junkie names."

"Good," Fabrizio said. "We could use some help."

We went to the kitchen, made espresso, then went into the room we had used before and began to plan.

"The other night had to put a hurt on Viktor," Fabrizio said. "That was a lot of money, and he's now without a lot of drugs. He'll be running low before long."

"That's where we can hurt him," I said. "Viktor can take a hit on the money, but the drugs are a different story. The junkies he serves won't wait for him to get his feet on the ground. When they need their fix, they need it. And they won't wait until Viktor can deliver. They'll get their fix wherever they can."

"How do we take advantage of that the best way?" Fabrizio asked.

"By giving them what they need," I said. "And I do mean giving. We don't charge them anything, or we charge them half the normal price."

Fabrizio smiled. "And to enhance the effect, we should get the police to pressure Viktor's dealers and junkies further putting a scare into them," Fabrizio said. "Between lack of supply and getting pressure from the cops, pretty soon Viktor won't have any dealers."

"That may be difficult—getting the police to dance to our tune."

Fabrizio smiled. "I'm counting on you for that, Niccolo. I have confidence you can do it."

"Yeah, well before we worry about getting the cops involved, let's talk about how we're going to do it from our end."

"I'm listening," Fabrizio said.

"I say we take some of the drugs and give them away to Viktor's customers. If we provide them a fix free of charge, they won't be spending money with Viktor. That will further erode his money stockpile."

"Maybe we only give the drugs to some of his customers, and at the same time, we get the cops to bust as many of his remaining customers as they can. Word will spread quickly that it's not good to do business with Viktor."

"I like that, Fabrizio, and I think I know who we can get on the force to go along with this."

I leaned to the side and called for Manny, who was in the other room. "Manny, can you come here, please?"

Manny damn near filled the doorway. "What do you need, Rat?"

"Fabrizio and a good idea, but for it to work properly, we're gonna need a cop uniform for Freddy. I'll fill you and Freddy in once we get it ironed out."

"A uniform like I got for you will work?"

I nodded. "That'll be fine. It only has to pass for a uniform with junkies, but I need it by tomorrow. Will that be a problem?"

Manny shook his head. "No problem. I'll have it by end of day tomorrow. Count on it."

"All right, Fabrizio, I'm heading out."

"Where are you going?"

"I have to see about arranging our police part of the plan, remember?"

"That works. I've got things to do for Dominic. I'll talk to you tomorrow."

I LEFT Manny's and went looking for the one cop I felt I could trust.

I parked outside the station and waited for lunchtime. Sure enough, she exited the building just before noon. Fortunately, she headed my way. I rolled down the window when she was passing by.

"Miller, you got a minute?"

Startled, he looked my way, then upon what I assume was recognition, cast glances to all around.

"Nicky! What are you doing here?"

"If you mean New York, I came for Bug's wedding. If you mean why am I in this parking lot, it's because I need to talk to you."

She cast more worried glances as if I were poison. "Don't worry, Miller. Nobody knows me but you and Bugs, and he's not here. Get in."

Sherri looked as if she didn't like it, but she got into the car on the passenger side. "What do you need?"

"Bugs told me that you were in on this plan to get Viktor, who we're pretty sure killed Lou. Are you? If you are, I need your help. If you're not, I'll ask for your silence."

"If it's for Lou, I'm in. I told Frankie that."

"All right, here's what I need." I then laid out the plan that Fabrizio and I had cooked up, telling her what we planned on doing with the bags and how we would count on her to bust what remained of Viktor's dealers."

"That's it? That's all you want? Hell yes, I'm in. I thought you were gonna ask me to do something illegal."

I smiled. "Miller, you don't know me well, but I'd never do that. I might do it myself, but I wouldn't ask you to break your oath. There is one catch though; you can't put this on the books as an ongoing operation. I don't mean you can't log it in, but make it seem as if you stumbled across these guys during regular duty."

"It'll look suspicious if there's more than one or two of them."

"It'll have to look suspicious then. Besides, I can't imagine they'll get too upset over you bringing in dope dealers who work for the number-one suspect in another detective's murder."

Miller smiled. "You're right about that. The brass may not be happy, but I'll have the rank and file on my side. I'll figure it out, don't worry."

Miller wrote down a number on a card and handed it to me. "Here's my private cell. Use this when you need me."

"Will do," I said. "It will be a couple of days, but I'll call soon."

"All right, Fusco. See ya then." She got out of the car and continued on her way.

As I drove back to Manny's house, I smiled. Things felt right. Everything was in place. As soon as Manny got Freddy's uniform, we were good to go.

I called Fabrizio on the way to Manny's. "We're set with the cops. All we need is to bring Freddy up to speed so he can do his part."

"You think he can handle it?"

"I think he better handle it. If he doesn't, he won't be around long. Manny already has him in his sights."

"I thought I detected something," Fabrizio said. "I can't imagine Manny was happy about Freddy doing business with Viktor."

"Not only was he not happy, he was ready to take him out. I asked him to at least wait until this was over. Maybe if Freddy does good, he'll get a reprieve."

"You gonna tell him?" Fabrizio asked.

"No, he'll sink or swim on his own. I'm guessing he suspects though, based on the way he acted when Manny and I were in the kitchen with him."

"You should tell him what's at stake," Fabrizio said. "He deserves to know. He helped us."

"If I tell him, he may get too nervous," I said.

"It's up to you," Fabrizio said. "If it were me, I'd tell him."

"All right, I'll think about it. Stop by tomorrow at lunchtime, and we'll put the finishing touches on this."

LET'S GET ON WITH THE PLAN

anny called Freddy once he got the uniform, and Freddy showed up a little before noon. He seemed to be in good spirits, not nervous like he was before.

I took him into the kitchen and put on some espresso. "Freddy, this is an important role you're playing for us. You know that?"

"Yeah, I figured. Don't worry; it's right up my alley. I'm used to dealing with junkies and dealers. I ain't gonna screw it up."

I had made up my mind to tell him, but Freddy's confidence had me questioning my decision. Maybe I should let it occur naturally.

I decided he may benefit from a little motivation. "Freddy, if you do this right, there will be something in it for you."

"Like what?"

"The money you lost with Pavel. How's that sound?"

Freddy set his espresso down and stared. "You shittin' me? Mother of God! I'll make sure it goes right. Just tell me what to do. I'll do anything."

I smiled. It seemed as if that was the motivation he needed. "Drink your coffee, and I'll fill you in."

"You gave us the names of a few of Viktor's customers. I want you to get in touch with them and give them free dope. Free. And tell them that we're gonna give free dope to anyone who—"

"Bags," Freddy said.

"What?"

"Bags. They don't refer to it as dope; it's 'bags.'"

"Okay, thanks. So we're gonna give free bags to anyone who brings us a new customer—but the customer has to have been one of Viktor's previous customers."

"Excuse the expression, Nicky, but you're half nuts. You'll have junkies flocking to you. You're gonna need a lot of bundles to keep this up."

"What's a bundle?"

"A bundle is ten bags, and if you're giving bags away for free, a bundle won't last long."

I nodded. "I hope it won't. And don't worry about the supply. I've got plenty of bundles."

"When do you want me to start?"

"I want you to start as soon as you're ready, but we need this to go as planned. And one more thing, I want you to hand out the bags dressed as a cop. Manny's got the uniform, that's why he wanted your measurements."

"What? No shit? I thought—"

"You thought he wanted to buy you a suit to bury you in?"

Freddy forced a smile. "Yeah, something like that. He had me worried."

"I need you in uniform so word gets back to Viktor that it's the cops doing this to him. I want him to think it's because of him killing the detective."

Freddy nodded. "Sounds good."

"That's not all," I said. "We need to make more incentive for people to stop buying drugs from Viktor. Tell them that whoever stays with Viktor will be busted. It's not a question of if they'll be busted, just when."

"How are you going to make sure that happens?" Freddy asked.

"Don't worry about how. It will happen. You make certain that the junkies and dealers know this."

"Viktor's dealers aren't going to abandon him for a few bags. They'd be crazy to. Viktor would kill them."

"I know they won't for a few bags, but make it a few bundles and show them the cops are serious about busting Viktor's men, and it won't take long. All I need from you are the dealer's names and the best place to find them."

"I can do that. You got it. I don't know all his dealers, but I can find out most of them."

"One more thing, Freddy. Make sure to stress the importance of timing. Tell the junkies that you're giving away bags for two weeks only, then you'll sell it for half price for another two weeks, but after that, it's back to normal."

I took another sip of espresso. "And make sure they understand that if they don't sign up in one week, they don't get in on the deal."

Freddy wrote notes on a pad in front of him. "And what about the junkies? What do they get for bringing me customers?"

"Every junkie who brings a new customer—from Viktor—gets a bag for free. But they have to have been one of Viktor's customers."

"Suppose they bring ten customers," Freddy asked.

"Then you get a bundle free."

"No shit? Really?"

"No shit," I said, then handed him a burner. "You can use this to have them get in touch. I'm leaving it up to you to verify the junkies are who they say and not a cop."

"I thought the cops were in on this?"

"They are, and they aren't," I said. "I've got one cop who's going to handle busting the dealers who stay loyal to Viktor, but I haven't told her about what we're doing."

"Shit, that makes things complicated."

I grabbed Freddy under the chin and lifted. "Freddy, I didn't say this was without risk, but you stand to come out of this with a lot of money. Remember that."

"Okay, yeah. Got it. I'm on it, starting today."

"I expect customers quickly."

"You got it, man. Be ready to hand out bags because my phone will be ringing soon."

"Sounds good, Freddy. Get going and don't forget your uniform."

"I won't," he said. Before leaving, he turned. "Nicky, thanks. I appreciate what you're doing."

I nodded. "Just do your job, and don't forget to call me every time you get a dealer's name. I want them busted quickly. The faster we take Viktor's business away, the more it will hurt."

Manny walked in after Freddy left. "You still using him?"

"Manny, I told him if he did a good job, he'd be all right. I even told him I'd give him back the investment he had with Pavel."

"What? You're fucking crazy. That's a lot of money. I'd just as soon let Giorgio take him for a ride to Jersey."

"I know what you'd rather do, Manny. But Freddy's done a good job so far. If he keeps it up, he'll be worth it. Besides, once Viktor is gone, you might find he's a valued member of your team again."

"Once Viktor's gone? Is he gonna be gone?"

"I made a promise, Manny. I always keep my promises."

AN EARLY RETURN

Frankie and Kate took the first flight out, but being a six-hour flight and coming from the west coast, they didn't arrive in New York until after work hours.

Frankie thought about going home to spend the night but decided against it in case Viktor still planned on getting to him. Instead, he went to Manny's, and knocked on the door. It was almost midnight.

Nicky answered the door. "Bugs, what the hell are you doing here? I thought you were gone until Saturday."

"I was supposed to be, but something came up."

"Something came up? What?"

Frankie pulled Nicky to the side, whispering. "Somebody hit one of Viktor's drug shipments dressed as cops. They not only took his drugs and money, but they killed his men. You know anything about this?"

Nicky shrugged. "News to me."

"And you expect me to believe that? That it's news to you?"

"That's what I said."

"I know what you said, but I asked if you expected me to believe it."

"You should have stayed in San Francisco, Bugs. I had things covered here."

"Had things covered? Then why did my lieutenant call me four times? *Four fucking times.*"

"You want some espresso?" I asked.

"Espresso? It's almost midnight for Christ's sake. And you still haven't answered my question."

I put some water on to boil and turned to face Bugs. "We didn't intend to hurt anyone, but they started it."

"*They started it?* That sounds like an excuse for a playground scuffle, not the scene of a drug bust with dead bodies littering the docks."

"Bugs, settle down. We've got this covered, and Miller has her end."

"Who the hell is *we?* No, don't tell me. I presume it's you and Fabrizio. And what do you mean by 'Miller has her end'? Did you get Sherri involved in this?"

"She wasn't before, but she is now," I said. "We're finishing up what we started."

Bugs lowered his head and mumbled. "Corrupting the whole goddamn force."

"Bugs, I'm not doing anything but helping you to survive. Viktor is a lunatic. He'll keep coming after you unless we do something. I'm doing something."

Bugs shook his head. "All right. Tell me what's going on."

I sat at the table and filled him in on what had happened so far, and on what Freddy and Miller were doing. "If this goes according to plan, Viktor will be pissing blood within two weeks."

"You're not going to be here in two weeks," Bugs said. "I'm supposed to drive you home this weekend."

"Going home will have to wait," I said. "You'll have to make an excuse for Angie."

Bugs laughed. "Like hell. That's your department. I've got enough to worry about with the lieutenant."

I slugged the last of the espresso and took the empty cup to the sink. "Then I'll continue with my plan."

"What's Miller got to do with your plan?"

"Bugs, I already told you, all she's doing is making a few busts from names I give her. She's not doing anything wrong."

Bugs nodded. "Okay. I just wanted to have my ducks in a row before seeing Morreau tomorrow."

I headed for the stairs, but Bugs called to me. "Nicky, before you go, what happened to the drugs?"

"I told you, we're giving free bags to Viktor's customers."

"I know what you said, but that doesn't account for the whole shipment; in fact, that doesn't account for hardly any of the shipment. Where's the rest?"

"You probably don't want to know," I said.

Bugs nodded. "The nightly charge for Manny's hotel?"

"No way! Manny never asked for a thing. I volunteered to give him and Dominic some of the shipment for the help they provided, but neither one of them ever asked."

"And the money?" Bugs asked.

"It's still being used."

Bugs nodded. "All right. I'm going to bed too. It's been a long day, and I imagine tomorrow will be worse."

Frankie drove into the office early. He hoped to see Morreau before his calendar filled up. Even more so, he hoped he could catch Miller.

As he walked into the station, he spotted her talking to a few uniformed cops. "Hey, Miller. You got a minute?"

Sherri turned, smiling when she saw Frankie. "Donovan, what are you doing here? I thought you were on your honeymoon."

"I was, but the lieutenant kept calling about some trouble with the Russians. You know anything about that?"

Sherri lost her grin. "I don't know what you're talking about. I guess you better ask the lieutenant."

"I intend to ask him," Frankie said. "I'm on my way up there now. By the way, have you busted any drug dealers lately?"

Sherri had started to walk away, but she stopped and stared, then she lowered her voice. "Since you seem to know what's going on, there's no sense in beating around the bush. Yes, I'm working with Fusco. And yes, I'm helping him get Viktor. I'm doing it for Lou. I liked Lou, and I'm not letting his killers get away with his murder."

"I understand that," Frankie said. "Lou was my partner, but—"

"No 'buts' about it. They killed him at his front door, for God's sake. Left him for Marie to find. We can't let them get away with that shit."

"All right. All right. Just be careful and watch your ass."

Frankie went upstairs. As he passed Carol's desk, she said, "Donovan! What are you doing here? Kate get tired of you already?"

"Real funny," Frankie said. "I'm going in to see Morreau."

"I'll let him know," Carol said.

The door to Morreau's office was open. Frankie walked in without knocking and took a seat. "You wanted to see me, Lieutenant?"

Morreau finished whatever he had been writing, then looked up at Donovan. He gestured to the door. "Close that, please."

Frankie stretched and flung the door closed, then focused on the lieutenant. "What's so urgent?"

"I've had numerous reports that the Russians had a big drug shipment busted. One of Viktor's shipments."

Frankie sat up. "Sounds good so far."

"The reports say that it was NYC policemen who did the busting, and four of Viktor's men were killed."

"I still don't see the problem, Lieu."

"Some of the men were executed, not just killed during the bust. And the drugs and money are missing. Missing, Donovan, as in we don't know where the hell it is."

"Lieutenant, we went through this when I was in San Francisco. I told you then that I didn't know anything, and I'll repeat that now. *I don't know anything.*"

Morreau leaned forward. "I need to be honest with you, Donovan. I find it difficult to believe that the man you have been hell-bent on investigating for Mazzetti's murder suddenly has a drug shipment stolen and his men killed, and you know nothing."

"Difficult to believe or not, that's the way it is. I was in San Francisco, and I have no idea what happened. Besides, if I had anything to do with seeking revenge for Lou, I'd simply put a bullet in Viktor's head."

"I wouldn't joke like that if I were you."

"Two things, Lieutenant. You're not me, and I wasn't joking. I've thought about it more than once."

"I didn't hear that," Moreau said. "Now let's get back to the matter at hand. If you know nothing about this, who does?"

Frankie shrugged. "You think it really was cops?"

"I don't want to believe it, but reports say they were dressed like cops."

"I don't know," Frankie said. "Why would cops dress in uniform if they intended to steal drugs. And if they were going to kill some of the people why not kill them all? It doesn't make sense."

"It does if those cops wanted to send a message to Viktor," Morreau said. "A message meant to convey retaliation for Mazzetti."

Frankie looked at Morreau, then leaned back. "Wait a goddamn minute, Lieu. If you're thinking I had something to do with this—again—you're crazy. I want this prick Viktor as much as anybody but not that way. I'll get him the right way; otherwise, I'd have shot him in the head, like I said."

"I'm not saying it was you, Donovan, but *somebody* did it. And I want to know who. It's bad enough we had a damn cop killed. We can't have a vendetta. This isn't Dodge City."

"Sometimes I wish it were Dodge City. It would make things simpler."

"It's not a simple world, Donovan, so get your head out of your ass and find out who did this. I want this to be top priority."

"Anything new on Lou's case?" Frankie asked.

"There's nothing new, and you shouldn't be worried about it. There's a reason we don't let detectives investigate the deaths of people close to them. Try to remember that."

"I remember," Frankie said. "And it pisses me off. Nobody knew Lou better than I did. I should be the one investigating."

"Maybe in the next life, Donovan, but for now, do as I ask. And stay away from Mazzetti's case. If I hear that you're poking around there, I'll—"

"Yeah, I know. You'll cut off my dick and feed it to the dogs."

"Christ's sake, Donovan.That wasn't what I was going to say. You're a sick son of a bitch."

"I may be sick, but that's what you *should* have said. It would have had more impact."

Morreau shook his head. "Just get the hell out of here, Donovan. I don't know why I let my day start with you."

"Because you didn't have a choice. I walked in."

"Now you're making it worse. Just go. And stay away from Mazzetti's case."

Frankie got up and walked toward the door. "I'm leaving, but the other isn't going to happen. I intend to find out who killed Lou. I'm not leaving it up to the jerks running the case now."

"Goddamnit, Donovan, I—"

Frankie left the office and closed the door behind him.

THE PLAN IS WORKING

$\mathcal{V}$iktor focused on Vlad as he finished his drink. "What do the reports from last week look like?"

Tension covered Vlad's face. "I told you on the phone, Viktor, sales are down to almost nothing."

"Why? We still have supplies. We can use them while we wait on the next shipment."

"No one is buying from us. Our dealers are being arrested and ..."

"And what?"

"The word on the street is that the cops are giving bags out free. Nobody's seen them yet, but that's what people are saying. I've got men looking into it. But if it's true, no one is going to pay when they can get it free."

"That doesn't make sense. Why would cops give free drugs to people?"

"It makes perfect sense," Vlad said. "...if they want to destroy our business."

Viktor nodded while he poured another glass of vodka. "And the gambling?"

"The cops are still busting the bookmaking operations too, and they've increased the pressure on the loan sharking. We've lost most of our patrons in both areas. And we're losing the people who worked for us. Everyone is afraid of being arrested."

"We need to do something."

"There's more," Vlad said.

"What?"

"Our supplier from Asia said they want a guarantee on the money before they ship anything. After losing so much last time, they said it's not worth it."

"Are other people experiencing this trouble with the cops?"

"A few were in the beginning—the Italians and the Mexicans—but now it seems to be just us. And the cops are spreading the word to make it worse. They're telling people that working for Viktor will get them arrested."

"How bad is it?" Viktor asked.

"Bad. We've lost almost 80 percent of income from our drugs, and probably half of our dealers have deserted us."

"Only half? Based on what you told me, I'm surprised that it's not more."

"It might as well be. About a third of the half that stayed have been arrested, and if we can't help them get out, word will spread and we won't have anyone for long."

Viktor smacked the top of the table. "It's that fucking Irish detective, the one who just got married. Is he back yet? I want something done about him."

"We have tried several times, Viktor. We lost two men at his house and three more at the hotel. And when we sent men to the church, Manny's men were there."

Viktor brushed Vlad's comment aside. "Manny said he was only there because the priest asked him."

"Do you believe that?"

Viktor gazed at Vlad beneath furrowed brows. "Yes, I believe him. Why wouldn't I? Does Manny have a reason to be in bed with this cop? If he does, I can't see it. He's not even Italian."

"I don't know, Viktor, it seems to be a pretty big coincidence."

Viktor gulped the last of his drink. "It doesn't matter. If Manny's involved, he'll pay the consequences. I want this man taken care of."

"You want him done like the other cop?"

"What do you think, Vlad?"

"Since you're asking, I think you shouldn't kill him. Look what happened after killing the other cop. We're still feeling retaliation. And orders for that kind of pressure had to come from above. The detective could not have done it himself. That means if you kill him, the same people who gave the other orders will still be there. There's a good chance the pressure will be even greater."

Viktor thought for a moment, then said, "You may be right, Vlad. I'll go along with you. We won't have him killed, at least not yet. I want him to suffer, and I want my businesses back. Instead of killing him, take his wife but don't harm her. Not yet."

"What do you mean by 'take her'? Do you mean kidnap her or kill her?"

"Kidnap her. We need leverage."

Vlad breathed easier. "I think that's a good move, Viktor, but taking his wife may be just as much trouble."

"You said the orders came from up top. I think you're right about that, so we'll have to make sure they don't know about us taking his wife."

Vlad looked confused. "Are you hoping to use her to get your operations back?"

Viktor nodded. "It may be our only way to get them back. I'll have to plan this out so that the detective tells no one. Get a few men ready to take her. And plan on sending extra men in case she's guarded. I doubt she can be guarded all day, but take them just in case."

KATE GOES BACK TO WORK

"Where do you think you're going?" Frankie asked as Kate came down the stairs.

"It's not where I think I'm going, I know I'm going to work."

"You should stay here a few more days," Frankie said. "It's not safe yet."

Kate kissed him on the cheek. "Frankie, I love you, but this is not my idea of a honeymoon. Remember, we were supposed to be in one of the most romantic cities in the country, enjoying ourselves; instead, I'm in Brooklyn and sleeping in a gangster's house."

Frankie laughed. "Sorry for laughing, but when you think about it, it is funny."

Kate laughed with him and kissed him on the cheek. "You're right, dear. It is funny, but it's not tolerable; therefore, I'm off to work."

FRANKIE WAS TALKING to Franco about the next stage of the operation when his phone rang.

"Donovan."

"Frankie, it's Kate."

"What's up? Are you okay?"

"I'm fine, Frankie. I was calling to let you know that Lou was shot with the same gun as Shawna, which makes it the same gun as the professor also."

"All three were shot with the same gun?"

"That's what it looks like," Kate said.

"You're sure?"

"I didn't do the autopsy, but I read the report. That's what it says."

"That's what I figured."

"I know you 'figured,' but I'm confirming it. I hadn't seen the results before we left."

"Okay," Frankie said. "I needed to know that. It convinces me more than ever that Viktor is the one doing this."

"One more thing," Kate said. "For what it's worth, Lou was shot from three to five feet away. I'm guessing whoever killed him was waiting in the hall."

"Why do you say that?" Frankie asked.

"Because if someone followed Lou into the building, he'd have turned around and confronted them, but he was found on the floor as if he had been trying to get in his apartment. In fact, Marie said she heard his key in the lock."

Frankie thought for a few seconds. "You're probably right about that."

"The same logic applies if the killer was in the hall and Lou saw him.

If he didn't recognize the man, he wouldn't have turned his back and gone inside. You know Lou. He'd have asked who he was and what he was doing in there."

Frankie didn't need to think about this statement. "Right again, Kate. Thanks."

"You need to get used to that, you know," Kate said.

"Used to what?" Frankie asked.

"Used to saying 'right again, Kate,' because it's going to happen a lot now that we're married."

Frankie laughed. "You mean all these years you've been playing dumb just so I'd marry you."

"You bet. I was after your money. Now that I've got it, I'm going to show you who you really married."

"Damn, but you're a wicked woman," Frankie said. "But that's what I love about you. See you tonight."

"What are you working on?" Kate asked. "Still messing with those Russians?"

"Unfortunately, yes. We've put a dent in their business, but we haven't broken it. While we were gone—someone—and I think you know who, managed to make a bigger dent than I had."

"Nicky?"

"I'm not mentioning names. Let's just say it was an unsanctioned bust that I'm catching shit for. I can't be too mad though, because what he did seems to be doing the job."

"You mean getting to Viktor?"

"That's exactly what I mean. Someone took out one of Viktor's major drug shipments, and he not only stole the drugs and the money, but he killed several of Viktor's men in the process."

"Viktor must be mad about that."

"I doubt he gives a shit about the men, but they're not something he can continue to replace. It's gotta hurt. Remember, two were taken out at our apartment also."

"How can I forget? I was right there, scared to death."

"I never did hear what happened that day."

"That's because you kept telling me to be quiet about it," Kate said.

"Well?"

"The men busted in and made vulgar threats against Angela and me, and said they'd hurt Alex also. Then Nicky came out of the bedroom, and in a flash, he shot them both. They never had a chance to even draw their guns."

Frankie smiled. He wanted to laugh, but he didn't. "That's Nicky for you. I should have set him on Viktor long ago."

"Frankie! You can't do stuff like that."

"I know I can't, but I should have anyway. It's what Viktor deserves."

"Nobody deserves the kind of justice Nicky delivers."

"I bet you didn't think so that day in the apartment."

"Don't make me think too hard, Frankie. You've already got me sleeping in the bedroom of a charming gangster."

"If you knew Manny better, you might think more of Nicky."

"Really?" Kate asked.

"Really," Frankie said. "He can smile at you while you share a meal or a drink, then cut your throat a minute later. Don't let his jolly demeanor fool you."

"I'd have never known."

"Hey, I gotta go," Frankie said. "I've got to brief everyone on what we're doing."

"All right, see you soon. Love you."

"Love you too," Frankie said.

"Frankie, wait."

"What?"

"One more thing. We've got enough DNA from the floral van the killer used at Shawna's. If you get me a suspect, I can match it up."

"Fantastic. I knew there was a reason I married you."

WHO KILLED LOU?

Frankie walked into Morreau's office and sat in a chair across the desk from him.

"Have a seat, Donovan. It's not like you weren't invited."

"I know I wasn't invited. I'm not one of the privileged, so I need to create opportunities when I see them."

Morreau rolled his eyes. "All right, what the hell do you want?"

"I want to know what's going on with Lou's case. Have they made any headway?"

Morreau wagged his finger at Frankie. "Detective, I told you. Stay the hell away from that case."

"Is that supposed to mean I can't ask about it? If it does, that's bullshit. Lou was my goddamn partner."

"I know who he was. I'm your goddamn boss, remember? But there are rules about this. Partners cannot investigate partners."

"I wasn't asking to investigate. I simply asked about the status of the investigation."

"And I've been your boss for five miserable years. Long enough to know that what you ask about and what you have in mind are different things."

"You didn't even tell me that Shawna and Lou were killed with the same guns."

"Since you are prevented from investigating, I view that decision as a wise course of action. I didn't want to tempt you."

"How thoughtful of you, Lieutenant! From now on, though, let me make decisions that affect my life."

"I didn't tell you who to marry, Donovan, just who not to investigate. Now get out of here and let me get some work done."

Frankie stood. "Fine, I'm leaving, but I want to know what's going on."

"Yeah, sure. And you quit asking questions about his death."

Frankie mumbled as he walked out the door. "Snowball's chance in hell of that happening."

"What?" More asked.

"Nothing," Frankie said, and continued down the hall.

"I miss the old shit," Carol said as Frankie passed.

Frankie turned. "Sorry, Carol. I didn't hear you."

She smiled. "I said, 'I miss the old shit.' He was a pain in the ass sometimes, but it doesn't feel the same without him. Know what I mean?"

Frankie nodded. "I know exactly what you mean," Frankie said. "I miss him too."

"By the way, Frankie, someone called for you. I think their name was Franco."

"Tell him I'm busy today. Tell him and anyone else who calls to do something else today."

"Where will you be?" Carol asked.

"Nowhere," Frankie said. "I'll be nowhere, and I'm going nowhere. Tell anyone who asks that I'm a Nowhere Man."

"Nowhere Man? That sounds like a song from the 60s."

"It is," Frankie said. "Whoever figures out the song will find me."

Carol shook her head and mumbled. "Donovan, you're bat-shit crazy."

Frankie almost ran to get his car. He was going to find out what was going on with Lou's case no matter who it bothered. First, he talked to the detective—Hawkins. He had been assigned to the case, but he said he had nothing.

"No witnesses?" Frankie asked. "Nobody saw or heard anything?"

"Donovan, you know how it is. This is a city of blind people. Nobody sees anything."

"What about ballistics? Anything there?"

Hawkins shook his head. "Nothing yet. I'll let you know though. You'll be the first to know."

"All right. Thanks," Frankie said, then headed for the door.

Lying piece of shit. No ballistics yet my ass.

Frankie got in his car and drove to Lou's old apartment. He fought his way through a small group of kids hanging outside smoking, then knocked on the door. Marie answered right away.

"Frankie! Oh my God, it's so good to see you. How is married life?"

"Too early to tell," Frankie said. "But I didn't come here for that. I'm trying to find out some things about the day Lou got shot. I know it hasn't been that long ago, but are you up to it?"

"I'm fine, Frankie. Lou would have been the first one to tell me to stand up and speak my mind, say what I heard or saw."

Frankie nodded. "You're right about that, Marie. He told everybody that."

Frankie pulled out his notepad and a pen. "Marie, I know you told the other cops what you saw, but if you don't mind going over it again. They won't let me investigate the case because Lou and I were partners, but I don't feel as if they're making it a priority, so I wanted to do some work on it."

"Thank God," Marie said. "I've been wondering that myself. You and Lou always did things so quickly."

"Tell me what you saw or heard that day. You said you heard him put his key in the lock. Start there."

"I only heard the key hit the lock for a few seconds, then I heard gunshots. I think there were three of them."

"Go on."

"After I heard the shots, I ran to the door and opened it." Marie pulled out her handkerchief and sobbed. "He was on the floor bleeding. There was so much blood. And his face…they shot him in the face."

Marie got up and walked to the kitchen. "I'm sorry, Frankie. I can't help it."

Frankie had followed her to the kitchen and now had his arms around her. "It's okay, Marie. Don't worry. I'm gonna get these people. I promise. If nothing else happens in life, count on the fact that I'm going to find Lou's killer." He patted her back as he spoke.

"One more question. Did you get a glimpse of the man who shot him?"

Marie shook her head. "Nothing. When I opened the door, he was gone, ran out the front door, I assume. And when I saw Lou…" She began crying again. "Oh my God, Frankie, what am I gonna do? He was all I had."

"That's okay, Marie. It'll be okay. Did your sister ever come down?"

She nodded and tried to stop crying. "Yes, she came down but she can't stay long; she's leaving tomorrow. I thought of going back with her because I can't stand to be by myself or even leave the apartment. Every time I try, I open the door, then just stare at the spot where he was lying. I can still picture him there, Frankie. I can still see the blood."

"I know. I know. When is your she leaving?"

"Tomorrow, but my other sister is coming down."

"All right, listen. If your other sister doesn't get here in time, you need to pack up and come to stay with me. Kate and I will keep you company until she gets here."

Marie shook her head. "You can't do that, Frankie. You don't have room for an old lady."

"You're right, I don't, but I'm not talking about my place. Kate and I are staying with a friend in case there's more trouble. He's got plenty of room, and he won't mind."

Marie dried her eyes and looked at me. "For real? You don't think he'd mind?"

"I"m sure he won't. He knew Lou, and he liked him."

"Who is it?" Marie asked.

"I don't know how to answer this because I don't know how much Lou told you about our cases."

"Spit it out, Frankie."

"His name's Manny. He—"

"Manny Rosso? The gangster?"

There was no escaping it now. "Yes, Marie. Some people consider him a gangster, but he—"

Marie swiped her hand in the air. "You don't have to tell me about him. Lou told me plenty of times. Lou liked him. He said he was a gangster, but that he was a stand-up person."

Frankie breathed easier. "He was right. Manny's been letting Kate and I—and even some other friends—stay at his place for protection. He won't mind if you join us."

I called Manny on the way and told him I was bringing Lou's wife.

"Hey, no problem. Tell her I liked Lou."

"I didn't ask, but do you have enough room?"

"I got plenty of room. I'll kick one of my guys out or make him sleep on the couch. She can have the bedroom down the hall from Nicky. That son of a bitch never makes a sound anyway. He's like a ghost."

When Frankie got to Manny's house, Kate was already there. She and Nicky were in the living room, and Manny was in the kitchen cooking dinner. Frankie took Marie to the kitchen and introduced her to Manny.

"Mother of God," Manny said, "You look just like my family's neighbor back in Napoli."

"Naples? Where in Naples? I was born in Naples."

"Forcella, where else?"

"Forcella is where I was from," Marie said.

"Then you have to be related to the Piscano's. You look just like Sofia."

"The Piscano's are my cousins," Marie said. "I can't believe you know them."

Frankie grabbed Kate by the elbow and pulled her aside. "Looks like Marie will do fine. Let's go in the other room to talk."

"What's Marie doing here?" Kate asked.

"I stopped by her house to ask a few questions, and I think I got her worked up. Well, I know I got her worked up. She was crying so hard, I couldn't leave her by herself, so I brought her here."

"And Manny's all right with this?"

Frankie gestured toward the kitchen. "You tell me. They're like old friends after five minutes."

"What were you doing asking questions about Lou's killing? You know you're not supposed to be."

"I know I'm not supposed to be, but somebody needs to do it. Whoever they've got trying to solve Lou's murder isn't doing their job."

"Why? Because they haven't caught the killer yet?"

"It's not just that. When I talked to the detective handling it, he didn't even acknowledge that the ballistics were the same as Shawna or the professor."

"Maybe he didn't want to say anything to you. You are officially not on the case, you know." Kate smiled after she said it. "And you have a new wife who's happy about that."

Frankie kissed her on the cheek. "Happy or not, I'm not giving up until I get the son of a bitch who did it. I have a good idea who it is. All I have to do is prove it."

Kate took Frankie's hand and walked to the stairs. "Proving it will have to wait until at least tomorrow. You are required for marital duties upstairs."

Frankie smiled. "Damn, I can't say no to that." As he passed the hall leading to the kitchen, he could hear Marie and Manny gabbing away. Frankie shook his head. "Who would have thought?"

"By the way, Mr. Donovan, if your performance is above par, I'll try to find out a little more about that DNA evidence in the van."

"You've got a deal," Frankie said.

KATE IS MISSING

Kate left early so she could get a jump on her work. She had a hell of a backlog after being gone for almost a week, and she had promised Frankie to look further into Lou's killing.

By noon, she had read through dozens of reports, and she felt she had a handle on things, or at least enough of a handle to give Frankie a run-down on what she knew. With that in mind, she called him as she exited the building to sit on a bench and have lunch.

"Donovan."

"This is Mrs. Donovan. I don't have much, but here's what I know so far. The DNA that was found in the driver's seat matches DNA found on the driver that was tied up in the back of the van. What's significant is that it was not the driver's DNA. I'm talking about the real driver, not the guy who stole his van."

"Which means you assume it's trace evidence that came off the killer when he tied up the driver and then again when he made his escape?"

"Exactly. You're not bad for a lousy first-grade detective."

"That still leaves me nowhere—unless I can find a suspect and we match his DNA to what you found."

"Even that is only going to get you a car hijacking. We've still got nothing to tie it to the scene at Shawna's. Her place was clean. And we've got no DNA evidence that was found on the professor or Lou either."

"Maybe we should make another run at the scene, see if you can find anything they missed."

"I already did that today, but there were so many kids running in and out of there that any DNA evidence would have been long gone or tainted beyond use."

"What were you hoping to find?" Frankie asked.

"I don't know. Something—anything. Maybe a cigarette butt around the corner where the killer may have waited, or an empty bottle of water. I don't know. Maybe I was hoping to get lucky."

"You used up all your luck when you landed me. You'll have to get by on smarts now, and that may be tough."

"You really are an ass; you know that?"

Frankie laughed. "Yeah, I know. See you when you get home."

"When I get home? Manny's place is home now?"

"You know what I mean. Just get here early. Manny's cooking his famous ravioli tonight."

"I wouldn't dare miss it. See you then."

Frankie began analyzing everything he had on Lou's death, at the same time, he wondered why the detectives handling the case seemed to be nowhere.

Nicky walked in the front door. "Bugs, what are you doing home? I thought you'd be burning the midnight oil after missing so much time."

"I didn't go in. I"m working on Lou's case."

"I thought that was taboo," Nicky said.

"It is but what the hell."

"You want to go over there?" Nicky asked.

"Kate was there today and said they kids were as thick as mosquitoes in the summer."

"Speaking of Kate, where is she? In the shower?"

"She's working," Frankie said.

"This late? She should have been home long ago."

Frankie stopped and looked at the clock on the wall. "You're right. Where the hell is she?" He pulled his phone out and dialed, but the call went to voicemail.

"Not answering?" Nicky asked

"No, and that's odd. She almost always answers her phone. Where the hell is she?"

Frankie called her office phone. It was answered by her assistant. "Hello?"

"Jess, this is Frankie. Is Kate there?"

"No, she left an hour or so ago. She said she you were having something good for dinner."

"Did she say she was stopping anywhere?"

"Didn't say anything to me, but I'll let you know if I hear from her."

"All right. Thanks," Frankie said. He hung up, then dialed her cell. It went to voicemail again.

"You want to take a drive to check the route she uses?" Nicky asked.

Frankie shook his head. "I'll check with the local hospitals first and see if there were any accidents."

Frankie was still calling hospitals when Nicky said, "Bugs, why don't you use that 'find my phone' thing and see if it shows where she is?"

"I hadn't thought of that," Frankie said, then he navigated to Apple's site and initiated the search. After entering Kate's data, the app located her phone.

"There it is," Frankie said, pointing to a blip on the screen.

"Where is that?" Nicky asked. "I can't tell from here."

"Hang on. According to 'find my phone,' Kate is near the corner of 18th and Ocean Parkway."

"What's there? Why would her phone show up at that spot?"

Frankie stared at the screen. "It shouldn't. That's on her way from work, but there'd be no reason for her to stop."

He dialed another number. "Sarge, this is Donovan. See if you have anyone near 18th and Ocean Parkway. I'll hang on."

"Fernandez is only about a block away. What do you need?"

"Tell him to go to the corner and listen for either a phone ringing or beeping. In fact, have him call me so I can talk to him."

About five minutes later, Fernandez called. "Donovan, the sarge asked me to call. What do you need?"

"I'm showing my wife's phone at that location, but she's not answering the phone. I'm going to call it, but it may not ring. If it doesn't, I'll ping it, and it will make a beeping sound."

"Okay, go."

Frankie dialed, but it went to voice mail right away. He then got the phone to beep using the app.

"I hear it, Donovan. Hang on and let me look."

A minute later, Fernandez came back on the phone. "I got it, Donovan. Found it in the grass by the sidewalk."

"See anything else? Any signs of an accident or anything?"

"Nothing. Clean as a whistle."

"Fuck!" Frankie said. "All right. Can you bring the phone back to the station?"

"Got it, Detective. If you need anything else, let me know."

Frankie hung up and stared. "Nicky, what the hell is going on? You don't think anything happened to her, do you?"

Nicky put his hand on Bug's shoulder. "Nah, don't worry. She'll show up. Probably stopped for pizza or something and dropped her phone."

"You don't believe a goddamn word of what you're saying, and neither do I," Frankie said.

Nicky nodded. "Okay, who's driving?"

Frankie got up from the table. "I am. I know exactly where it is."

Nicky grabbed his arm as they walked out the door. "You need to think straight on this. Don't lose your temper and go berserk, that's exactly what Viktor would want. Assuming this is Viktor."

"You know damn right well it's Viktor. If he does anything to Kate, I'm going to cut his balls off and stuff them in his mouth. Then I'll crucify him on the door of his club."

WHERE IS KATE?

*N*icky climbed into the passenger seat while Bugs got behind the wheel. "Buckle up, Nicky."

"I'll buckle up, but remember that you can't do Kate any good from the morgue."

Frankie raced off, turning right to get on a route that led to Ocean Parkway. He hadn't gone three blocks when his phone rang. "Donovan."

"Detective, how are you?"

"Who's this?"

"This is Victor Polenko. You—"

"Victor! Did you do anything to my wife? If you did, I'll—"

"Your wife? Is she missing? Didn't you just get married?"

"Where's Kate?" Frankie asked.

"The last time I saw her, she was tied to a chair with a gag in her mouth."

"You motherfucker. If anything happens to Kate, I'll—"

"Yes, I'm sure I know all the things you will do to me. I'll be trembling all night after we hang up."

"If you touch a hair on her head, I'll—"

"You can ensure that she remains safe—if you do as I say."

"What do you want?"

"It's simple. I don't want anyone to be hurt, and if you follow my instructions, no one will be hurt."

Nicky tapped Frankie's arm for the third time. He turned to Nicky and mouthed, "Victor's got Kate."

"Tell me what to do, Victor," Frankie said.

"You will stop bothering my gambling and loan-shark operations. You will immediately cease interfering with my drug operations, and you will protect future deliveries."

"That's not all in my control."

"I'll leave it up to you to figure out how to accomplish this, but it must be done."

Frankie didn't respond for a moment, then said, "Okay. I'll get it done."

"One more thing," Victor said. "If anyone finds out about this, all deals are off. I'll have to hurt her. And just to be clear, by 'hurt her' I mean I'll have three or four of my men fuck her before I kill her."

Frankie gritted his teeth and squeezed his phone. "I already told you, I'd get it done."

"That's good. It's what I wanted to hear. Now understand this. If you stop all the pressure on my operations for two days, I'll release your wife. But you still won't be safe. If you go back on your word, I'll find you, and I'll take your wife. The next time I won't be so polite."

"It may take a day or two to get everyone to lay off, but I'll get it done. You just make sure nothing happens to Kate."

"It won't. I'm sure you don't put much faith into it, but you have my word as long as you keep to your end of the bargain."

"Let me talk to Kate."

"I'm afraid I can't do that."

"I need to talk to her," Frankie said.

"When I see signs of you cooperating, I'll call you, and you can talk. Until then, you have my word that she is safe."

"This isn't over, Victor."

"I know it isn't. It won't be over until you complete your end of the bargain. I'm hanging up now. You better get busy if you want your wife back."

Frankie hung up the phone and looked at Nicky. "That motherfucker has Kate."

"Don't worry, Bugs. We'll get her no matter what he does."

"I've got to get with the special team I put together. I need to stop the heat on Viktor so he lets Kate go. The problem is they'll want to know why we're slacking off, especially when we've been doing such a great job."

"Tell them you're giving him a reprieve so that he thinks the heat is gone. Then, when he builds back up, you start in again."

"But he said he'd get Kate if we did that."

"He can't get Kate if he's not around."

"What do you mean?"

"I mean I plan to take him out, Bugs. I know you don't want to hear that, but that's what I'm doing."

Frankie placed his hand on my arm. "Nicky, I may not like hearing that, and I shouldn't like it because I'm a cop, but it's what I wanted to hear you say."

"You serious?"

"Dead serious. I'd do it myself, but I don't think I'm good enough. I may have been good enough once, but not now. Viktor's too well-protected."

"I'm glad to hear you say that, Bugs. This is a tough decision for me. I don't take killing people lightly."

"What? You find religion?"

Nicky stared. "In a sense, I guess I did. I've sworn not to hurt anyone, but I keep getting put in situations where I'm forced to. It's almost like I'm supposed to do God's work."

Frankie laughed. "You're shitting me, right?"

Nicky shook his head. "No, I'm not. I don't want to kill people, but I'm not going to stand by and let them hurt other people. It's like what happened with Borelli's kid or Monroe's cousin. They were innocent kids. The people I took out to resolve the problems needed it, and I'd do it again if I had to."

"The avenging angel, huh?" Frankie said.

"Maybe," Nicky said. "Maybe that's what I'm supposed to do. Who knows? I know that when I have to do something like this, I get bothered at first, but then a calm settles over me, and I feel good."

"Don't do this for me, Nicky. I'm not asking you to—"

"I know you're not asking, but this is the happiest I've seen you since we were kids. I'm not letting some scumbag Russian destroy that."

"Nicky, I—"

"Case closed, Bugs. Viktor's a dead man."

"How are you going to do it? You said yourself that he's guarded by too many people."

"I plan to ask Dominic for some help."

"He already gave you Fabrizio. What more do you think he'll do? He's not going to go to war with Viktor over some me."

Nicky nodded. "You're right, but he might give me the information I need if I do something for him."

"Whoa! Don't go there, Nicky. It's not good to owe Dominic favors. You don't know what he'll ask you to do."

"No, I don't. But I'm willing to bet whatever he asks of me won't be as bad as doing nothing in this situation. I told you already—I'm not letting Viktor hurt Kate. Not now. Not ever."

TIME TO GET VIKTOR

I was leaving Manny's house when Bugs came down the stairs.

"Catch you later, Bugs."

"Where are you going?"

"To do what I need to do. There's a lot to plan for."

"Nicky, you don't have to do this," Bugs said. "I'll get her back."

"I know you'll get her back. I have no doubt about that. But something needs to be done about Victor. He can't be allowed to go on and do things his way. And you and Kate have the right to feel safe, not wake up every day wondering what's going to happen."

"I know that, Nicky, but I don't want you doing anything. It's not your problem."

I grabbed Bugs and hugged him. "I've known you almost all my life. It is my problem, and I'm going to take care of it," I said, then turned to leave.

"Nicky —" Bugs said, but I was already closing the door.

I called Dominic to let him know I was coming, then headed for the Bronx. I'd already popped in on him several times so I figured I better call beforehand. I parked down the street, walked up and knocked on the door. Dominic's "assistant" answered. I called him an assistant, but I didn't know many assistants who carried Beretta's in their waistband.

Dominic met me in his sitting room, impeccably dressed as always. He gestured to the assistant, then asked, "Espresso?"

"Thanks," I said. "I'd love some."

"Now tell me what you need today. In case you don't know, you're amassing quite a few favors that you owe me."

"I'm well aware of what I owe, Dominic. One more won't make it any worse."

"How is Fabrizio doing? Are you getting along?"

I smiled. "Fabrizio knows his business. I like him."

"Yes, he does. You should be working together all the time, not just on this."

"I've got a family, Dominic. I can't put them at risk."

The assistant brought espresso, set the cups on the table, then departed. Dominic picked up his cup and sipped. "Niccolo, what can I do for you?"

"Victor has kidnapped Frankie's wife., and I need to do something about it. Where would Viktor take his wife and kids if they're not at the house?"

"Did he move them?"

"I don't know, but I think he might, so I need to know where he'd take them."

Dominick leaned back and looked to be giving thought to the question. "I can't be sure, but if I had to guess, I'd say it would be his sister's house in Queens."

I sat up. "Do you know where in Queens?"

Dominic shook his head. "I'm not sure, but it wouldn't be wise to presume that's where he'd take them. I'd make certain you know by forcing his hand."

"What do you mean?"

"Find a way to make him worry about their safety, then either you or Fabrizio follow whoever moves them to see where Viktor takes them."

I listened to Dominic's suggestion, thought about it, then nodded. "I like that Dominic. I think a simple break-in attempt at Viktor's house may provoke him."

"I agree," Dominic said. "But be careful. Viktor is not just a suspicious man; he is a vindictive man. If he thinks you are associated with the detective, he may do something to harm Donovan's wife."

"I'll make sure he doesn't know."

"Making sure he doesn't know isn't good enough. He must not even suspect."

"All right," I said.

"What do you plan on doing?" Dominic asked. "Do you intend to take his family?"

"I noted the disgust in your voice, Dominic. Don't worry, if I take his family it will only be for negotiations—in case he doesn't live up to his end of the bargain. I would never harm a man's family."

"That's good for me to know, but don't let anyone else know that. If your enemies know what you won't do, you have given them an advantage."

"I won't. But I won't hurt his family either."

"That's fine, Niccolo. I understand, but you must understand that Viktor is not to be trusted. He will break his word in a minute. My suggestion is to get what you want from him, then kill him."

"I don't know, Dominic. I don't like resorting to killing, but …"

Dominic nodded slowly. "I understand that too. If it bothers you, then I would suggest you get what you want and let Fabrizio kill him. But under no circumstances leave Viktor alive, or you'll be walking down the street one day, or eating lunch, and a bullet will find it's way to you. Trust me. I know this man."

"You think it's that bad?"

"I know it's that bad. Kill Viktor, Niccolo. It's the only way."

"Why don't you kill him?" I asked.

Dominic sighed. "If I have to, I will. But if I do it, word will get out, and that will start a war between the Russians and us. It won't be pretty. If you do it, you're just an unknown man who killed Viktor. Even if they blame it on the cops, they can't do anything. What are they going to do—go to war with the police force?"

Dominic reached for his espresso and sipped. "Besides, Niccolo. You owe me a favor, or did you forget? In fact, you owe me several favors."

I looked at Dominic, trying to judge him, but it was like trying to read a stone. "Are you asking for that favor?"

"I might be."

I thought a moment and then decided. Things had gone as I hoped, and since I owed Dominic a favor, this was probably as good as it was going to get. "If this is the favor, consider it done. I'll kill him."

Dominic smiled and set his glass on the table. "Good," he said. "I was hoping you'd say that."

Dominic looked at me and cocked his head. "But I think you knew that's what I wanted. I think you had already made up your mind to kill him and you just wanted to use one of your favors." Dominic laughed. "You're a clever man, Niccolo. I like that."

"When can you get the information you mentioned, about where Viktor might hide his family? Just in case the tail doesn't work."

"I have the information, Niccolo. I just wanted to see if I should give it to you. I'll get it to Manny tonight."

"Manny?"

"You're staying at Manny's aren't you?"

I smiled. "I should have known you'd know. When did you find out?"

"About twenty minutes after you went there. Manny and I have no secrets. He wanted to let me know in case I didn't approve. Remember that day we spoke? He told me you were staying there then."

I stood and shook hands. "Okay, Dominic. You've got a deal. You won't have any trouble from Viktor again. Nobody will."

"Do I need to give a message to Fabrizio?"

"I'll take care of it. He's expecting my call," I said.

"And you can tell Detective Donovan that this one's on me. No favors are expected from him."

"Getting soft, Dominic? Or just getting a heart?"

"I owe your friend for his help in Houston. Your Houston friend did me a small favor for my niece. For that, I owe him greatly."

"Bugs told you where Paulie was?"

"What he did for me is between the detective and me, Niccolo. Let's keep it that way."

I laughed as I headed for the door. "No problem, Dominic. And he'll be thrilled about the 'no favor owed' part. Not like you'd get a favor, but he'll still be thrilled."

~

A FEW HOURS LATER, I met Fabrizio so we could plan a strategy. I filled him in on the details and asked what he thought.

"We know where he lives," Fabrizio said. "I say we wait for him to come home and pop him."

"I love your direct approach, Fabrizio, but Viktor is too well protected. Even if we used enough men there would be a lot of casualties. We don't need people dying."

"Breaking in is probably not an option," Fabrizio said. "I'm sure he has a good security system."

"Not to mention plenty of guards," I said.

"But there is always a fake break-in," Fabrizio said.

"Considering that Viktor's security system is probably first-rate, I like the sound of fake break-in."

"Good. I say we go there during the day, take it far enough to trip the alarm system, then sit back and wait. Knowing Viktor, he'll waste no time in moving his family. Especially since you threatened to take them before."

I nodded. "And when he moves them, we follow."

"Exactly," Fabrizio said. "No matter who he has doing the transfer, if we work together we won't be seen. Viktor will think his family is safe, and we'll know exactly where they are."

"More importantly, he'll send his men to protect the family and leave his house unguarded."

"That only helps a little," Fabrizio said. "He'll still have a security system that we have to get past, and like I said, it's probably a good one."

"We'll figure that out when we get to it, Fabrizio. For now, let's focus on finding out where he takes his family. And remember, we can't do anything until he lets Kate go."

FIRST STEPS

Frankie got ready for work. He had asked the team to meet him at the station, and he didn't want to be late.

As he was leaving, Manny stopped him. "Bugs, none of my business, but I say we put a few in the back of Viktor's head and forget about it."

Frankie shook his head. "I can't, Manny. Not while he's got Kate."

Manny shrugged. "If that's the reason, I understand. I thought you were gonna spew some nonsense about being a cop."

"No, I need to see Kate released first," Frankie said. "Speaking of which, I'll try to come back later and take Marie home. Her sister should be in today."

"Way ahead of you. Giorgio's taking her home after lunch. I'm making her my gnocchi with tomato-basil soup."

Frankie laughed despite his situation. "You're going to spoil her, Manny. I didn't know you were such a softie."

"Hey, everybody should taste my gnocchi before they die."

Frankie headed out and got to the station minutes before his team did.

"How's married life?" Ronan asked.

"How was the honeymoon?" Franco asked.

Frankie fidgeted. All this talk about Kate was putting him on edge. "Marriage is fine, Ronan. You should try it. As far as the honeymoon goes, it was too short."

Frankie cleared his throat and raised his voice. "Now to get on with things. We're going to ease off Viktor for a while. He—"

"What for? What we did is working."

"Yeah, and we heard someone was helping us too," Ronan said. "I heard people were posing as cops and giving out free bags in his territory."

"Must have been whoever ripped off his drugs," Jasper said. "You don't know anything about that, do you, Donovan?"

"No, I don't know anything about that, Jasper. The reason I think we should ease off is to make Viktor feel safe. I've been getting a lot of pressure to lay off. If we quit, and he thinks that pressure is working, he'll go right back to his routine. When he does, we'll hit him again, and harder."

Morgan pounded his fist on the table. "I like that," he said.

Ruiz laughed and chimed in with his approval. "Me too, and the sooner the better."

"All right," Frankie said. "Then it's settled. Go back to your old jobs until I call. It will probably be a week or so."

"That's all? You called us all the way down here to tell us this? You could have done it over the phone," Franco said.

"I'm sorry," Frankie said. "This is important, and I didn't want to do it by phone. I wanted everyone here at once."

A couple of them grumbled as they left, but within a few moments, they were gone. Once that happened, Frankie called Nicky.

"Did you get Freddy to lay off on the drugs?"

"Yeah, I had to promise him his payment, but he's stopping as of today. No more free bags. And I asked Miller not to bust any more of Viktor's dealers or junkies."

Frankie panicked. "You didn't tell her why, did you?"

"Don't be an ass, Bugs. You know I wouldn't do that. I said I needed it done for a plan I was working on."

"Okay. Sorry. I was nervous."

"It's understandable."

"And one more thing, Nicky. If…if this goes down as you said, They're going to have phone records showing me and Viktor talking, and for more than a few seconds."

"Easily explainable. Tell them you were working on a team to tear his operations apart, and he kept calling to threaten you. Tell them the calls lasted as long as they did because you kept him on the line to taunt him. You'll be able to back up the part about your team, and it will be your word against assumptions regarding the other."

"And you think that shit will work?" Franke asked.

"It doesn't matter what I think," Nicky said. "They're going to be faced with a dead Russian mobster who was suspected of multiple murders, and who was talking to a decorated detective. They'll buy it. Trust me. I'm sure you've seen far worse."

Frankie sighed. "All right. Thanks."

After hanging up, Frankie thought of what to do, which got him pondering Lou's murder. It struck him what he'd been thinking of that didn't add up. Lou always complained that '10,000 kids were outside making noise.' And Kate said the kids were 'like mosquitoes in the summer' when she stopped by. But if that were the case, why didn't they have any witnesses?

Frankie turned at the light and headed toward Lou's place. It was time he did some of his own investigating. Hawkins wasn't getting anywhere.

Frankie knocked on three doors before anyone answered. He showed his badge and told the lady what he wanted.

"I already told the other cop everything I knew, and my kid did too."

"I understand, ma'am, but perhaps you can repeat it for me. It might help."

"If you want to hear it right, you should talk to my son. Him and Darvel saw the man."

"Saw the man? You mean the killer?"

"Yeah, the killer. I told that other detective. The killer ran right past them."

"The other detective? Was that Detective Hawkins, a skinny white guy about my height?"

"That's him," she said, then swung the door wider. "You might as well come in and sit. My name's Nagle. Barbara Nagle."

Frankie sat in a chair that looked as if it may collapse at any minute. "First let me explain that there is a reward for information that leads to an arrest. Did the other detective tell you that?"

Mrs. Nagle shook her head. "Nobody said anything about a reward. If they had, I'd have been sitting' outside your office."

"What do you mean by that?" Frankie asked.

"I mean my boy saw that man plain as day. He ran right past them."

"Them?"

"Yeah. Tucker and his friend Darvel," Nagle said, then she cocked her head and stared. "I'm not splitting this reward money just because I told you about Darvel. And how much reward is it? How much will I get?"

"No, you won't have to split it. If we use the information from your son as well as Darvel, we'll make sure he gets something too."

"Well?" she asked. "How much?"

Frankie looked at her to judge her reactions, then said, "Ten thousand dollars."

"Ten thousand dollars! Are you shitting me? I didn't know they paid that kind of money for solving crimes. Shoot, I could have a full-time job just by lookin' out my window."

"We don't pay that much for everything," Frankie said. "But this was a detective who was killed."

"A detective? Now see, I didn't know that either. That other cop didn't tell us shit. I'm glad you came by."

So am I, Frankie thought, then leaned toward Mrs. Nagle. "Ma'am, I need to tell you that the men who we believe did this are dangerous men. They've been known to hurt people in the past."

"Honey, for ten thousand dollars, I'll risk a little hurt."

"That's just it; it's not just a little hurt. These men have killed people, a lot of people."

"They won't know who did it right? Don't you have something to make sure they don't know who told on them."

"We do," Frankie said. "But it doesn't always work like it should. I can probably get my boss to issue witness protection though."

"What's that?"

"We'd give you a new identity and a new place to live. It's the best way to stay safe."

"Sounds good to me," she said. "About time we moved anyway."

"I'll have someone come down here and tell you all about the program once I get it approved. It's a good program, but it does have its drawbacks."

"Like what?"

"A lot of things, but they'll explain it to you. Probably the biggest is you'll have to cut off everyone you know now. No calls to your friends or relatives, no visiting them…"

Nagle scoffed. "If that's all it is, I got no problem. I'm tired of talking to people around here anyway."

Frankie stood to leave. "One more thing, Mrs. Nagle. The information your son gives me has to be good. I don't want bullshit. Bullshit won't be enough to earn the reward. I need information that will let me catch the son of a bitch who did this."

"Don't you worry about that. My son can tell you," Mrs. Nagle said. "He told me he saw the guy. Even told me what he looked like."

"Is your son home? Or is he at school?"

Nagle raised her eyebrows and looked at Frankie. "Where do you think? He's at school. We could go down there and talk to him though."

Frankie drove to the school that Tucker attended, and Mrs. Nagle had them call her son out of class so they could talk.

Frankie leaned down and spoke to him. "Tucker, your mom told me that you saw the man who shot that person in your building?"

"Sure did," Tucker said. "Me and Darvel got a good look at him. We heard the shots, then the man ran right past us when he came out of the building."

"What happened after that?" Frankie asked.

"Nothin'," Tucker said. "He got in a car that was waiting for him, and it sped off."

"What did he look like? Can you remember?"

Tucker nodded. "I ain't gonna forget that. He was a big white guy with dark hair and a tattoo on his arm. His left arm."

"A tattoo? What did it look like?"

"That's easy. It was a picture of some guy with a beard and mustache, and he was wearing a uniform."

Frankie thought for a moment then walked to where Mrs. Nagle stood. "Would you mind if we took a drive and I had Tucker look at some people to see if he recognizes them? I'll make sure they don't see him."

"Will it help us get that reward?" she asked.

Frankie inhaled deeply, then held his breath. "Yes, ma'am. If he recognizes the man who did the shooting, it will go a long way to earning you the reward."

He went back to Tucker. "We're going to take a ride, Tucker—you, your mom, and me. I'm going to point out a few men, and you need to tell me if any of them were the men who shot Detective Mazzetti, the man who was shot in your building."

"When are we gonna do this, because I'm supposed to play baseball after school."

"If your mom okays it, we can go now."

Tucker looked to his mother, and she nodded as she walked to him. "Let's get it done," she said. "No sense waitin' on this any longer."

"You mean I'm getting' out of school for this?" Tucker asked.

"It looks like it," Frankie said.

Frankie drove by the station and picked up a car with heavily tinted windows, then he headed toward Brighton Beach.

He parked across the street from Viktor's club, and they waited until some of Viktor's men came outside.

"Take a look at those men," Frankie said. "Was it any of them?"

Tucker put his face to the window and stared. "No, none of those guys."

About fifteen minutes later, Viktor came out with three men accompanying him. They walked toward a limo parked near the front door.

"That's him," Tucker said, "…the one near the front of the car with the tattoo on his arm."

"You sure?" Frankie asked, but he could tell by the way the kid was trembling that he was sure.

"It's him," the kid said. "I remember that tattoo. Never saw a tattoo like that."

"Okay, good," Frankie said. "That's going to help."

"I want to go home, now. Can we?"

"You get what you need?" Mrs. Nagle asked.

As disgusted as he was, Frankie smiled. "I think we did, Mrs. Nagle. Thank you."

CATCHING LOU'S KILLER

*B*y the time they finished, it was almost the end of the school day. Frankie dropped Mrs. Nagle and Tucker off at her apartment.

"Remember," he said. "Don't say anything to anybody about this. We don't want word getting out that Tucker knows anything. It will put him in danger if the man who did the shooting finds out."

"We ain't saying nothing," Mrs. Nagle said. "Don't worry about that. You just worry about gettin' me that reward."

Frankie watched them enter the building, then he drove back to the station to see Morreau.

He took the stairs two-at-a-time, then walked into Morreau's office and took a seat.

Morreau stopped what he was doing and looked up slowly. "Come on in, Donovan, and while you're at it have a seat."

Frankie smiled. "Thanks, Lieutenant. I think I will. In fact, I think I did."

Morreau laid a pencil down on his desk. "What is it? What are you trying to con me out of now?"

Frankie stared. "I need the okay for a ten-thousand-dollar reward on Lou's murder, and I'll need authorization for witness protection for a mother and her child."

Morreau's eyes widened. "Really? Is that all? Nothing else? Don't need a new car or a raise?"

Frankie leaned back and shook his head. "No, I think I'm good there."

"All right, Donovan, tell me what's going on. It's not like I thought you'd stay away from Lou's case, but I was hoping you wouldn't stir things up."

Frankie looked to make sure the door was closed. "Listen, Lieutenant, I'll fill you in on everything, but you have to promise to keep it quiet."

"Quiet?"

"That's right. Quiet. And I mean from everybody. No one can know."

"All right. I'm listening."

Frankie sat up straight. "You know I had Viktor Polenko pegged for the murder of that professor and also for Shawna?"

Morreau nodded. "I remember. I had to authorize the team you put together that you used to bust his operations."

"After Lou and I started putting on pressure is when Lou got killed."

"Go on."

Hawkins has been working on this since the beginning, and he says he's got nothing. He said he didn't even have the ballistics that matched the killing to Shawna's.

"And?"

"And I worked on it for two days, and I not only have the ballistics match, I have an eyewitness who saw the killer running out of the apartment."

"What?"

"Yeah, that's what I say. I know being seen running from the scene of a crime isn't proof that you did it, but it is pretty damning evidence, especially when you have no reason to be at the scene of the crime."

"Interesting," Morreau said. "And why is it that this has to be kept secret? And while you're telling me that, explain why you're looking into this when I told you that wasn't allowed."

Frankie looked at the door again, then whispered, "Viktor kidnapped Kate."

Morreau shot up. "What? Why didn't you tell me?"

"Calm down, Lieutenant. Viktor said he'd kill her if we tried anything, and he said if we didn't lay off his business he'd kill her too. I stopped all team activities this morning, and with nothing else to do, I looked into Lou's murder. I figured that maybe if we could get him on this, we could put him away, but I can't do anything until I get Kate back."

"Donovan, I don't like it. I say we get a couple of dozen men and swarm his place. Besides, you know these Russians. Even if you get the killer, he isn't going to roll on Viktor."

"I know that," Frankie said. "That's why I need Kate back first, then I'll figure out what to do about Lou's killer. Which brings up the subject of what are you going to do about Hawkins?"

"You think he's dirty?" Morreau asked.

"He's not incompetent, and what I've done so far any rookie would have done. I think he's on Viktor's payroll."

Morreau made a few notes. "I'll look into it. I can have his phone records and bank records checked. Hell, I'll have everything checked."

"Good. And make sure you don't say anything about Kate."

"I won't, but let me know when you get her back. Then we'll get that son of a bitch. And, Donovan, take off for the remainder of the day. Get some rest."

Frankie glanced at his watch. "Gee, thanks, but it is the end of the day, Lieutenant."

"Then take the night off. Either way, get the hell out of my office."

Frankie was driving home when his phone rang. "Hello?"

"Detective, you're off to a good start. If tomorrow is the same, I'll let you wife go."

"Let me talk to her," Frankie said.

"I said I would, so I will."

"Frankie?" Kate said.

"Kate, are you all right? Has he hurt you?"

"I'm scared, but I'm not hurt. Are you getting me out of here?"

"Damn right, I am. I'm working on it now. You should be home tomorrow."

"Make sure I am, Frankie. Like I said, I'm scared."

"I know you are, and you should be. I'm getting you home though."

"It's me again, Detective. You'll have to wait until tomorrow to talk to her again."

"I thought you were letting her go tomorrow."

"I will, Detective. I'll call you near the end of the day. Just remember, your job doesn't stop tomorrow; it starts."

PLOTTING A BREAK-IN

I rushed breakfast then started toward the front. Bugs caught me at the door. "Nicky, where you going?"

"Going to meet Fabrizio. I'll catch up with you later."

"Make sure you don't do anything that would upset Viktor. He's supposed to let Kate go today."

"I'll call you later, Bugs. I'm late."

I met Fabrizio at a diner close to Manhattan. "You ready, Niccolo?"

"I'm ready, but for what?"

"I was thinking of what we had to do, and I have an idea," Fabrizio said.

"I'm listening."

"Back in Sicily, there was a wealthy man who no one liked, but his home was very secure. Then one day, the police found him dead, and no one knew how. No alarms had gone off, and no one had reported anything."

"How did they do it?"

"No one knows for sure, but the rumors were that someone broke in during the day and hid inside the house. Then after the wealthy man went to bed, they came out and killed him."

I thought about it. "Sounds good, but the cameras would show us going in and not coming out. Viktor would know we were inside."

"I checked with who installed his system, and there are several blind spots that we can use to our advantage."

"Blind spots won't help, Fabrizio. Even if we can access a blind spot, the alarm will go off when we go in."

"I have a way to fix that," he said.

"How?"

"We go in the front door while wearing masks. While we are going in, two other people wearing masks will follow us."

"The camera will catch them," I said.

Fabrizio shook his head. "The cameras at the doors rotate to detect motion once the alarm is set off. So when we go in the front, the camera will turn to follow our movement. When it does that, the other two people can come in behind us."

"And then what?"

"Once we're all in, we can take advantage of the way the cameras follow the movement and eventually make our way upstairs. Once we're up there, we can hide while the other two take our place. When they leave, whoever is watching the tape will assume it is us."

"But Viktor will come to check on things, or at least send people to check on things," I said.

"Exactly," Fabrizio said. "And when he gets there, the system will be turned off. We'll have to stay in the attic for a long time, but later that night, we can come out and take care of business."

"So you're saying we trick Viktor into getting his family out of the house, hopefully sending the guards with them, and then use this plan to hide in his house?"

"Exactly," Fabrizio said. "He won't search the attic. He won't expect someone to be hiding there."

"And if it doesn't work?"

"Then we kill everybody and leave."

"Fabrizio, sometimes I don't know when you're joking."

"Sometimes I don't either."

I laughed. "Looks like we're set, Fabrizio. Remember, nothing until we get Kate back. That probably means we go into action tomorrow."

"I'll get what we need as far as masks. We should have a few jars for the attic too. Just in case."

"The jars will be needed if we're going to be in the attic that long. As well as bottles of water. And don't forget we'll need the decoys. They'll have to be similar in build to us."

Fabrizio nodded. "Already have the men, and they're ready to go. I can get a few bottles of water before we go in."

"I think we're set then. I'll call you in the morning."

TWO HOURS LATER, while drinking coffee in Manny's kitchen, Bugs came in.

"Well?" I asked.

His face was all smiles. "Viktor just called. He's letting Kate go now."

"Where?"

"We need to meet him the same place we found her phone, over on Ocean Parkway."

I gulped the last few sips and said, "I'm coming with you."

"No need, Nicky."

"Maybe there isn't a need, but I'm coming anyway. You want me to drive?"

"No, let me drive. And Nicky, I want in on this. I want that son of a bitch. I can have twenty cops raid his place and haul his ass down here."

"You can't, Bugs. This is a job better for one man. Let me do it."

"We can get him, Nicky. And I'll nail him for Lou's murder too."

"And you know damn right well that you won't find anything when you got o his place. Then you'll have nothing to hold him on, and he will eventually kill Kate. I'm telling you, let me handle it."

"What are you going to do? I can't have you fucking this up."

I stared at Bugs without speaking. Kept staring for maybe thirty seconds. "Bugs, have I ever let you down? Do you think I'd screw up something so important?"

Bugs calmed down and lowered his head. "No, I guess not. Sorry, Nicky. But you know how I feel. I married her for Christ's sake."

"I know, Bugs. Just let me take care of this. I promise that Viktor won't bother you anymore."

"I don't know why I'm doing this, but okay, I'll trust you."

"You do know why you're doing it, Bugs. You're doing it because it's what you really want without breaking your oath as a cop. Tell me I'm wrong, and I'll stop. Tell me you don't want Viktor dead and I'll go home tomorrow."

Frankie turned onto Ocean Parkway. "Do you know what a pain in the ass you are?"

"The question is: do you know what a pain in the ass you are?" I said.

Frankie drove about half a mile, then said, "There she is. There's Kate."

Kate stood on the corner as if she were waiting for a bus. Frankie pulled to the curb and jumped out.

"Kate! Kate, are you all right?"

She ran to him, and they embraced. Kate cried while Frankie consoled her. "It's all right now. Nothing's going to happen."

"What if he does it again? He said if you did anything wrong, he'd do it, and he said…Oh my God, the things he said he'd do to me."

I got out of the car and held the door for Kate so she could ride up front with Bugs, then I got in the back seat.

"Don't worry, Kate. It won't happen again."

"How do you know, Nicky? How does anyone know?"

"Because I'm going to make sure of it, Kate. I promise."

She turned her head and stared. "You promise? For real?"

I nodded. "I promise, Kate."

A BREAK-IN THAT ISN'T A BREAK-IN

I finished my second cup of espresso, ignored yet another call from my wife, then said goodbye to Manny.

"Headin' out, Nicky?"

"Got a few things to do," I said. "I might be a while too so don't expect me back until late, maybe even tomorrow."

"Yeah, I'll keep that in mind. Just be careful and let me know if you need anything."

As I headed out, Bugs came down the stairs. "Going out, Nicky?"

"Yeah, and I may not be back tonight."

Frankie looked at me sideways. "Why?"

"Don't worry about why, Bugs, but you *should* make certain to have an alibi tonight. Take Kate to a hotel or something, one with good security cameras. And make sure not to leave the building."

Frankie stared for a few seconds, then nodded. "All right. I can manage that."

I did a few errands, then met Fabrizio, who had our decoys with him. We went over the details with the decoys so that they understood their part in this.

"We're going to do a fake break-in, hoping that will spur Viktor into moving his family somewhere else. We're assuming he'll send the guards along, leaving the house empty or near empty."

"How long will that take?" one of the decoys asked. I believe his name was Artie.

"We're hoping it won't take long. Maybe an hour or so. Viktor is a paranoid man, and he responds to threats quickly."

"Then what?" Artie asked.

"We were planning to follow them and see where he hides his family, but now we don't need to. It will be enough to know that they're not at home and not coming home."

"Okay, so the family's gone, and the guards are gone. Now what?"

"Nicky and I will go in and head straight for the door. The cameras will pick us up, but we'll have masks on so it won't matter."

"And what do we do?" Artie asked.

Fabrizio pointed to a sketch he had of Viktor's house.

"You approach the left side of the house, the one with no windows. It also has a huge blind spot dead center of the wall that extends all the way to the fence. When you reach the house, hug the wall and come around to the front door."

"Sounds good so far," Artie said.

"Nicky and I will go inside. Once we trip the alarm, the camera at the front door, which is the one that will be alerted, will switch to a motion camera and follow our movements. When we go inside, you wait a few seconds, then follow. The camera will not pick you up."

"How do you know this is gonna work like that?" Artie asked.

"Because that's what the security expert who installed it told me. And I trust him because he doesn't want to die."

We went over the rest of the plan, then went over everything again. When Fabrizio and I were convinced they had it right, we left to go to Viktor's house.

∼

VLAD RUSHED up to where Viktor was sitting. "Alarms went off at your house."

Viktor stood quickly. "What? When?"

"Just now. The front gate was triggered."

Viktor pounded the table. "Son of a bitch! I *knew* I shouldn't have let her go."

"Let who go?"

"That cops's wife. It's him doing this. I know it."

"I don't know," Vlad said. "I doubt he'd do something like this. He—"

"It's him. I know it is." Viktor took a cigarette out and lit it. "Tell Ruko to take my family to my sister's house. And tell him to take everyone with him. I want them protected."

Vlad hesitated, then said, "Is that wise, Viktor? To leave the house unprotected, I mean."

"If my family isn't home, there is nothing to protect. No one can get in the safe. And besides, you said it was the front gate that was triggered, right?"

Vlad nodded.

"It was probably some kids, but I'm not taking chances. Get them to safety."

~

WE WATCHED as Viktor's men moved his wife and kids out of the house. They were carrying overnight bags, which we presumed to mean they intended to stay a while.

"Looks like it's working," I said to Fabrizio.

"Of course it's working," he said and smiled. "But that was the easy part." He then handed me an empty jar and a bottle of water. "Now we have to make sure this part goes as planned."

We waited twenty minutes before putting the plan into motion, but once we started, it went quickly. Within a half hour, Fabrizio and I were inside the house and in the attic hiding. Artie and his partner, ransacked the bedroom dressers and a few other places, then they did some unnecessary damage to make it look good, then they left.

Now the difficult part came. Fabrizio and I went into the attic and settled into a spot behind the AC unit where we couldn't be easily seen—and waited.

~

VLAD RUSHED INTO THE CLUB, panting. "Viktor, it's the alarm again."

"Is my family gone?"

"Yes, they left when you said, but this time the front door alarm triggered. Someone is in the house."

Viktor shook his head. "Get a few men and let's get out there. Hurry."

Viktor and his men spent half an hour searching the house but found nothing.

"It looks like an amateur robbery attempt," Vlad said. "They went through the bedroom dressers, and your wife's jewelry box has been emptied. Other than that, mostly just destroying things."

Viktor gritted his teeth. "I want you to find who did this, Vlad. And when you do, we won't turn them in to the cops. I'll take care of them myself."

"Yes, sir," Vlad said.

"Reset the alarms and let's get going."

"You want me to leave some people here?" Vlad asked.

"What for? My family isn't here, and whoever did this already got what they wanted. We'll know if they come back."

Vlad nodded.

I heard the front door close and tapped Fabrizio on the arm. "I think they're gone now."

He moved to the attic stairs and listened. "They're gone," he said. "We can rest a while."

"It'll be a few more hours until Viktor gets home," I said. "Make sure you don't take your gloves off. We don't want to leave prints for them to find."

We waited until almost seven o'clock before Viktor came home.

"Get comfortable," Fabrizio whispered. "It's going to be a long wait."

And long it was. It was almost midnight before the house was still and during that time, all we could do was whisper.

"I heard one other person," I said. "How about you?"

Fabrizio nodded. "Me too. And it sounded like he went into the bedroom at the end of the hall. We should take him first."

"Wear your mask," I said. "I don't want to kill him if we don't have to."

Fabrizio took the mask from his pocket and slipped it on. "Ready," he said.

We waited another fifteen minutes, and when we didn't hear any noises, we opened the attic stairs quietly and descended. Many attic stairs made a creaking sound when they were opened, but Fabrizio had thought of that and brought oil to lubricate the joints.

"It's a good thing you thought to bring that oil for these steps, Fabrizio. Otherwise, the springs always make noise."

Fabrizio closed the steps again, then we tiptoed down the hall to the guard's room. Fabrizio sneaked in and placed the gun barrel to his head. I was right beside him. The guard woke up at once.

Fabrizio had his finger to his lips. "Shh. No noise or I'll have to shoot. Understand?"

The guard looked at us with his eyes wide, then nodded.

"Do as we say, and nothing will happen to you," I said. "Now sit up. We're going to tie you and gag you, then we'll leave you alone."

He nodded again.

Fabrizio tied him to the bed, then taped his mouth shut. "Don't make noise," I said. "If you do, I'll come back in and put a bullet in your mouth. Understand?"

He nodded once more.

Fabrizio and I left and tiptoed to Viktor's room. The door was closed but not locked.

As he had done with the guard, Fabrizio placed the gun barrel against Viktor's head. He opened his eyes, staring at us.

"Stay still; I'm going to turn on the light so Viktor can see who's doing this to him."

"No need," Viktor said.

He probably realized that once he saw us, he was dead, but it was too late. The light went on.

"You?" he said.

"Yes, Viktor. It's me. In case you don't recall, my name is Nicky, and I'm a friend of Detective Donovan."

He scowled. "I knew he was behind this."

"I wish I could say that he was, but he's not. I'm doing this. And I'm doing it because I made you a promise in your club when I came to see you. You threatened my family. Then you made things worse by trying to harm the detective's family. Now you'll pay."

"I'll make sure you pay for this," Viktor said.

I laughed. "No, you won't, Viktor. Perhaps you don't understand. I'm not just going to hurt you; I'm going to kill you. You're not going to make sure of anything."

When I finished saying that, I shot him in the left knee. The shot was silenced but still loud, though not as loud as his screams.

"Should I shut him up?" Fabrizio asked.

I shook my head. "Let him scream. He's got a long way to go."

I shot him in the other leg, just below the knee. His scream grew louder, and he mixed this one with more threats.

Then I shot both ankles. He screamed a few more times, then passed out.

Fabrizio looked at me. "Shall we get it over with?"

I nodded. "Might as well. You can do it if you want."

Fabrizio shoved the barrel of the gun into Viktor's mouth, breaking a few teeth as he did. Once he had it inserted, he fired twice into the back of his throat.

"That should do it. Let's wipe down a few things and go."

I shot Viktor once more in the heart to make sure, then we took the blankets off him and rolled them up to take with us.

"Get the blankets from the guard's room," I said. "No sense in leaving DNA around."

"DNA might be anywhere," Fabrizio said.

"Yeah, but DNA in the bed covers would be more difficult to explain."

FABRIZIO WALKED BACK to the guard's room and removed the covers. "We just killed your boss," Fabrizio said. "You will not cooperate with the police in any way. Tell them two masked men came in and tied you up, then they went and shot Viktor. You know *nothing* else. If you tell anything else, we will find you and kill you too. Do you understand?"

He nodded.

Fabrizio rejoined me, and we went a few blocks to a spot we had decided on earlier. On the way, Fabrizio called Artie and asked him to pick us up.

"Fabrizio, is that you?" Artie asked.

"We're ready," Fabrizio said. "Don't delay."

"Be there in five minutes," Artie said. "I've been hanging out at a friend's house close by."

"Tell him to bring some lighter fluid or anything that burns quickly."

"I heard," Artie said. "I'll bring it."

Fabrizio turned as I was piling the blankets on top of one another, separated by sticks I'd gathered from nearby woods.

"I presume you're planning to burn those," Fabrizio said.

I nodded. "As soon as Artie gets here."

Artie arrived in a few minutes and handed me the fluid. I sprinkled it on the blankets, lit it, then got in the car. "Let's go," I said.

THE NEWS ISN'T GOOD—OR IS IT?

ate rolled over and kissed Frankie on the lips. I can't believe what a great night that was. Hell, I can't believe I'm still alive."

Frankie rolled her over and got on top of her. "You better start believing in everything, including knights in shining armor because you married one."

Kate stared over Frankie's shoulder at the TV that was playing. "Or at least married someone who has a friend like that."

"What do you mean?"

"Look at the TV," she said. "Viktor Polenko is dead."

"What?"

Frankie sat up and turned the volume higher just as the Channel Two reporter was starting.

"Viktor Polenko, a well-known Russian immigrant who was often spoken of as being associated with the Russian mob, was murdered last night in what appears to be rival gang violence or a coup by his own people. He was shot numerous times while lying in his bed, and the shots appear to have been designed to inflict pain."

"That's why he wanted us here," Frankie said.

"What?" Kate asked. "I couldn't understand you."

Frankie cleared his throat and turned off the TV. "I said that's why Nicky suggested we come here, so we'd have an alibi."

"Are you saying this was planned? That you knew it was going to happen?"

"I'm not saying anything, but we better get going. Morreau is going to have a fit."

"Where am I going? I'm not staying here?"

"You can come with me. I'll only be a few minutes, then we've got to drive Nicky home and pick up Alex."

Frankie walked into the station a little late, but there were a lot of people mulling around downstairs.

Sherri walked up to him, all smiles. She held out her hand in a gesture to bump fists. "Way to go, Donovan. I didn't think you'd do it."

"Do what?"

Sherri moved closer and whispered, "Viktor's dead. Don't tell me you didn't know it."

"I just saw it on the television, but I had nothing to do with that."

"Is that right? Your friend Fusco still in town?"

"He is, but I'm taking him home today."

"Coincidence?" Miller asked.

"Go to hell," Frankie said, then walked up the stairs, dreading his session with Morreau.

He walked into Morreau's office after knocking lightly on the door.

"I heard Polenko's dead," he said.

"You heard? That's all, you just heard? You didn't have anything to do with it?"

"Lieutenant, I had nothing to do with this. I didn't even know where he lived. Besides, Kate and I were at a hotel last night. We were there the whole night."

"Kate's back?"

Frankie nodded. "I got her last night. That's why we went to the hotel, to celebrate."

"Pretty coincidental that you get Kate back and later that night, Viktor dies."

"And coincidence is all it is. I'll state it again. I had nothing to do with this."

Morreau smiled. "All right. I'm glad to hear it. Why don't you and Kate take a couple of days off to enjoy married life, then pick up the ball and try busting these Russian bastards while there's a power struggle going on."

Frankie smiled and offered a mock salute. "You got it, Lieutenant. See you later."

Bugs and Kate picked me up at Manny's house mid-morning. I'd had my espresso, but I still didn't feel awake.

"Bugs, how are you," I said when he walked into the kitchen. "Kate, good to see you."

Bugs embraced me and whispered, "Thanks," then he took a seat at the table.

Kate kissed me on the cheek, offering her thanks as well.

"Looks like you heard the news," Manny said.

"What news?" Bugs asked.

"What news my ass. Viktor's dead, and you know it."

"I guess that is good news," Bugs said.

"You bet your ass it is," Manny said, then he went to Kate and kissed her cheek. "I'm happy for you, doll."

Kate blushed. "Thank you, Manny. I won't even object to you calling me 'doll.' "

Manny laughed. "It's a good thing because that's what I call all the beautiful women."

I got a text while sitting at the table. It was from Dominic.

All favors are paid. Thank you.

I smiled. Not much could have made me happier. The "thank you" may have been because I had Fabrizio give the rest of the money and dope to Dominic and Manny to split—most of the money anyway. I gave Fabrizio enough to send him home to see his family, and I saved some for me. Dominic and Manny got the bulk of it, but they had earned it, after providing so much help.

It didn't matter. If it was the money and dope that did it, it was worth it. I was off the hook. I wouldn't have been comfortable spending the money anyway.

"You ready to go, Rat?" Frankie asked.

I put my phone away and looked up. "Give me five minutes. I need to pack a few things."

Five minutes later we stood at the front door, packed to go. Manny walked over and hugged us all. "Okay, great to have you guys as guests. Now it's back to business. Bugs don't let me catch you trying to bust my operations."

Bugs laughed. "You know I'll try, Manny, so watch out."

"Well don't try so hard then," he said. He reached to shake hands. "Nicky, good to see you again, and thanks for everything."

He leaned over and kissed Kate's cheek. "Kate, take care of that Irishman. Keep him safe."

"I will. And thank you, Manny. You were a magnificent host, and you were a great chef."

Manny laughed. "I don't know about the host part, but you're right about the chef."

We got in the car and left. Sixty miles later, as we were heading south on I-295, Kate said, "Nicky, I don't know what to say. Thank you isn't enough, but thank you. I didn't understand what you did until…"

"Kate, you're a medical examiner. You understood what I did. You just didn't appreciate it. But that's all right. Nobody appreciates the garbageman until their trash needs to be emptied, or the plumber until their toilets won't flush."

Two hours later, when Frankie pulled up to the house, Angela, Rosa and Alex came running. She was carrying Dante, but set him down halfway down the sidewalk.

"Daddy!" He screamed and ran toward me.

We went inside, me carrying Dante, and sat around the kitchen table. Angela put on some coffee and served a tray of cookies she and Rosa had made.

"You should stay the night," Angela said. "You've got to be tired."

"Thanks, Angela, but we need to get back. I've got to get Kate to work before she gets lazy."

Angela reached over and took Kate's hand. "Nicky told me what happened. How did you deal with that? That must have been horrible."

Kate glanced my way, and I shook my head, a signal for her not to say anything. "It was horrible, but thanks to Frankie's quick action, I'm here and safe."

Angela smiled. "That's what's important. Thank God for that."

"Listen," Bugs said. "I hate to break this up, but we have a long drive ahead of us. We need to go."

I got up and hugged Kate and Bugs and said goodbye. "Drive safely," I said. "Take your time."

Kate leaned in and kissed my cheek. "Thanks again, Nicky. I owe you."

I smiled. "I've warned you about favors, Kate. Be careful."

After Bugs and Kate left with Alex, I sat in the chair to relax. It had been a long and tiring trip, and I was eager to take it easy.

Rosa got me a glass of wine and set it on the table next to me.

I looked at her. "What do you want, Rosa?"

"What makes you think I want anything?"

"Because you're never this thoughtful unless you want something. Now spit it out."

"I want to talk about what happened at Bugs's apartment when you shot those men."

"Not going to happen," I said. "I'm tired, and I've got a lot to catch up on at work."

"You said when we got home—"

"Yes, I said when we got home, but I didn't say the moment we got home. We'll talk about it when I decide."

I leaned my head against the chair and closed my eyes.

"But—"

"Rosa! There are no buts. Do I need to call your mother?"

She stood and stormed off. "You promised," she said.

What she said caused me to sit up straight. I had promised. "Rosa, come here."

She came back, standing with her hands positioned on her hips, identical to how her mother stood.

"I'm sorry. I *did* promise. I'll tell you about things but not tonight. We'll do it this weekend."

She smiled. "Okay, Dad. Thanks." Then she leaned toward me and kissed me on the cheek. "You're the best."

I hope you think so when I'm done talking.

I read a few pages then closed the book and sipped on the wine. Angela came in, sat on my lap and rested her head on my shoulder. "I'm so glad you're home and safe."

I kissed her cheek. "Me too. Now I'm eager to get back to work and see what needs to be fixed."

"I thought you said Johnny had things under control."

"I did. But I guarantee you there will be something to fix. I don't know what, but something."

Angela sat up. "You'll fix it, babe. I have confidence in you."

"Aside from all the trouble, did you have fun?" I asked.

"I did. It was nice to spend time with Kate, but I'd love to go somewhere with just you, or with you and the kids."

"Where do you want to go? Name anywhere."

"Like you'd take me."

"I can't take you if I don't know where you want to go."

"Okay, smart-aleck, I want to go to Boston."

I squeezed her tightly and kissed. "If you want to go to Boston, we'll go, but how about Rome?"

Angela laughed. "Yeah, like we could go to Rome."

"You never can tell," I said.

THE NEWS IS GOOD

I came home from work with one of the people who worked for me following in another car.

"Drive my car home," I said. "I'll get a ride in with someone."

I went inside and saw Dante hiding behind the door, preparing to attack me. I acted scared and surprised when he jumped out, and he laughed like hell.

"Dante, you didn't fool anybody," Rosa said. "Dad knew you were there."

"Did not," he said.

"Leave Dante alone," I said. "He hid well, and I didn't know he was there."

Rosa rolled her eyes and shook her head, then she leaned toward Dante and said, "Spoiled."

"Where's your mother?" I asked.

"Right here," Angela said as she came down the stairs.

"I need everybody to come outside with me," I said. I bent over and scooped Dante into my arms. "That means you too, little guy."

"What are we going outside for?" Angela asked.

"You'll see," I said.

I walked outside followed by the rest of them.

"Well?" Rosa asked. "What's the deal?"

I handed her a set of keys. "Will you please get my briefcase out of your car?"

"What?"

"Hit the button to sound the horn," I said. When she did, I pointed at it, "That's your car. That's for being such a perfect daughter."

She screamed, ran down the sidewalk, unlocked the car door, then jumped behind the steering wheel. She rolled down the windows and shouted, "I can't believe it. Is it really mine?"

"It's really yours," I said, "But you have to drive me to work tomorrow."

"Oh my God, of course. Can I drive it to school? Can I pick up my friends?"

I nodded while smiling. "Yes, you can pick up your friends. Now get my briefcase and bring it in."

Rosa continued to gush about her car while I sat in my favorite chair. "You could at least pour your tired father a drink," I said.

"Coming right up," Rosa said, "but then I'm going upstairs to call people."

Angie sat on my lap and whispered, "Nicky how can we afford a car?"

"I had some big contracts come in. Real big."

"I hope they were real big. Car payments aren't cheap."

"There are no payments, babe. We own it. Paid for."

"What? Are you kidding me? That's a lot of money."

"It is, but Rosa is worth every penny. She's a doll."

Angela kissed me softly. "You're a great dad."

"You should reward great dads. I'm thinking a nice bottle of wine and an early bedtime."

"I guess I could do that. I would have definitely done that if the car was for me."

"Really? How about if I take you to Rome?"

She kissed me again and giggled. "That would do it too, but we can't go to Rome."

I pulled an envelope from behind me. "We could with these."

Angela quickly opened the envelope. Inside were four first-class tickets to Rome. "What the hell! Are you shitting me?"

Rosa came running downstairs. "Did Mom just say 'shitting'? What was that all about?"

Angela jumped off my lap and ran to hug Rosa. "We're going to Italy. All of us."

"What?" Rosa asked.

I nodded. "We're going to Rome, Florence, and Venice. We're going to have fun."

"I can't believe it!" Rosa said, and she and her mother jumped up and down.

"Please be quiet, or you'll wake Dante," I said.

"Like it matters to you," Rosa said. "Mom's the one who watches him."

"Maybe I had other activities in mind," I said. "The kind that might keep your mother occupied."

Angela blushed. "Nicky!"

Rosa laughed. "Oh, my God, that's my cue. I'm going to bed."

LET'S GO ON A TRIP

For two weeks, Angela packed, then repacked. She'd put one thing in the suitcase only to take it out the next day.

I walked in on her during one of her drills. "Angela, I already told you. Pack lightly. Whatever we don't have we'll get over there."

"Don't be ridiculous. We can't be buying clothes and things like that. We have them."

"Then pack them and forget about it. We leave in less than an hour."

"Did you check with Rosa? Is she ready?"

"Angela, Rosa has been ready for a week. You're the only one holding things up."

Angela walked over and shut the bedroom door. "All right, Nicky. I have to know. Where did this money come from? And don't give me any line about new contracts."

"You'd worry too much if I tell you the truth."

"Just tell me."

"Dominic and Manny gave it to me."

"What? Dominic Mangini? And the Manny we stayed with?"

"They're the ones," I said.

"Why would they…what did you do?"

I held her by the shoulders. "You asked me where the money came from, and I told you. Nothing happened and nothing will, so please just enjoy yourself in Italy. I've even got plans to go to Campania to see your family."

Her face lit up. "My family! I've never met them."

"I know. That's why I planned it. They can meet Rosa and Dante too."

She threw her arms around me. "Nicky, you're the best. But when we get home, you're going to tell me what you did to earn this money."

Forty minutes later, we were on our way to the airport, and half an hour after that, we were standing in line at security.

Rosa looked over and shrieked. "Alex, what are you doing here?"

Ten feet in front of us, Bugs, Kate, and Alex waited in line to go through security.

Angela was almost as exuberant as Rosa. "Kate, what are you doing here? Where are you going?"

Kate beamed. "You won't believe it. Frankie is taking me to Italy."

"What!" Angela yelled. "That's where we're going."

Bugs stared at me, one of those "I knew it" looks were in his eyes. "Is this your doing, Rat?"

"I don't know what you're talking about," I said.

"Really?" Frankie said. "I get three tickets to Rome in the mail, and I *happen* to meet you here, and it's just a coincidence?"

"Guess so," I said.

"Pretty big coincidence," Bugs said. "Especially since the tickets were for a flight departing from Philly."

"Bugs, sometimes you have to take what happens in life and run with it. And don't forget to enjoy it."

I gestured to Kate and Angela chatting next to Rosa and Alex. "Some people learn to enjoy things quickly."

Bugs shook his head. "You're a character, Rat. Thanks."

"What are you thanking me for? I didn't do anything."

"Yeah, you never do," Bugs said. "But thanks anyway."

We were flying to Italy in first class, and everyone was having a good time. Angela and Kate were chatting like old school chums, and Alex and Rosa had become good friends despite the age difference.

I was sitting next to Bugs. I reached into my pocket and handed him a small gift box.

"What's this?" he asked.

"A birthday present," I said.

"It's not my birthday."

"I know, but as bad as you are at protecting yourself, I didn't know if you'd make it that far, so I'm giving it to you early."

Bugs laughed. "You're a dick, Nicky."

"Just open the gift," I said.

Bugs unwrapped it. It was a coin of solid silver with images the likeness of me and Bugs. Engraved across the top was written: *Friendship and Honor*.

"Oh my God, that's beautiful, Nicky. Where'd you get it?"

"A guy who Johnny Moresco knows did it. He used to work for Jimmy the Gem."

"Johnny Moresco—the Whale's nephew?"

"That's him. He looked after my business while I was in New York; in fact, he's looking after it now."

"Son of a bitch," Bugs said. "Thanks, Nicky. This means a lot."

"You're welcome. Now, sit back and enjoy the trip. Life is meant to be enjoyed."

"Even when there are mysteries?" Frankie asked.

"Especially when there are mysteries," I said, and smiled.

ACKNOWLEDGMENTS

It is with great honor that I give eternal gratitude to my wife and all four of my grandkids. They give me the inspiration to keep going.

ABOUT THE AUTHOR

Giacomo Giammatteo is the author of gritty crime dramas about murder, mystery, and family. He also writes non-fiction books including the No Mistakes Careers series, No Mistakes Publishing, No Mistakes Grammar, and No Mistakes Writing.

When Giacomo isn't writing, he's helping his wife take care of the animals on their sanctuary. At last count they had forty-five animals—eleven dogs, a horse, six cats, and twenty-six pigs.

Oh, and one crazy—and very large—wild boar, who takes walks with Giacomo every day and happens to also be his best buddy.

nomistakespublishing.com
gg@giacomog.com

More Grammar:

No Mistakes Grammar Bites, Volume I, Lie, Lay, Laid, and It's and Its

No Mistakes Grammar Bites, Volume II, Good and Well, and Then and Than

No Mistakes Grammar Bites, Volume III, That, Which, and Who, and There Is and There Are

No Mistakes Grammar Bites, Volume IV, Affect and Effect, and Accept and Except

No Mistakes Grammar Bites, Volume V, You're and Your, and They're, There, and Their

No Mistakes Grammar Bites, Volume VI, Passed and Past, and Into, In To and In

No Mistakes Grammar Bites, Volume VII, Farther and Further, and Onto, On, and On To

No Mistakes Grammar Bites, Volume VIII, Anxious and Eager, and Different From and Different Than

No Mistakes Grammar Bites, Volume IX, A While and Awhile, and Envy and Jealousy

No Mistakes Grammar Bites, Volume X, Could've and Should've, and Irony and Coincidence

Writing:

No Mistakes Writing, Volume I—Writing Shortcuts

No Mistakes Writing, Volume II—How to Write a Bestseller

No Mistakes Writing, Volume III—Editing Made Easy

Publishing:

How to Publish an eBook, No Mistakes Publishing, Volume I

How to Format an eBook, No Mistakes Publishing, Volume II

eBook Distribution, No Mistakes Publishing, Volume III

Print on Demand—Who to Use to Print Your Books, No Mistakes Publishing, Volume IV

Other nonfiction

Uneducated

Whiskers and Bear—Volume I, Sanctuary Tales A Collection of Animal Stories, Volume II, Sanctuary Tales

More Animal Stories, Volume III, Sanctuary Tales Surviving a Stroke—or Two

Life and Then Some

Fiction:

Friendship & Honor Series:

Murder Takes Time

Murder Has Consequences

Murder Takes Patience

Murder Is Invisible

Murder Is a Promise

Blood Flows South Series:

A Bullet For Carlos: A Connie Gianelli Mystery

Finding Family, a Novella

A Bullet From Dominic

The Good Book

Redemption Series:

Necessary Decisions: A Gino Cataldi Mystery

Old Wounds

Promises Kept, the Story of Number Two

Premeditated

Rules of Vengeance Series: (Fantasy)

Light of Lights (the beginning, a novella)

A Promise of Vengeance

Undeniable Vengeance

Consummate Vengeance

Note. The Light of Lights is a novella. It's about 100 pages long and sets the stage for the series. The other books in the series are about 800 pages long.

~

OTHER BOOKS

You can always see the current and coming-soon books on my website.

Fiction:

Memories for Sale (mystery/sf)

The Joshua Citadel (SF novella)

Children's Books:

No Mistakes Grammar for Kids, Volume I—Much and Many

No Mistakes Grammar for Kids, Volume II—Lie and Lay

*No Mistakes Grammar for Kids, Volume III—*Bring and Take

No Mistakes Grammar for Kids, Volume IV, "Would've, Should've" and "Your and You're"

No Mistakes Grammar for Kids,Volume V, "There, They're, and Their" and "To, Too, and Two"

Shinobi Goes to School—Life on the Farm for Kids, Volume I

Fiona Gets Caught, Life on the Farm for Kids, Volume II

Coco Gets a Donut, Life on the Farm for Kids, Volume III

Squeak Gets a Home, Life on the Farm for Kids, Volume IV

Biscotti Saves Punch, Life on the Farm for Kids, Volume V

Coming Soon:

The Adventures of Adalina, Volume I, Adalina and the Five Tiny Bears

The Adventures of Adalina, Volume II, Adalina and the Underwater Bears

Get on the mailing list and you'll be sure to be notified of release dates and sales.

<u>Mailing list</u>

And don't forget to leave a review!